THE SHROUD

(A Techno-thriller)

Pierce Evans

and

Frank DuPont

Cover Design by: Sandra Evans

ISBN 0-7414-0891-0

Published by:

INFINITY
PUBLISHING.COM

Infinity Publishing.com
519 West Lancaster Avenue
Haverford, PA 19041-1413
Info@buybooksontheweb.com
www.buybooksontheweb.com
Toll-free (877) BUY BOOK
Local Phone (610) 520-2500
Fax (610) 519-0261

Printed in the United States of America

Printed on Recycled Paper

Published December, 2001

THE
SHROUD

CHAPTER ONE

They could not have had a worse night for what they were about to do.

Jewish months begin with the new moon and it was now a little more than half way through the Jewish month of Nisan. The moon would be bright, very bright, dangerously bright.

"It is time."

"We must hurry. There are Roman soldiers everywhere. Take full advantage of the dark alleys and recesses. We will meet at the start of the foot path."

The individual members of the group darted one by one out into the moonlight and moved furtively among the shadows, ducking into this doorway and that alley, as they made their way through the warren of twisting and turning streets that zigzagged through Jerusalem.

The Roman soldiers were not as much of a problem as they had supposed. The clatter of their weapons and armor signaled their presence but the sharp angular turns and the reflections of the sound off the hard walls sometimes gave the illusion that they were where they were not. One of the group almost stepped out of a dark doorway right into the path of the changing guard but recovered in time. The officer in charge of the guard detail assigned his legionnaires one at the time. Each relieved a soldier who joined others assembling at this location and only when the last guard had been changed did the officer call them to attention and march them off. The figure hidden in the shadows had to wait for the soldiers to clear the area before he could leave his hiding place. His late arrival at the chosen assembly point at the base of the foot path caused some concern among his group but with his safe arrival, they immediately went about their business.

They would be exposed, at times, as they climbed the tortuous path up the hill but as they got closer to the top their confidence grew. It was not likely that there would be any Roman soldiers up here.

To what purpose? There would be no need to guard the dead. What could *they* do?

Nevertheless, the group moved cautiously, senses acutely tuned to any sign of danger. They conversed only in whispers.

They reached the spot, finally, and heaved a collective sigh of relief upon finding that there were no Roman guards at the site of the crucifixion.

They quickly went about the task of taking the body down from the cross. It was not easy. They could have used some more help but a larger group moving about the city at this time of night might have attracted attention.

This was not a time to reflect on what they had done. There was much still left to do and the return to the city would be much more difficult. They would have to stay together to carry the naked body to its destination. Several times they had to duck into dark recesses and make themselves invisible as the changing guards marched within feet of their hiding places.

They were out of breath, adrenalin pumping, and hearts pounding as they reached their destination. The door opened to their secret knock and they silently moved inside with their burden.

The sparse room had been carefully prepared. The only window had been covered with multiple layers of thick dark fabric to prevent the slightest glimmer of light being seen from the outside. A single smoky oil lamp flickered on a sconce mounted on one wall. A long low table was centered in the room and it had a long linen cloth lying on it with one end hanging down to and rolled up on the floor.

They gently laid the body on the linen with the head toward the long end of the cloth.

Even in the bad light it was clear what terrible things had been done to this person. There were multiple puncture wounds all over the head where a thorn bush had been brutally jammed on his head, a large wound in the side from a Roman lance, the holes through the wrists and feet made by the nails that had secured him to the cross, and scourge marks cut into the back, sides, buttocks, and legs.

The scourges used by the Romans had small dumbbell-shaped metal or bone *torchillia* attached to the end of each thong. The *torchillia* had sharp projections on them intended to tear and lacerate the flesh and they had done what they were designed for. Imprints of the *torchillia* were all over the areas that they had contacted. Those present wept at the sight of the body.

"We must clean him up and anoint his body with oils."

"Yes, we should do that but there isn't time. Any moment now, they will discover what we have done. Soldiers will be searching everywhere. We must finish our work and put him where the Romans can never find him. Hurry."

Ezra, one of the group, had apparently anticipated this and before dark, had picked a variety of flowers from the area. Almost as an afterthought, he laid the flowers along both sides of the body. The free end of the linen shroud was gently lifted over the naked body and rolled down to the feet. The shroud was then carefully folded around the body and bound in place.

Ezra went to the door and slipped outside to check for the sound of soldiers in the area. He did not hear any. He came back inside, extinguished the oil lamp, and held the door open. The rest of the group lifted the enshrouded body onto their shoulders and moved out again into the moonlight.

They silently cursed the moon for the peril that it added to their task that would have been perilous enough under any circumstances. The delays had made it necessary to proceed with less caution than they would have liked. The sky in the east would be lightening soon and the coming of dawn could prove to be a disaster.

The distant sound of a cock crowing in anticipation of the dawn put an exclamation point on that unspoken thought.

They quickly made their way through the twists and turns of the helter skelter streets. Tiredness from their earlier efforts and the weight of their present burden coupled with the stress of dodging the roaming soldiers was taking its toll.

They finally cleared the last buildings and moved across a low stone wall into an olive grove. They were less likely to encounter Roman soldiers here. Appearing like specters out of the night, they were right on top of a pair of lovers lying on the ground under the branches of an olive tree before either was aware of the other. The terrified lovers startled them as they scrambled to their feet, and bolted like a pair of frightened rabbits. The lovers raced back toward the city dragging their blanket behind them.

They carried their burden through other groves, out into open country, and then into the surrounding hills. There was no path here and the way was covered with small rocks and boulders that cut into their sandaled feet at every step. Exhaustion overcame them but they struggled on until they reached their destination. It was now light enough to find what they were looking for, a large boulder half buried in the side of a hill. They laid the shrouded body on the ground and with their bare hands dug the loose sand and rocks away from the boulder. Moving the rock away from the hill was a formidable chore but despite the tiredness of mind and body, and the lack of anything that might be used as a lever, they put their backs into it and the stone moved, almost imperceptibly, but it moved. Redoubling their efforts the stone grudgingly gave up and rolled away from the hillside revealing the entrance to a cave. The opening was small but it widened into a somewhat larger chamber. They could stand up in here.

Gasping for breath in the stale air, they wrestled their burden into the cave and laid it carefully on a flat rock that was roughly in the center of the chamber.

There were rituals that should be performed but they had neither the materials nor the will to perform them. They straightened out the shroud as the light of dawn streamed into the chamber through the tiny cave entrance. There was no time for ceremony. They could not, they must not, be discovered after coming this far. The work must be completed, and quickly.

It was not according to Jewish burial protocol but it was the best they could do. It would *have* to do.

Could they muster up enough strength to roll the boulder back into place?

They *must*. There was no way that they would let their mission fail after they had risked so much.

It took all that they had left in them to do it but the stone was eventually back in place. Again, with their bare hands they dug the loose sand and rocks and packed them around the boulder. They ached to the very marrow of their bones and their fingers bled from the task but they persevered until the job was finished. One of the group jerked a bush out of the hillside and used it as a broom to smooth the sand and brush away their hand and foot prints. In the morning light, it did not look quite the way they would have liked, but hopefully, the wind would smooth out the remaining imperfections and in a day or so there would be no telltale signs of what they had done this night. The Romans would never find him here.

And so it was. Their secret remained hidden for over a hundred years. The body putrefied and decayed to yellow bones, but the dark and the virtually unchanging temperature and humidity within the cave preserved the shroud and its remarkable image.

Then the unthinkable occurred.

An earthquake caused the boulder to roll away from the cave entrance and it was not long before a shepherd, looking for a lost lamb, stumbled upon it and discovered its incredible contents.

CHAPTER TWO

The shepherd took the shroud back to his tent. All of the members of his family were Christians and when they saw the image on the linen, they were bewildered and prostrated themselves before it. The father, eldest member of the family, timidly touched the large blood stain on the side and was immediately cured of a painful and crippling affliction.

"This is the image of Christ," he cried out, "It is the burial cloth of our Holy Savior," and they all marveled at the miracle of his healing.

The power of this relic was undeniable so they selfishly hid it and kept it to themselves but the marvelous healing of the father of the shepherd could not be kept secret for long. The members of the congregation asked about it, for nothing like this had ever happened in their community. Eventually, the shepherd could not keep the secret for another second. This was too important. He had to tell someone. He went to the small building where he and other Christians met and blurted out the whole story to all of them.

Many were dubious but when the father showed up to attend a meeting, apparently in good health, they were amazed because it was known throughout the community that he was a cripple who also suffered great pain at the slightest movement.

Naturally, they all wanted to see this wonderful linen. Many of the true believers, upon seeing it, were cured of all sorts of illnesses and the shepherd's family agreed that this precious cloth should be shared with all Christians and consented to the display of the Shroud in their tiny church.

This soon proved to be inadequate as word of the miracles spread about the countryside and pilgrims came from all corners of Israel to see it with their own eyes. Conversions to Christianity occurred in huge numbers. Membership of the congregation exploded accordingly and soon became so large that the elders decided that the small chapel should be replaced with a much larger and more suitable structure in which to display the Shroud.

The congregation tithed and made special offerings so the Chapel of the Shroud would be a spectacular place in which to display the sacred relic.

Soon, a special group within the congregation was elected to tend, care for, and protect the Shroud from all who might try to steal or damage it. Only those who had demonstrated holy and virtuous behavior for their entire lives were elected to this elite group. This assignment elevated their standing and placed them among the most respected citizens of the community.

These men became known as the Holy Order of Defenders of the Shroud. A cult emerged who gradually shifted their devotion from Christ to the Shroud, and gave to it the reverence that formerly had been directed toward Jesus. The church built to house the Shroud became the center of activity of this cult in Jerusalem.

There is no telling where this might have gone but, in the year 614 AD, a historical event occurred that would change everything forever.

In this year, the Persians attacked the Christians in Jerusalem. Stories of the rape of Jerusalem abound with terrible atrocities. When the carnage was over, surviving Christians were taken by their conquerors into Persia.

The surviving members of the Holy Order of Defenders of the Shroud mingled with the other Christians taken captive by the Persians and the Shroud was hidden among the scant possessions that they carried with them to Byzantium.

Byzantium was a paradox. While the Persian soldiers had been vicious and vengeful in the attack on Jerusalem, the Persian leaders of this city were extraordinarily more tolerant of religious diversity than most contemporary governments. They began the system in which each religious group was permitted to govern itself in family and religious matters.

This system was continued for a long time, even under the Turks.

It was in this permissive environment that Christianity gradually recovered, gained converts, and eventually flourished. There were obscure periods in the early centuries after Christ's death in which the Shroud disappeared. Undoubtedly, it had to be concealed from time to time. Certainly, it would have been hidden during the period in which millions of Christians were killed in the arenas from Rome to Corinth. There were also periods when it had to be protected from destruction by the Romans, Medea, Persians, and Parthians who pillaged and destroyed Christian churches everywhere. It is not a great mystery that there are inconsistencies in the dates of various events regarding the Shroud. During the periods when it was hidden, no records were kept of its whereabouts so much of the story of the Shroud must be classified as legend.

CHAPTER THREE

By the year 1074 AD, the Saracens had overrun much of Christian Greece, devastating everything in their path, and were threatening Constantinople. They were tyrannically governing all of the conquered lands. Christians were being slain by the thousands.

The Byzantine emperor, Alexis Commenus, sent letters and his ambassador to the West asking for military aid to combat the Turks in Asia Minor.

While the Emperor's request was relatively modest, it fired a more grandiose plan in Pope Urban's mind. He called a church council for November 1095 at Clermont in southern France and announced that he planned to close the council meeting with an important speech.

Urban was an eloquent and captivating speaker. He called for all to embark on a great crusade and indicated that rich and poor alike should do their duty. He charged that poverty should be no excuse for shirking one's duty. He directed this remark, not at the serfs and peasants, but at some of the knights who were not wealthy, and in some cases, literally, penniless. He could not have dreamed that his speech would stir the poorest of the Medieval peasantry to leave their fields and embark on a Crusade of their own.

Pope Urban's speech resonated through the next half millennium.

The peasants and commoners did not delay. A large well-disciplined army cannot be organized and equipped overnight for such a huge undertaking, but this did not deter the peasants. They started out armed only with pitchforks, scythes, woodsmen's axes, and pointed sticks, to walk, in sandals and even barefoot, all the way to the Holy Land, freeing Christians along the way from the yoke of the infidel.

One of the most influential leaders of the peasants was a hermit called, appropriately, Peter the Hermit. Peter was a firebrand who roused thousands to his cause. From Flanders his ragtag band marched up the Rhine River valley, gathering strength. They were joined by other preachers with their recruits. By the time he reached Cologne, there were 15,000 peasant Crusaders. A number of poor knights like Walter the Penniless joined his band at Cologne. These knights added a much needed, though inadequate, military skill to the endeavor.

Poorly provisioned, the People's Crusade was forced to forage and live off the land.

The largest force in the peasants' army was lead by Peter and Walter, and this army entered Byzantine territory in the summer of 1096. It was not at all what the emperor, Alexis Commends, had envisioned. Alarmed by reports of looting and pitched battles, Alexis sent an army to escort the Crusaders into the Byzantine capital. Along the way, disagreements escalated to conflict and by the time he reached Constantinople, Peter had lost a quarter of his army.

Peter tried in vain to gain the backing of Alexis for a march on Jerusalem. In an abortive attempt to capture the city of Xerigordon, Peter's main army was ambushed by the Turks. Most of the Crusaders were killed. Many more were enslaved, and only about 3,000 out of a force of 20,000 managed to escape.

Thus ended the so-called People's Crusade.

The *real* Crusader army had not yet arrived. They were still getting organized back in Western Europe.

Alexis Commenus wanted warriors, but, naturally, he wanted to control them himself. Further, he wanted to employ them in pursuit of his *own* goals, not *theirs*.

For Alexis, the arrival of the People's Crusade had been unfortunate and embarrassing enough, but the arrival of the *real* Crusaders also did little to impress the emperor.

When they arrived, the *real* Crusaders were demanding, loud, unruly, and unconscionably rude. They argued with Byzantine merchants and got into fights with the local citizens . . . *and* they were very well armed, a point that could not be easily ignored.

Alexis needed them, but experienced great difficulty controlling them without arousing their anger. He had to walk a very fine line.

Despite the shakiness of the alliance, the campaign to capture Jerusalem continued. The siege started on June 7, 1099 and lasted for more than a month.

What followed when the Crusaders finally breached the walls was an orgy of murder. The Crusaders fired by stories of the rape of Jerusalem by the Arabs in 614AD spared no one, regardless of age, sex, or religion. The killing went on all that night, through the next day, and into the following night. Order was finally restored the next day.

When the slaughter was over, all Muslims and Jews had either been killed or driven out of the city. The Crusaders had liberated Jerusalem, but the streets ran with blood and the entire city had become an empty carcass.

The Muslims would never forget the sacking of Jerusalem. This was the crowning event in a string of incidents that convinced the Arabs that the European Christians were ferocious barbarians. Any Arab leader seeking to rally his people against the Christians had only to remind them of Jerusalem.

This was only the first Crusade. Hatred smouldered on both sides. In the next four to five hundred years there would be many more Crusades, eight of them major, some ending in total disaster.

Despite the virtuous goals of the Crusades, they often degenerated into unconscionable pillaging and looting.

The Crusaders poured into the eastern Mediterranean regions in waves, and the Crusades lasted for several hundred years. There were good and bad times for those in whose keeping the Shroud had been placed. At times it was openly displayed and venerated. At times it had to be hidden away to protect it from the Saracens. It eventually took its place in the basilica in Constantinople that had been specifically constructed to house it.

In 1203AD, a French Crusader, Robert De Clari, wrote of seeing the Shroud in the basilica of Saint Mary of the

Blachernae in Constantinople. This is believed to be the earliest known *written* mention of the Shroud by an eyewitness.

Unfortunately, some Crusaders lost sight of their lofty objectives and at times the Shroud had to be hidden from marauding Christian Crusaders as well.

The Knights Templar were prominent in the Fourth Crusade, participating in the looting of Constantinople. In the weeks preceding capture by the Crusaders of the Arab held portions of the city, Templars had been unwelcome guests, roaming the city. They were certainly aware of the great prize, the Shroud, that had been seen by Robert de Clari and doubtless many others, especially the leaders of the Templars.

According to legend, the holy linen Shroud was seized by the Templars and taken to Athens.

The significance of the Shroud, to medieval people, cannot be overstated. The Christians of that period would have considered a blood relic of Jesus to contain the essence of His soul. Many relics purporting to contain a droplet of the blood of Christ were said to have great, even unlimited, healing power. To *see* one of these relics was to have direct knowledge of God. Veneration of the bleeding Divine Heart of Jesus led to a cult within the Roman Catholic Church that survives to this day.

The churches of Europe are full of relics. It is claimed, by some, that if all of the relics purported to be pieces of the "True Cross" were collected in one spot, they would weigh many tons. Blood relics of Christ similarly abound. Most are in icons containing no more than a tiny droplet of His blood. Nevertheless, droplets add up and soon amount to buckets full.

However, If one truly believes the story of the loaves and fishes, is it that much of a stretch to believe that the True Cross could yield enough fragments or that Christ's body could yield enough droplets of His sacred blood to go around?

THE SHROUD

One of the unfathomable questions is, how could a blood relic as sacred as the Shroud of the Lord Jesus Christ disappear for long periods of time only to emerge in another place and another time with no record of the miracles that surely would have been attributed to it in the interim? It was, obviously, hidden away for protection from time to time but the fact that there were periods in which no miracles were attributable to it is one of the abiding mysteries of the Shroud.

It has been conjectured that the Shroud benefitted only those having clean hearts and did nothing for those who would attempt to profit from its possession or use.

The Shroud somehow found its way from Constantinople to Athens and hence to Lirey, France. There is no record of how it got there. It may have happened like this.

There was no honor among the thieves of the Crusades. Réymonde de Sugét, a Knight Templar, was taken with a serious and prolonged illness. He had made his way to Athens and was preparing to return to his home in France. Réymonde had a plan to steal the Shroud and use its miraculous powers to heal his affliction.

He brought a skin full of wine to the place where the Shroud had been hidden away. After a bout of drinking with the Templars who were guarding the Shroud (during which Réymonde filled *their* cups several times to his one) the guardians fell into drunken stupors. Hoping for a cure of his debilitating illness, he folded the Shroud carefully, packed it among his things, and departed.

It was many hours before the wine wore off and by that time Réymonde had such a head start that it was impossible for the enraged Templars to catch him. Nevertheless, Réymonde did not tarry, rising early and traveling well into the following night before stopping, primarily to give his horse a rest. He continued this pattern of flight all the way home to Lirey in France.

It was an exhausting trip and the fear that he might be caught weighed heavily on him. Upon arrival back at his castle, he told no one of his prize but, rather, hid it away among his little-used possessions in the cellars beneath the castle.

He went straight to his bed where he developed a high fever and became violently ill. He cried out about his tormentors who were pursuing him but his family and priest could not make any sense of his ravings. Soon, he slipped into a coma and succumbed during his third night at home.

His possession of the Shroud certainly did nothing to cure the illness of Réymonde de Sugét.

———————————

CHAPTER FOUR

Returning Crusader, Knight Templar, Réymonde de Sugét was laid to rest in the family mausoleum. His prize lay unnoticed among his moldy possessions in the dark cellar of Château Sugét for nearly 50 years before it was rediscovered. The Shroud came into the hands of the de Charney family who owned the church at Lirey and who had close ties to the Templars. It was taken to the basilica in Lirey by Geoffery de Charney where it was believed to be an authentic relic.

Three separate papal bulls recite the fact that Geoffrey de Charny placed the Shroud of Our Lord Jesus Christ, bearing the effigy of our Savior, in the church of Lirey. Clearly, the Shroud was in the church at Lirey before Geoffrey died in September 1356 because on May 28, 1356, Henri de Poitiers, Bishop of Troyes, sent Geoffrey a letter of approval regarding the ceremony of dedication that took place earlier that year.

While the Shroud was not publicly displayed, word spread throughout the countryside that the sacred linen resided in the reliquary. The presence in the basilica of such a sacred relic drew large crowds of the faithful who paraded past the reliquary. The mere presence of the Shroud is said to have brought about many miraculous healings but the Vatican was skeptical about the reports of miracles.

While the term "psychosomatic" would not be defined for another thousand years or so, the officials of the Church knew well that many illnesses were imagined and that any charlatan could talk a receptive patient out of an imagined illness. It happened all the time and, if there were no charlatans around, the psychosomatically ill would often cure themselves in the presence of a "healing power" like the Shroud.

In 1357AD, the first known public exposition of the Shroud occurred. When shown to the public, It was held full length by the Canons of Lirey. Many who viewed it were awestruck by the image and prostrated themselves before it. Again miraculous healings were reported.

Of course, the Church was quick enough to take credit for a miracle if it had happened during some officially sanctioned event. However, the deposition of the Shroud in the reliquary and its subsequent display did not have the full seal of approval of the Vatican, even though the three papal bulls had attested to its presence there.

A letter from Bishop of Troyes, Pierre d'Arcis, to Pope Clement VII, written in 1389, complained about a scandal uncovered in his diocese at the church of Lirey, France. According to the bishop, the church canons had " . . . falsely and deceitfully, being consumed with the passion of avarice and not from any motive of devotion but only of gain, procured for their church a certain cloth, cunningly painted, upon which by clever sleight of hand was depicted the twofold image of one man, that is to say the back and front, then falsely declaring and pretending that this was the actual Shroud in which our Savior Jesus Christ was enfolded in the tomb."

In his letter Bishop Pierre d'Arcis stated that, evidently, the cloth had first been exhibited at Lirey some thirty years early by Bishop Henri de Poitiers. But, according to Pierre, Poitiers eventually discovered the fraud. He revealed the fact that the linen had been cunningly painted. An Inquisition had been convened to question the artist who purportedly painted it. He confessed to the Inquisitors that it was a work of human skill and not miraculously wrought or bestowed.

Nothing is known of the fate of the artist confessor but one can surmise that, at the very least, his hands were in no condition to perpetrate such mischief again.

———————————————

CHAPTER FIVE

After the exhibition in Lirey, little is recorded about the Shroud for nearly a hundred years. Presumably, Geoffery de Charney did not *give* the Shroud to the church in Lirey but rather, *loaned* it to them for display there. At some point in time, perhaps right after the accusing letter of Bishop Pierre d'Arcis, the Shroud appears to have been recovered from the church by the de Charney family. Geoffrey's granddaughter, Margaret de Charney inherited it. Margaret and her husband, Humbert de Villersexel, kept the Shroud at Hippolyte sur Doubs. In her later years, Margaret took the Shroud to Liege, Belgium where it was exhibited to large crowds. Surprisingly, there were no reports of miracles in Liege.

In 1453 Duchess Margaret de Charney, a childless widow having no direct descendant to leave it to, ceded the Shroud to a relative, Duke Louis of Savoy.

Roughly 50 years later, in 1502, The Shroud was deposited in the chapel of Chambréy Castle. A beautifully embossed silver box was fabricated for the storage and preservation of the Shroud and it was neatly folded in forty-two layers and placed in the container.

In 1532, a fire in the Castle of Chambréy damaged the Shroud. The Shroud was stored, folded, in the silver box. The fire was so intense that it actually melted one corner of the box and, because of the way the Shroud was folded, caused two long scorch marks that ran essentially the full length of the Shroud. There are patches in several spots where the Shroud was burned through. The Shroud was handled so carefully after the fire that it would have been difficult to obtain a piece of it unless the trusted person chosen to reweave it snipped out an unburned piece and wove a patch there to conceal the removal.

Here, Godfrey Du Luc, a devout Christian, had an opportunity to purloin a sample of his Savior's own blood. What power he must have believed that tiny scrap of blood stained linen to possess! The most skilled weaver in the nearby city of Troyes, Godfrey was commissioned to repair the Shroud.

There was, in Troyes, a sneakthief named André, whose last name is lost in the cobwebs of antiquity. André hoped to steal the Shroud and obtain a large ransom for it. He thought that his best chance to steal it was while it was in the possession of Godfrey the weaver but found that Godfrey guarded the Shroud very carefully.

While André was spying on Godfrey, watching for a chance to steal it, he saw him remove the snippet and reweave the spot with linen thread. André, giving up on the idea of stealing the Shroud, informed on Godfrey, hoping for a reward. He got no reward, but Godfrey was accused by the Church of removing a small piece of the original fabric and concealing his theft by weaving a repair over the hole.

Godfrey was subjected to an Inquisition.

An Inquisition is *supposed* to be convened to arrive at the truth but this one was not. It was designed to force the defendant appearing before it to confess to whatever charges the Inquisitors had brought against him. Desecration of a holy relic was a most serious charge.

Godfrey's eyes were burned out with hot irons. His fingers were chopped off, and he was stretched on the rack, slowly, painfully, and when he asked for water was given vinegar. He fainted when the joints of his arms and legs were pulled apart. They poured buckets of water on him to bring him around. He cried out in agony as his arms were eventually pulled from their sockets. Mercifully, he passed out and never again regained consciousness.

Godfrey died on the rack but he had so much faith that he and his family would receive salvation through that sample of the Savior's blood that he preferred death on the rack rather than reveal the location of the snippet of linen to the Inquisitors.

In notes to his family, written before his seizure by the Inquisitors, Godfrey gave cryptic clues as to the whereabouts of the scrap of linen but his immediate family was in mortal fear of the Inquisitors. They should have burned his notes but, inexplicably, hid them and made no attempts to find the relic.

The scrap of linen would remain hidden for nearly three hundred years. A distant cousin, of Godfrey, Francis Halpern, who dabbled in codes, found a note scribbled by Godfrey which contained a veiled reference to its location and Francis deciphered it. He recovered the snippet but, being unsure of his rights in the matter, put it in a safe place and waited. He died and the snippet passed from generation to generation but remained safely and secretly hidden away along with a copy of the decoded message left by Godfrey which conveyed the significance of the snippet.

Meanwhile, word spread about the miraculous healings associated with the Shroud and on May 4, 1535, it was exhibited in Turin. The sick, the demented, and the lame came from all over the surrounding countryside and once again there were reports of miraculous cures . . . not everyone, but then not everyone has *ever* been miraculously cured.

The Vatican, doubting the authenticity of the Shroud, was suspicious of the alleged miracles and made the local clerics put the cloth back into the reliquary with instructions to *keep* it there.

The following year, 1536, the Vatican yielded to public pressure and once again permitted the Shroud to be put on display, this time in Milan. The streets of Milan were filled with the faithful pressing forward for a look at the image of their Holy Savior and once again, miraculous cures were attributed to the Shroud.

On September 14, 1578, the Shroud was moved by Louis de Savoy to its permanent home in the Cathedral of John the Baptist in Turin but ownership remained with the House of Savoy.

The Shroud was handed down through Louis' descendants to Umberto of Savoy who willed it to the Vatican, the transfer of ownership occurring in 1983 after

Umberto died. Amazingly, ownership had been in private hands up until that time. With this change of ownership, the Shroud began to lose, with great rapidity, its fraudulent reputation.

———————————————

-20-

CHAPTER SIX

On May 28, 1898, Secundo Pia, an Italian lawyer, a photographic buff, and prize-winning amateur photographer asked for and was grudgingly given permission, by King Umberto I, to photograph the Shroud.

The equipment that he used was similar to the equipment used by Matthew Brady to make his remarkable photographs of the American Civil War. In this camera, a glass plate coated with a light-sensitive substance was exposed and then developed. The plates were capable of very high resolution but usually required a long time exposure or a flash obtained by igniting flash powder (essentially the same material used in firecrackers) in a long tray often held in the hand of the photographer, at great risk to himself.

Secundo Pia did not use a flash but, rather, took two very long exposures, late in the day and it was nearly midnight when Pia got back to his apartment and developed the plates. Pia's plates were the equivalent of the negatives of black and white photographs today. On a negative, portions of the picture that will appear dark in the printed positive are light on the negative and vice versa.

When Pia developed his plates of the Shroud, he got a surprise. Instead of a *negative* image, what he saw was what he would have *expected* to see on a positive print, not on a negative. The bloodstains, on the other hand, were not part of the *image* per se. The blood came out as one might expect. On the Shroud, the bloodstains were very dark and on Pia's plates, the stains came out white.

Pia concluded that, the bloodstains aside, the *image* on the Shroud was a *negative* image.

How could that be?

Surely, no artist, hundreds of years before the principles of photography were understood, could have imagined how to paint a negative image to be revealed centuries later by photography.

THE SHROUD

One of the triggers of the debate was a device known as a *camera obscura.*

This is a simple device that was probably discovered quite by accident at some very early date. *Camera obscura* literally means, in Latin, *dark room.* In its simplest form, it consists of a dark room with a tiny hole in one wall. It was a very large version of the pinhole camera that was popularized in the early 1900s. In the pinhole camera, light from a distant object passed through the pinhole and was projected onto a sheet of photographic film. A tiny aperture behaves like a fixed focal length lens. The smaller the aperture, the greater the depth of field but the dimmer the image and, in the case of the pinhole cameras, the longer the exposure required to activate the photosensitive chemicals on the film.

In a *camera obscura* there was, of course, no film. The image was projected onto a white wall opposite the aperture.

The image on the wall was in full color and had spatial perspective, something that artists of the early medieval periods knew nothing about.

Unfortunately, the image on the wall was upside down. It is also upside down in a film camera but all we have to do to make *that* right is to rotate the finished picture 180 degrees. A person inside an early *camera obscura* would have to stand on his head to achieve the same result.

Eventually, experimenters learned to use a system of mirrors to turn the image right side up. When lenses were invented, experimenters found that the aperture could be greatly enlarged permitting a much brighter image but a lens was needed to focus the image sharply. In some *camera obscuras,* the aperture, lens and mirror are mounted in a small cupola atop the dark room. This permits the image to be projected downward onto a white tabletop permitting viewers to stand around the table and look down on the image. Artists, particularly, Vermeer made extensive use of the *camera obscura.* They stretched their canvasses on the wall or table top, projected the images onto them, and then painted right over the projected images in the colors of the actual subjects. It was in a sense, a "paint by numbers" operation but for the time the results were sensational and Vermeer is ranked as one of the greatest painters of his or any other time.

Such devices could be found in many European cities in the late 1800s. A *camera obscura* was usually situated in a location having a good view of the city or its harbor and was large enough to accommodate a number of tourists at one time. The public was therefore familiar with them but these devices were far superior to anything available in medieval times. The modern *camera obscura* had a bright image because its wide aperture and lens permitted the collection of large amounts of light that could be focused to produce a sharp image as well. The modern *camera obscura* also had a mirror system to turn the image right side up.

People tended to assume that the *camera obscura* of *their* experience was the kind being discussed in scientific circles.

Not so.

It is conceivable that a medieval artist of great skill chanced upon a primitive *camera obscura*. Perhaps, he was in a dark room that had a tiny hole in the wall, and noticed the dim inverted picture on the opposite wall. It is also conceivable that he might have obtained a cadaver and hung it up, feet up, thereby obtaining an upright image on the wall. (But then the hair would have been pointing the wrong way, wouldn't it?)

It is even conceivable that he worked out a means for moving the cadaver forward and backward in order to obtain a full scale image on the wall and, like his counterparts many centuries later, stretched his canvas, or in this case a linen shroud, on the wall and started painting.

At this point, the argument falls completely apart. The image projected on the linen would be a color positive. How could an artist transform this into a *monochrome negative* painted image? And why? If it was his intention to perpetrate a fraud, couldn't he just as well have done it with a fake positive image . . . and a lot easier? If we accept the premise that this was a painted image we must also accept the fact that the painter anticipated by a thousand years the invention of photography and our ability to finally see what his subject really looked like.

Those who considered the image to be a fake, changed direction and postulated, not a painter, but a primitive photographer, an alchemist who somehow knew a millennium ahead of the invention of the photographic camera that certain chemicals changed when subjected to light and that these changes could be frozen by the application of other chemicals leaving a permanent record of the recorded light patterns. To these skeptics, it was simple. Someone coated the linen with a light sensitive chemical. The image was projected onto the linen. Other chemicals were then applied to it to develop and fix the image to make it permanent. In their view, the image on the Shroud is truly a photographic negative . . . and that explains everything.

Attributing this remarkable finding to the application of some unknown photographic technique in medieval or earlier times seems to be out of the question, but surely scientific tests might be conducted on the Shroud to detect the chemical residue which defined the image. It would be nearly eighty years before such tests could be made.

Scientific curiosity was piqued at that time and ever since. Arguments, pro and con, raged for roughly forty years. Then Gieuseppe Enria obtained permission to photograph the Shroud with a much more modern camera than the one employed by Secundo Pia in 1898. Enria photographed the shroud in May of 1931 using very fine grain film. His photographs confirmed Pia's earlier findings and were of exceptionally high quality. Enria's photographs have been blown up to produce full size images of the Shroud that show remarkable detail. The Enria photographs settled nothing but yielded enticing details that only served to further stoke the fires of debate.

Meanwhile, the drums of war were beating in Europe and the attention of the world turned to more serious matters. When World War II broke out in earnest, the Shroud was removed from the Cathedral of John the Baptist, the only time this was done since it was deposited there in 1578, and stored in a safe place until the end of the war. Europe's recovery from the war's devastation and the Cold War had the full attention of many scientists. The Shroud of Turin was not high on anyone's agenda.

CHAPTER SEVEN

Natalie Goodenough, a teenager, watched a pair of cardinals building a nest in a rose bush outside her bedroom window. The nest the cardinals were building was distinctly different from the oriole nest in her back yard.

At first, this did not set off any bells. All of the homes on her block were quite dissimilar. Why should it be any different for the birds? Eventually, however, she noticed that the nests of other cardinals in her neighborhood were identical to the nest of *her* cardinals and the nests of other orioles were identical to the nest of *her* orioles. Why?

She watched as the bulging eyes and ravenous mouths attached to fat little bellies developed into recognizable little birds which were quickly pushed out of the nest and on their own in just a matter of days.

The nest had been built before the eggs were laid. There was no training period . . . no time when the mother or father bird said, "Collect bits of string and twigs of this size and weave them together, just so, to build a nest so distinctive that one would not hesitate to say, 'A cardinal lives here.'"

And it was the same with the orioles. Their unique nests would never be mistaken for cardinal's nests.

"How do they know?"

In her childlike innocence, she concluded that when the time came to build their first nest, God would show them how to do it.

When she was older and began to learn about heredity and genes, her ideas began to mature. She marveled at the variety of color in the plumage of the various species of birds and their distinctive song patterns. Why did cardinals always look and sing like cardinals? These were obviously characteristics that they had inherited from their parents, but how?

Then it struck her and the ideas came gushing forth, the astounding amount of information conveyed in the genes . .

. the entire blueprint for how, from a single fertilized egg cell, the stem cells must divide and differentiate to become bones and claws and feathers and eyes and arteries and blood and a beating heart to pump it through the body and a reproductive system to start it all over again . . . and this blueprint was not for a generic bird but for a specific kind of bird . . . like her cardinal.

The enormity of the amount of information needed to do this overwhelmed her and Natalie sank into her favorite soft chair beside her bed, her head spinning. It was like the entire universe had suddenly revealed itself to her in all its glory. It was just too much to absorb all at once.

And the nests?

Why not?

If a single fertilized egg contained enough information to do all of that, why not the instructions for building a nest, a distinctively *cardinal* kind of nest? What other information might the fertilized egg carry?

Natalie wondered if anyone else knew what she had just discovered. It was like a revelation from God and the excitement of the event kept her awake for most of the night. She was not the only one who knew, of course, but, for now, it was *her* secret.

When she went out the following morning, her whole world had changed. She was acutely aware of the essential characteristics of every plant and animal that came into her view.

She saw large lumbering dogs and tiny nervous prissy little dogs but they all had a characteristic that she coined a term to describe. She called it, "dog-ness." Cats regardless of size, shape or color all had the essence of "cat-ness" and trees, despite their many differences, all had the essence of "tree-ness."

Natalie ran about the neighborhood mentally cataloging everything she saw. She was confused at first by the houses in her neighborhood that all had the essence of "house-ness" and by the "car-ness" of cars but soon realized that these things had been designed and manufactured by man, whereas living things had been, in a sense, designed and manufactured by God.

Natalie had been exposed, in Sunday School, to the concept of a soul. On this day, she wondered if all of God's creatures, the birds, the dogs, or, for that matter, the trees, had souls.

Natalie had no way of knowing it at that moment, but the revelations of the past 24 hours, her brief theological meditation, and the flood of questions they raised would profoundly change her life and propel her unerringly toward her lifetime career . . . and it would become more than just a job, . . . it would become a passion.

In high school, Natalie was a straight-A High-Honor-Roll student. She was accepted into the National Honor Society and was active in many extra curricular intellectual endeavors. She played first violin in the school orchestra, was in the drama club, won first prize in a national poetry contest, was state spelling champion and, in fact, excelled in anything she put her mind to.

On the tennis court she was a formidable adversary for anyone, male or female.

She also had a soft natural beauty that made her stand out in any crowd. Everyone noticed her, The girls envied her, and the boys . . . well, they did what boys do when fantasizing about such a gorgeous face and figure.

Natalie was blissfully unaware of her beauty, but she was getting stirrings inside about some of the handsome boys in her class.

She was comfortable in groups and fun to talk to but, in a one-on-one situation with a boy, things usually did not go well at all. She dated occasionally but her dates were so awestruck by her intimidating combination of brains, beauty, and athletic ability that they rarely asked her out on a second date. By the time she was graduated from high school, only two boys had even tried to kiss her.

High school was not all that Natalie had hoped that it might be but it established good study habits and laid a solid foundation for the important events to come.

With her outstanding grades and extracurricular record she was a shoo-in for any college she wanted to attend and when she chose The University of California, Berkeley, she was welcomed with open arms.

Those were turbulent times on college campuses everywhere . . . experimentation with drugs, and sex, political activism urged on by left wing professors, . . . demonstrations . . . even riots . . . and Berkeley was at the heart of it all. This was not a good environment for an innocent and naive beauty.

Natalie managed to stay clear of the drug scene but celebrated her 19th birthday with one too many beers at the campus pub and lost her virginity on the shag rug floor of a student's psychedelically decorated van. It was a very brief and most unpleasant experience and she had two anxious weeks afterward but was very relieved at the time for her menses. She did not expect to repeat the experience but, better safe than sorry, so she went on the pill.

College boys boast and word got around. For a while she was pursued by everyone in his fraternity. In that free-sex environment, girls who didn't do it on the first date never got a chance for a second and interest in her soon waned.

She did have an occasional date but they usually ended in one minute of sex. College boys treated it like a race which *they* inevitably won. This did nothing to make her want more, so whatever interest she might have had in sex went on the back burner and her studies dominated her days and nights.

The college experience, like high school, was not all that she had hoped for but on the plus side it helped keep her focused on her goals.

Both of Natalie's parents were killed in a tragic automobile accident in her senior year and she had no other living relatives so there was no one to watch her receive her baccalaureate degree.

CHAPTER EIGHT

In June of 1969, The Shroud was shown to members of a special Scientific Commission but the brief study raised more questions than it answered. Despite the distraction of the Viet Nam War and the Cold War, not all scientists lost interest in the Shroud.

In November 1973, The Shroud was exhibited for television and the press in Turin. The press was consistently skeptical and gave short shrift to the story. It made the front pages only in Turin and Rome. The rest of the world relegated the story to "Page 8 ". It simply was not news. Italian television gave it full coverage. After all it was a local story. However, in the United States, CBS, ABC, and NBC were preoccupied with the Viet Nam War. European television scanning standards were different from the NTSC standard used in the US and this gave the networks all the excuse they needed to essentially ignore the event.

At the time of this exhibition, Dr. Max Frei, a prominent Swiss botanist and criminologist, used sticky tape to sample surface particles for analysis. Today, Dr. Frei would probably be called a forensic scientist. As a botanist he was particularly interested in the pollens recovered from the Shroud on his sticky tape. He identified pollen from 25 flowers indigenous to Jerusalem or within a radius of twelve miles from Jerusalem. Investigation proved that all of these flowers bloom in the March-April time frame suggesting the interment took place in the Spring. This is consistent with the time of the crucifixion. He further identified pollens from the area around Constantinople suggesting that the Shroud had been in that area at some time as well.

Work eventually got under way in the scientific community, under the watchful eye of the Vatican, to organize and conduct a thorough study of the Shroud. The Vatican sanctioned the study, approved the test protocol, and in 1978 this mysterious strip of linen was subjected to the most exhaustive set of tests ever applied to a single archeological artifact.

Before the 1978 tests were conducted, there was a public exhibition of the Shroud in Turin. The streets around the cathedral in Turin were jammed with the faithful waiting to see the Shroud. To protect it from vandalism, the Shroud was displayed behind a polycarbonate bulletproof frame mounted above the main alter of the cathedral.

A wooden platform was constructed about fifteen feet in front of the Shroud. Groups of thirty people at a time were ushered up onto the platform and they were given roughly fifteen seconds in which to view it. The fifteen-foot distance was chosen because details can be seen at this distance that cannot be seen close up. Anatomical features cannot be distinguished at all when the viewer is within arms length of the Shroud.

One of the scientists there for the tests quipped that if an artist had faked the image, he would have required fifteen foot long paint brushes in order to see what he was painting.

Eventually, the public exhibition ended and the tests got under way. Meanwhile, sticky tape samples were taken at various points around the cathedral in order to get background data on the contaminants that might have deposited on the Shroud during its long stay in this locale.

The Shroud was separated from the red and blue silk wrapping cloth and mounted on a plywood frame. It was carefully vacuumed to collect whatever minute materials as had been deposited on it during its existence. This collection yielded fragments of bugs, dust and dirt, pollens, bits of silk thread, some flecks of both blood and paint and other minutia.

It was photographed full size and, in whole and in part, at many different distances, micrographed, and X-rayed. More than 50,000 photographs were made.

With some difficulty, the picture negatives were developed in a lab set up in the cathedral for that purpose to avert any damage that might occur to the latent images during transport back to the United States.

Samples were lifted using a special sticky tape developed by 3-M to remove samples without damaging the Shroud and without leaving any residue. These were placed in hermetically sealed containers for later analysis.

Samples were also lifted from the Holland cloth that backed the Shroud and it was separated from this cloth in order to see the back side of the linen for the first time in 400 years.

The Vatican agreed in advance that a sample could be taken for Carbon-14 dating. It is not clear what authority the Vatican had to do this. While it was generally assumed that the Church owned it, the Shroud was still privately owned by the House of Savoy.

A group of carbon-dating experts, textile experts, chemists, and other specialists examined the Shroud and identified several locations from which samples of the linen might be taken to obtain a good statistical representation.

They all agreed that no sample should be taken from the lower right-hand corner because it was obvious that someone, in the remote past, had removed a snippet from this location and the area had been rewoven. They felt that samples might be taken from spots beneath patches that had been sewn over previously damaged areas. The experts also agreed that samples should be taken from the Holland backing cloth because the dating of that fabric was known. However, no samples were cut from the linen during these 1978 tests.

At the time, the carbon-dating experts were confident that a first century date would be found. Their confidence stemmed from the consensus of the archeological textile experts that the linen was woven using a method that was commonplace in the Middle East in the first century AD but virtually unknown in Europe.

CHAPTER NINE

1978 was also an important year for someone else. Natalie Goodenough obtained her doctorate in Biological Science, *magna cum laude*. She obtained a research grant and immediately dove into a study of genetics. Fruit flies were her subjects. They have a very short life cycle and many generations of flies occur in just a few short months giving her time to view the effects of her experiments on multiple generations.

She experimented with the alteration of certain gene sites in the DNA to produce abnormal physical appearance in the flies and then observes the transfer of these aberrant characteristics to offspring and the inheritance of these characteristics in subsequent generations.

She did not know what specific effect the gene manipulation might have but it did not matter. For her purpose, it was only necessary that the aberration be visible and obvious. In her experiment, the aberration met both of these criteria. The fruit flies were born with a seventh leg at the site where there should have been a wing. Subsequent generations of the flies all had the seventh leg.

Natalie was excited about the success of this first part of the study and was anxious to get on with the second, and in her view, the most important part. She replaced the gene producing the defect with a normal gene to correct the defect. There were problems with the cultures and the first six attempts failed but the seventh try worked perfectly. The result was an apparently normal fruit fly and the progeny appeared to be normal as well. Natalie finished her report, wrote the mandatory paper for publication, not that what she had accomplished was any big deal but she had gotten her feet wet on a research project with a successful outcome.

It was just a stepping stone. However, it made her next grant easier to obtain. She had much more ambitious goals this time. She hoped to successfully clone a fruit fly. The fruit fly experimentation was a necessary nuisance en route to her real objective, the cloning of a mammal. The cloning of the fruit fly was unsuccessful but she realized, toward the end, what she had done wrong and planned to correct it the next try. Her grant was running out so she tidied up and wrote a second paper that ended with a summary of the necessary steps to successfully clone a fruit fly (or any organism for that matter). Natalie's paper established the protocol for cloning.

That was important to her.

It was important to someone else, too. Even though her papers were published in an obscure scientific journal they came to the attention of Richard Halpern, a direct descendant of Francis Halpern who had decoded the cryptic messages of the weaver Godfrey Du Luc and found the snippet from the Shroud.

It was quite by accident. Halpern was one of those individuals with an insatiable thirst for knowledge . . . knowledge about anything and everything.

He was browsing in a library regarding one of his favorite pastimes, genealogy. He had worked for several years on his family tree and was fascinated by the many branches that he had uncovered. On one limb of the tree, he found the name Natalie Goodenough. He was surprised that while many such explorations led to dead ends, this was an unusual name and he found more information on Natalie in "Who's Who."

This led to her papers.

Gene research? Certainly, that was a field of science bearing indirectly on his genealogical research. It piqued his interest, especially with regard to the small snippet of linen stashed away in his safe deposit box.

He couldn't believe his luck. He had found a distant relative who did genetic research. He found her address and wrote her a long letter introducing himself, explaining his interest in her, and relating as much as he knew about the Shroud and the snippet of blood stained linen that had been passed down to him.

She replied, expressing her interest and suggesting that they meet somewhere, but where?

They were separated by the Atlantic Ocean.

That turned out to be no obstacle. Richard Halpern was coming to New York on business and had some time to spare. Natalie cleared time on her busy calendar and a meeting was arranged. They met for lunch at a midtown New York restaurant.

They instantly clicked and after about an hour of conversation, Richard had made up his mind. He had no idea what she might do with it but was certain that he had found the right person to entrust with his prize. He reached into his coat pocket and removed the flat jewelry case that contained the precious piece of linen.

Natalie could not explain the feeling she had when he handed the case to her, something she had never experienced before, an electric, almost orgasmic surge of excitement.

At that instant her future crystallized. There was no doubt in her mind. It would be the biggest challenge that she or anyone would ever face.

Suppose the Shroud of Turin really was the Shroud of Christ.

Suppose she was able to extract a viable DNA sample from this snippet.

Suppose sufficient progress would be made to seriously entertain the prospect of cloning a human being.

Suppose she could clone . . . she dared not even think it.

Wow!

Not since her awakening as a teenager to the mystery of the information carried in the genes had she felt like this. After the initial surge of excitement, she felt faint.

"Are you OK?"

"What?"

"Is anything wrong?"

"No, I'm fine. it's just that this is so... overwhelming."

Natalie's assistant in her fruit fly experiments was Sarah Buckley. Sarah was that "good right arm" that only comes along once in a lifetime. She was a graduate assistant, working on her Master's degree when first assigned to Dr. Goodenough. Sarah was a meticulous worker. She kept extensive and accurate notes on every aspect of Dr. Goodenough's work which became ever more deeply involved in the micro-mechanics of cloning technology.

They were breaking new ground with every experiment. There were no guidelines for anything. Working on the cutting edge of their profession, they had to make up the rules and establish the protocols as they went along. It was slow and tedious work but, for Natalie, the ultimate prize made it all worthwhile.

Natalie and Sarah were an extraordinary team, complementing each other in every possible way. Their relationship had started out with appropriate formality, *"Doctor"* Goodenough and *"Miss"* Buckley. Natalie was a basically friendly person under her businesslike persona and, when "Miss" Buckley began work on her Doctoral thesis, Natalie broke the ice and started calling her "Sarah" but Sarah did not reciprocate. In time Sarah received her Ph.D., *summa cum laude*.

"Look, Sarah, we are now *both* doctors. Don't you think it is time for you to call me Natalie?"

At that moment, what had been a strictly professional relationship turned into an enduring friendship, each considering the other more a sister than a colleague.

In all of the time they had worked together Natalie had never mentioned the snippet of blood stained linen that she had carefully hidden away in her safe deposit box. Nevertheless, Sarah developed a passion for this work nearly equal to that of Natalie. The deeper they got into it, the more there was to do and they both soon recognized the need for a research project of Herculean proportions, one which they would be unable to fund despite Dr. Goodenough's demonstrated fund raising competence in obtaining grants.

Human DNA is an extremely complex structure, the simplistic description of it as large molecule consisting of a double helix of protein made the idea of cloning *anything* a piece of cake in the minds of the press and most laymen but the genetic code turned out to be much more complex than even Natalie had ever imagined.

Just when they needed it most, assistance came from the most improbable of directions.

In 1986, the Department of Energy (DOE) undertook the Human Genome Initiative. This was the collective name for several projects begun by DOE to create an ordered set of DNA segments from known chromosomal locations, develop new computational methods for analyzing genetic map and DNA sequence data, and develop new techniques and instruments for detecting and analyzing DNA.

This DOE initiative is now known as the Human Genome Program. The national effort, led by DOE and The National Institute of Health (NIH) is known as the Human Genome Project.

The Human Genome Project had, what Dr. Goodenough considered to be, unlimited Federal funding. The DOE established a huge bureaucratic structure, established several laboratories, each to work on just one aspect of the problem but perhaps most importantly, provided each laboratory with several Cray supercomputers and allowed the laboratories to enlist the help of some of the best and brightest microbiologists in the world. However, in their zeal to grab up these experts and other specialists they filled their tables of organization too soon and overlooked many having skills equal to those of Natalie and Sarah.

Natalie and Sarah were taking a coffee break. Natalie stared into her coffee cup for a full minute before speaking.

"I find it very interesting that the human genome mapping project is funded by the U.S. Department of Energy. Does that seem strange to you? It does to me. What earthly interest could the Department of Energy have in genetics?"

Sarah thought about it and then replied, "I have been wanting to talk to you about this. I have heard unsubstantiated reports that within the inner sanctums of the government there is a group of statisticians who have been working on the productivity of human beings versus their energy demands. They are concerned that in our prime years we are heavy energy users . . . cars, other transportation, air conditioning and heating of expensive homes, refrigerators, freezers, electric ranges et cetera but this is more than offset by our productivity calculated from our contributions to the national economy, particularly through our taxes, and other factors. However, at some point in the aging process, not necessarily the same age for all individuals, a crossover occurs. Our energy demands may stay relatively constant or even decline but our societal contributions drop off even more. At that point in our lives, we are no longer *energy efficient* and we are becoming *less* so every day."

"I see," said Natalie. "Why should non-productive persons be permitted to waste energy that could be better put to other uses? Are they considering just terminating us when we reach that point? That is pretty cold, isn't it?"

"Well, these are statisticians. People are just numbers to them. They don't view us as human beings, just hard statistics."

"Do you believe that? Is your source reliable?"

"I think so, she is well placed in the DOE. According to her, the DOE has a specific agenda in funding the human genome mapping study. They want to find, among other things, the gene site that controls when our heart stops beating as a consequence of our aging."

Sarah continues, "In the future, the DOE plan is to control the fertilization of all eggs destined to develop into human beings at least in the US . . . and Uncle Sam obviously has a global interest as well."

"This is a DOE plan?"

"Yes, can you believe that? My source tells me that they already have, at least on paper, a Special Directorate of Eugenics, within DOE, to oversee this. Once their plan is in place, no longer will human conception take place 'the old-fashioned way'. They plan to fertilize each ovum in vitro and genetically engineer the DNA sequence in the ovum. Specifically, they intend to modify the gene site that controls the beating of the heart to cause the heart to stop when certain parameters are met . . . but these parameters will be correlated to correspond closely to the crossover of the energy use versus productivity curves."

Sarah paused for a moment then dropped a grenade, "If they pull this off, they can stop entertaining euthanasia as what was destined to be a very unpopular government program to accomplish the same end. Instead, it will all have been preordained at the moment of conception."

"How *neat,*" Natalie responded, with more than a small note of sarcasm, "Just talking off the top of my head, it appears to me the DOE has a very narrow perspective on this. They are only concerned with efficient use of energy . . . but other bureaucracies in and out of the government undoubtedly have their own agendas. For example, workers pay into health care plans but at some point they start taking out more than they are putting in and eventually reach a point where they are only taking out. I'll bet that health care and similar agencies are keeping a close watch on the DOE genome mapping project expecting to jump in at some point and modify the human DNA sequence to meet their *own* objectives. Social Security, for example. We pay in for many years, but just when we are ready to start taking out, bang, we get hit with the big one. Scary."

Sarah responds, "Think about this. Applicants might, at some time in the future, be required to submit blood samples for DNA analysis and be denied medical insurance altogether, or be granted limited insurance with the policies ruling out coverage for gene-specific illnesses."

"This is too big. I don't think the DOE has the political muscle to keep control of this once the mapping project is concluded."

"I agree," responds Sarah, "A bureaucratic fight is in the offing to see who will control our genetic destinies."

"I think so. My guess is that a cabinet post, Secretary of Genetics, may very well be in our future. That's pretty scary, but lets not look this gift horse in the mouth. Right now, we will need a lot of the DOE's findings for our own project."

When they got back to the office, Natalie invited Sarah in and closed the door.

Natalie had decided over coffee, to take Sarah into her full confidence, tell her about the snippet, and reveal the *real* objective of their research.

She laid it all out. The objective is to ultimately clone *not* just a mammal but a human being.

Then Natalie dropped *her* bomb. She went to her wall safe, opened it, and turned to Sarah with the jewelry case. It always excited her when she held this precious container. She fumbled with the catch and then opened it. Sarah stared for a moment and then appeared puzzled.

"Do you have any idea what this is?"

"No."

"This is a snippet from the Shroud of Turin. It is stained . . . stained with the blood of Jesus Christ."

"Oh, My God! . . . We are going to . . . ?"

"Yes."

Natalie snapped the case shut and placed it carefully back in the wall safe.

February, 1989 . . . The scientific world was buzzing with the reports of the exact duplicate sheep that had been cloned from DNA in Ireland. It had every characteristic of the donor even down to the freckles on its face and the unusual color and quality of its wool. As difficult as it was to believe, the new animal even responded to the pet name the lab workers had given the donor animal even though they had been separated since the original DNA sample had been obtained. The only discernable difference between the animals had been the growth rate of the new animal. It seemed to grow and age at a rate four times as fast as the donor. But even that difference faded as the animals approached the same physical capabilities. It was as if the new sheep somehow *knew* that it had caught up with the donor and now both could age and grow alike . . . like identical twins, which, in a sense, they were.

Both of these animals were destined for a life of ease and testing. The constant observations would continue and every minute variation in their behavior would be cause for a flurry of dissertations.

However, there was one thing that threw cold water on the general euphoria over the successful cloning. The clone developed an intense and unexpected animosity toward the donor sheep. There was no immediate explanation for this behavior and this was most disconcerting to all participants in the experiment.

Soon after the Irish success, there was a second sheep cloning in Scotland. This experiment also attracted world wide attention. It started out in a very similar manner with the clone developing at an accelerated rate. Like the Irish clone the Scottish clone also developed an intense and unexplained animosity toward the donor sheep.

There were, almost immediately, successful clonings of a chicken in Italy and a duck in France but these did not have the impact of the mammal experiments and were essentially ignored by the scientific community and the press.

Who *cared* about chickens and ducks. In the back of every reporters head was the thought that cloning a mammal was but a step away from cloning a specific species, a human.

Struck with the apparent early success of the two sheep clonings, other teams in Sweden and Germany pushed forward with their plans to clone various other mammals. The clonings were successful. The Swedes cloned a pig and the Germans cloned a dog.

No one wanted to say it but clearly it was now on all of their minds. The signs were all there pointing the way.

When would a human be successfully cloned?

There was something else that no one wanted to talk about, at least no one on any of the cloning teams. The animosity of the clones toward their donors was a worrisome aspect of every one of the successful clonings to date.

Well, if they didn't talk about it, maybe it would just go away.

The 1978 study of the Shroud in Turin had revealed enormous amounts of information about it and about its travels but had not answered the big question, "How *old* is it?"

In 1988 permission was obtained from the Vatican to take samples for carbon-14 dating. Succumbing to pressure from the church, scientists took only one sample instead of several from different parts of the Shroud needed to get a statistically valid set of data. Further, It was taken from a location specified by the church.

From the single snippet, three tiny samples were sent to separate independent laboratories at Oxford University Research Laboratory for Archaeology, the University of Arizona, and the Swiss Federal Institute of Technology, Zurich. They would have liked to have samples from several different locations on the Shroud, but that was not to be.

The labs had to do their best with the sample that the Vatican permitted then to take but it did not come from *any* of the areas the scientists had selected in 1978. All three laboratories dated the Shroud with a 95% certainty to the 1260 AD to 1390 AD time period.

With the announcement of this dating, the Vatican stated the Shroud was *not* authentic and scientific interest in the Shroud dropped off considerably but continued in some quarters.

Focused on her future direction, Dr. Goodenough attended the March 1989 United States Conference of Research on the Shroud of Turin. At first, she felt skeptical about the snippet but, after the conference, she got back in touch with Richard Halpern and made a quick trip to France to discuss it further. After two days of serious discussions and examination of Halpern family documents she knew in her heart that, while there was not an ironclad chain of custody, the snippet *was* from the Shroud of Turin.

The authenticity of the Shroud itself, of course, was another matter. What if it was not the Shroud of Christ, but, rather the shroud of one of the criminals who was crucified at the same time as Christ?

CHAPTER TEN

Natalie had not wasted any time finding a well heeled sponsor for her project. Potential donor, eccentric billionaire bachelor, Otto Kreist, wanted the cloning facility be located in Europe because all of the successful clonings to date had occurred there. He hoped some of that success would rub off on her project.

He asked questions, while interviewing her about the funding, that raised concerns that his primary interest was in ultimately cloning *himself.* Maybe he saw this as a way to make up for the missed opportunities for fatherhood. Natalie suspected that he was becoming aware of his mortality and that his *real* motive was to develop a supply of body parts to sustain his life when his original parts wore out.

After Natalie's passionate pitch for locating the facility in Los Angeles. Otto reluctantly agreed. Natalie had not inspected the mouths of a number of recent gift horses so she was not inclined to start now. She took Otto's offer at face value and within days, he donated a facility in LA that seemed to have been made precisely to their specifications.

"Sarah, it is imperative that we put our team together and get this under way with the utmost urgency. I have already prepared a list of the kinds of specialists we will require. Rather than have you simply review my list, please prepare a list of your own. Be thorough, but lets not make this team any bigger than we have to. The more people who know about this the harder it will be to keep it a secret. We will have to institute tight security over the entire area immediately."

The next day, they sat down and reviewed one another's lists. With one or two exceptions, their lists were the same. They started discretely "headhunting" that very afternoon.

It was also of the utmost importance that secrecy be maintained. Natalie contacted several companies specializing in high tech security systems. She prepared a working paper outlining the specific security objectives for the overall facility and for each of the specialized areas within it.

One by one the companies presented their proposals but none of them seemed quite right. They were all just *too* high tech. She soon realized that she needed a simple down-to-earth essentially-foolproof system and at that moment, John Pearsons, President and CEO of MAXXX Security Systems arrived on the scene.

Pearsons was a handsome, muscular, well tanned six foot . . . *Adonis*? Natalie was not sure when, if ever, she had seen such a virile specimen and was more than a bit flustered in his presence. She would have to get control of herself and handle this security matter in a business-like way.

John listened to Natalie's wish list, asked many pointed questions, and requested a week in which to prepare a formal presentation. Natalie asked if he could do it in four days. Pearsons agreed and was back in four days with a proposal that exactly matched Natalie's mental picture of the system.

"I will need a day to look this over."

Natalie had no idea why she said that. She was ready to award the contract immediately.

"Can you come by around four tomorrow?"

"Sure."

The following afternoon, Pearsons arrived promptly.

They signed the multiple copies of the contract and the Natalie blurted out, "Are you free this evening? If so, we could go to dinner, my treat, to celebrate the closing of the deal."

"I would be delighted. If you are treating, I'll drive. Where do you live and what time shall I pick you up?"

Natalie gave him her address and phone number and suggested 7:30.

"Fine, see you then."

"I don't believe I did that. I brazenly asked that man for a date and I don't even know if he is married or what."

Natalie hurried home, luxuriated in a bubble bath for a half hour then carefully prepared herself for the "date".

Natalie had lost none of her youthful beauty and when she got dressed up, she was a knockout.

When Pearsons arrived, Natalie had two candles burning and a bottle of Dom Perignon chilling in the ice bucket. There were two long stemmed champagne glasses on the buffet.

She removed the champagne from the ice bucket wrapped it in a towel and handed it to him.

"Will you do the honors? We have time, our reservation is not until 9:00."

Pearsons removed the wires, grasped the cork firmly in his palm and gently turned it from side to side. The sound of the popping cork was muffled by his hand. He poured a small amount in his glass, tasted it, half filled her glass, and handed it to her. He then did the same for himself.

They sat facing one another over the coffee table.

The conversation was casual but Natalie learned a lot about John Pearsons, the most important thing being that he was not attached. John learned a lot about her, too, and the more they conversed, the more aware he became of her stunning beauty. He wondered why he hadn't noticed it earlier. Perhaps it was the Ph.D. following her name. You just don't run across many of *those* with looks like Natalie's.

In a few weeks, John called her.

"How is the system working?"

"Great."

"That's not really why I called. This is social. I was wondering if you would let me take *you* to dinner tomorrow night."

"I would be delighted. What time?"

It was a wonderful evening. John took her to the dining room of the most elegant hotel in the city. There was an orchestra and they danced for hours. When John took her home, he kissed her gently on her lips, a warm moist kiss unlike anything she had ever experienced before. It was a kiss that made her nipples hard and caused a warm moist feeling elsewhere.

That was as far as they went on that date but as the security system installation proceeded they found reasons to be together on numerous occasions. Their evenings became more and more intimate and the night the system passed final inspection, they had an excuse for a really special evening that ended with Natalie spending the night in John Pearsons' apartment. The sex came naturally. It just seemed like the right thing for the moment.

All of Natalie's repressed frustrations and inhibitions dissolved in a surge of unleashed passion. Natalie was in love and so was John but neither of them dared break the magic of the moment by saying so.

After that night, Natalie saw John two or three times a week and they usually spent their weekends together, playing tennis, swimming, and enjoying one another's company in every possible way.

Most of the project positions were filled within a month. Offices and laboratory spaces were assigned and preliminary assignments were handed out. It wasn't exactly "make work" but it did not bear closely enough to the real work ahead to give anyone a clue as to why they were really there. Meanwhile it gave Natalie a chance to evaluate each of them and see how well they fit into the program. She was very pleased that at the end of her unstated probationary period, only one of their original choices had to be replaced.

Natalie called a meeting of the entire team in her conference room. There were place cards around the table indicating where each was to sit. She introduced herself. "I am Dr. Natalie Goodenough, Director of *The Project* (and that is what it would be known as from then on)".

She then asked them to introduce themselves.

Sarah, sitting on her right, introduced herself, "I am Dr. Sarah Buckley, Assistant Director of The Project." The introductions proceeded, counterclockwise, around the table. "Dr. Edward Fenton, Director, Genetics; "Dr. Wilhelm

Brüer, Director, High-Energy Physics";"Dr. Manfred Höltmeyer, Director, Forensic Hematology"; "Dr. Richard Mansic, Director, Microbiology"; "Dr. Lennart Jurgensen, Director, Genome Development and Evaluation"; "Dr. Henri Platinier, Director, Eugenics "; "Dr. Chin Won Chi, Director, Molecular Physics "; and last, "Lisa Hampton, Archivist and Project Librarian."

Dr. Goodenough then said, "I always like for things to be as orderly and consistent as possible. Please note your seating order. At future staff meetings, I would appreciate it if you would sit in the same seats as today and report in the same order."

Up to this point, they might have passed one another in the hall, but each had his or her job to do and Natalie was impressed that none of them congregated around the water cooler or coffee machine to chat or speculate about the reason for their presence here. It was exactly the kind of team she had fantasized about. Natalie looked up and silently thought, "*Thank you, God.*"

Natalie made a short speech explaining that each would be assigned specific areas of research. They would work in relative isolation from one another except for a staff meeting on the second and fourth Wednesday of each month, unless developments warranted otherwise. At those meetings, each would be expected to give an oral presentation on their progress and on the first working day of each month, each would be expected to submit a full written progress report on the preceding month's work. Each report must have a half page abstract for a cover sheet accompanied by a concise statement of goals for the following month. She would review the goals and modify them if there was a need to do so.

As if that didn't sound serious enough, Natalie paused, donned her most serious demeanor and said, "I suppose that you are wondering why we are here. Well, I am about to tell you but first I must get each of you to sign an oath of secrecy. Sarah, Please pass them out."

The oath was all inclusive. They were not to discuss *any* aspect of their work with *anyone* . . . not their wives, their parents, their children, their friends . . . their lovers, no one, . . . not a living soul.

Natalie watched as they read the oath for any signs of reservation but all unhesitatingly picked up their pens and signed.

However, Natalie wasn't quite finished. She asked each them to read the oath aloud.

This was to become a ritual. (In the future, every staff meeting would open with a recitation, in unison of this oath of secrecy. Before long, everyone knew it by heart, like the Pledge of Allegiance to the Flag).

"OK. One last thing before we get into the meat of this project. I would like to remind you that as each of you came on board, you were issued a single unique key. You are not to duplicate it, . . . but it cannot be duplicated anyway. In the Project Building, we have the most high-tech and pick-proof locks available anywhere. Your key fits into all locks in the Project Building. Each key has a *common* section which opens the front door and common areas like the library and restrooms. It has a *personal* section which opens only the areas for which you are personally responsible, specifically, your office and laboratory. Security is of the essence here so keep your key on your person at all times. It is not, under any circumstances, to be loaned to any of your assistants or to any one else. We will be working long hours but the schedules of your assistants must be arranged so they arrive after you and leave before you every day. Any questions?"

There were none.

Satisfied, she placed her briefcase on the conference table unlocked it, brought out the jewelry case, and told her astonished team what it contained. She didn't have to draw them a picture. They all immediately grasped the full implications.

There was stunned silence in the room.

Natalie let the import of her revelation sink in and then spoke earnestly to her entire team, "There is an enormous amount of information available regarding the 1978 tests of the Shroud . . . and there is an enormous amount of *mis*information out there, too. It may seem like a long time to devote to this but I would like for each of you to spend the next month surveying all of the information available in your areas of expertise. Your areas of expertise may overlap with one or more other members of the team. Don't worry about that. Right now, I want as many minds as possible trying to separate the truth from fiction, the real science from the pseudo science, and the historical facts from the religious mumbo jumbo surrounding the Shroud."

"When scientists work on a project like this it is hard to remain objective, particularly if they were raised in a religious environment which has implanted a core set of beliefs. The same is true of agnostics and atheists. All preconceptions and dogma must be set aside, here, if we are to get at the truth. You will find that many of the findings and conclusions regarding the Shroud are tainted with prior beliefs. We must cut through all of this and try our best to keep our own biases, whatever they might be, from diverting *us* in our search for truth. Be thorough. We don't want to get blind sided on this."

"I would like to have oral reports from each of you at the next two regularly scheduled staff meetings."

"That's all I have for now unless there are any questions."

There were none.

During the first two weeks of *real* work the team was bursting with enthusiasm. They all took their work home with them, studied into the early morning hours, and gave reports that riveted the other team members to their seats.

One of the most interesting reports was given by the Director of the High-Energy Physics Laboratory, Dr. Wilhelm Brüer.

Dr. Brüer was attracted to the image itself and the investigations into how it was formed. Initially, there were as many hypotheses as there were investigators but one by one the various hypotheses fell by the wayside as they failed to stand up to the scrutiny of the scientists and other experts. The investigators had to account for a number of facts. First, the image had no apparent distortions. There was an absence any significant amounts of detectable silver or chromium which would have resulted from any experimentation with photographic processes. There were no significant amounts of paint media of any kind. The intensity of the image was inversely proportional to the distance of the cloth from the body. Most importantly, the image appeared on only one side of the cloth and was due to different coloration of just the very tips of the linen fibrils.

Dr. Brüer discussed, in great detail, the premise that the Shroud was a fake. The investigators acknowledged that a few tiny flecks of paint were discovered among the sticky tape samples lifted from the Shroud, but after considering the number of times that artists were permitted to copy the image on the Shroud, often laying their paintings on top of the Shroud to verify dimensions and other details, it was surprising that there were so *few* flecks of pigment found.

Iron, in the form of iron oxide, a constituent of several different red pigments, was thought by some to be the source of red coloration in the blood stained areas, but the investigators found that there was iron in roughly the same concentrations throughout the Shroud. There was no greater concentration in the image than elsewhere on the Shroud and concluded that it had been soaked through and through when attempts were made to put out the fire in the Chapel of Chambréy Castle in 1532. The water in the vicinity of the castle is very hard with iron being a significant contributor to the hardness.

There was no evidence of the presence of tempera, egg albumin, or any of the other media used in medieval times, and earlier, to bind the pigments together and to the underlying surface. In addition, there was no evidence of gesso used to prepare the surface to receive paint.

Medieval paintings could not be rolled up or folded without cracks forming and bits of the painting flaking off the surface but the Shroud had been folded and unfolded many times and the image was still intact.

Dr. Brüer reviewed the hypothesis that a primitive *camera obscura* might have been use to obtain the remarkably accurate physiology. This hypothesis was demolished when it became clear that, while an artist like Vermeer painted incredibly accurate images and perspective using a *camera obscura,* an early medieval artist would have been confronted with a daunting challenge in converting the positive color image into a monochrome negative image. An artist attempting to fake the image would have to anticipate the invention of photography by 1000 years and our ability to finally see what he really looked like. The stake through the heart of this hypothesis was the question, "Why would he do this when a fake positive image would have done just as well and would have been a lot easier to do?"

Another hypothesis discussed by Dr. Brüer concerned the possibility that someone had, in effect, discovered the fact that certain chemicals changed their physical appearance when exposed to light. This hypothetical person would have had to coat the linen with such a substance, expose it in a *camera obscura,* and invent a way to fix the image to keep it from disappearing when the linen was exposed to light. Tests for silver and chromium, the substances known to have such properties, were negative. The only traces of silver were found along the scorch marks made when the 1532 fire in Chambréy castle melted a corner of the silver box in which the shroud was stored. There were no traces of these elements in the image itself.

Dr. Brüer reviewed the various hypotheses that the body itself, through physical contact with the Shroud had caused the image. Bodily fluids exuded through the pores of the deceased, contact with unguents and lotions applied to the body, and other possibilities were all examined and for valid scientific reasons were rejected.

When all of the hypotheses had been scrutinized, and subjected to challenge after challenge, only one was left standing.

Dr. Brüer paused for a moment to let all of this sink in, then continued.

"Think for a moment about the discoloration that occurs when objects are exposed for long periods to sunlight. A photochemical reaction occurs which permanently changes any surface so exposed. It is the consensus of the scientists who have studied this remarkable image that it was caused by flash photolysis."

"At some moment in time, perhaps at the moment that Christ's soul left his body, there was an intense discharge of energy . . . scientists studying 'near death' experiences describe this as a 'light shout', a measurable phenomenon. It is unlikely that it occurred while he was being carried because the friends might have seen or felt *something*, but perhaps not. It might have happened immediately after he was wrapped in the Shroud or even after he was laid to rest in the cave."

"The flash of energy was not necessarily in the visible frequency range. It could have been in the infra red or ultra violet range, perhaps even x-ray but, whatever its frequency or wavelength, it was intense and it permanently burned an image into the Shroud. Those who were caring for the body might have been there when it happened but would not necessarily have seen or felt *anything*."

"Most of the experts feel that Christ was probably already dead when he was taken down from the cross. So when, if ever, could such a flash of energy have occurred? Well, if not when he died and his soul left his body then it had to be when his soul reentered his body at the resurrection. This put a purely Christian spin on the explanation, but no one had a better idea."

"There are many aspects of the image that support this burst of energy hypothesis."

"You have all seen the photographs of the Shroud. There are no outlines. The image just sort of fades out at its edges."

"If we consider the mechanics of such a flash, it could not have been emitted straight up and straight down. Rather it would be emitted at right angles to the surface of the body at any point of emission. At any point at which the surface of the Shroud was precisely parallel to the emitting surface it would have received the radiation normal to the surface of the Shroud and at maximum intensity. However, since the Shroud was loosely draped over the body, radiation from the side of the nose, for example, would strike the surface of the shroud at a grazing angle and the surface would not have received the full intensity of the flash. The intensity of the image at that point would be less than the intensity along the bridge of the nose where the shroud and the flesh were in direct contact."

"This explains the lack of sharp defining outlines. It also explain the unnaturally long appearing fingers and limbs because only the parts of the linen parallel to the skin at any point received the maximum flash and the rest of the finger or limb was less distinct."

"There is something else worth noting. There is a common but incorrect public perception that the image is on the *outside* of the Shroud. It is understandable, then, that even some of the scientists who worked on this project are confused about certain aspects of the image. For example, the spear thrust in the side is described by some as producing a wound in the left side while others describe the wound as entering the right side between the fifth and sixth ribs, penetrating upwards, piercing the diaphragm, into the thoracic cavity, through the lung and into the heart."

"The image, with the exception of the heavy blood stains that soaked through the linen, is on one surface, only. In all of the hypotheses involving body contact with the Shroud, including flash photolysis, that surface would be on the *inside* of the Shroud. The image is, therefore, not only a *negative* image, in the photographic sense, it is also a *mirror* image of Christ. Everything about the image is *backwards*. The image on the Shroud is the *opposite* of Christ in every possible way."

The symbolic significance of this observation would haunt the team in the months and years to come.

Meanwhile, several world conferences on genetics featured papers on the possibility of cloning humans. One extremely disturbing paper proposed an alternative to cryogenics as a means of providing some semblance of immortality for those wealthy enough to afford it.

Specifically, Doktor-Professor Helmut Grünter, University of Applied Genetics, Berne, suggested that while sperm cells, zygotes, embryos, and similar microscopic bodies are routinely frozen and then thawed out and successfully resuscitated, it was altogether another matter to freeze and thaw out a solid body like an entire human being. It was his contention that irreversible cell damage occurs in the freezing of humans. No human had ever been successfully thawed and the successful freezing and thawing a human was viewed, by him, to be an unrealizable fantasy.

Nevertheless, many of the world's wealthy had spent extravagantly on cryogenic preservation in the hope that a way would be found at some future date to revive them and that, by that time, cures would have been found for whatever ailments they might have had.

Doktor-Professor Grünter then postulated that this obsession with immortality might be better satisfied through the mechanism of cloning. He pointed out that the fact that newts and other lower life forms had been cloned showed the way. Granted sheep had been cloned, albeit with dubious success, but, in his view, it was just a matter of time before a human would be successfully cloned. He envisioned a world in which endangered species, even those on the brink of extinction, would be saved by cloning. Successful cloning of endangered animals would inevitably lead to the cloning of humans. He expected that resistance to this idea, on moral grounds, would erupt and that human cloning would eventually be banned. That was an obstacle that would have to be overcome. His presentation was devoid of emotion. He might just as well have been discussing the number of beans in a can.

He went on to explain that those wealthy enough to afford it might donate their own blood and have a clone, or clones, of themselves produced. The purpose would not be to achieve some measure of immortality through the clones but rather to extend their *own* lives indefinitely.

The clones were viewed, by Grünter, as the possessions of the donors since they would be produced from their own cells. As *possessions*, the owners would simply use them for body parts to replace their own parts as they wore out. A clone would be a source of perfectly type-matched hearts, livers, lungs, kidneys, . . . even testes. In Grünter's view, replacement of some parts like the eyes and brain were not in the immediate future but given sufficient time, research, and funding, even that might be achievable.

Meanwhile, he postulated that with a suitable perfectly-type-matched spare parts supply, and barring serious virus and bacteria-borne "killer" diseases, a specific human life might be prolonged indefinitely, at least several hundred years, and perhaps a *thousand years* or more.

Immediately after the presentation of Grünter's paper, several things happened.

World leaders brought the matter before the United Nations and there was a universal outcry against human cloning but since there had never been a totally successful cloning of any mammal, much less a human, it turned out to be, like most UN matters, mainly talk and little action.

The world's wealthiest immediately grasped the significance of Grünter's remarks. The best and brightest of the world's genetic specialists dropped out of sight and there was a paucity of papers on the subject of cloning in all of the technical conferences in the area of genetics.

Rumors were rampant that new privately funded genetic laboratories were springing up all over the world for the express purpose of cloning the individuals who were funding the projects to provide them with an endless supply of body parts. There was no way that these rumors could be confirmed due to the high state of physical security at the new laboratories, but that alone suggested that the rumors were true.

There were, however, teams already in place with adequate funding and laboratories in several countries in Europe. These teams all accelerated their efforts to be the *first* to successfully clone a mammal and imposed tight security over their activities.

This was a race for fame and, perhaps, a Nobel prize.

In the face of 1988 carbon-14 dating which yielded a Medieval date, the Vatican had reported that the Shroud was *not* authentic.

This did not convince Dr. Goodenough. She believed that several errors were made in the 1988 Carbon-14 dating tests and firmly believed that properly conducted tests would give a first century dating. For example, the Vatican allowed the scientists to remove only a single small sample for carbon dating. She believes that this sample was taken from one of the areas that was rewoven when the Shroud was repaired after the fire in Chambréy Castle in 1532. Of *course* it would yield a medieval date if the flax was grown in the early 1500s. However, that would date it in the 1500's, much later than the date found by the three laboratories.

But suppose that whoever rewove parts of the Shroud has used a snippet of "old" linen fabric, perhaps 300 years old, to make the rewoven area less obvious to the eye? In those times, fabric of any kind was expensive and it was not a "throw away economy". People were frugal and it was not unusual for linen and silk to be cared for and preserved for centuries. Godfrey Du Luc the weaver might have done precisely that!

Also, while the Shroud had been vacuumed to remove any dust, pollen, tiny bits of insects, and other small particles that the Shroud might have collected in its travels, no attempt was made to remove any microbes, bacteria, molds, or other really minute organic matter and it is not likely that the scientists removed *all* of the pollen and other plant matter that might have become entrapped in the strands of the flax.

Residual organic matter of this sort would yield a later date even if the sample had come from the original Shroud fabric.

There were just too many questions regarding the radioactive Carbon-14 tests to take them at face value.

There was one last intriguing thing about the sample used for the C-14 tests, all of the micrographs of the Shroud that showed sufficient detail showed that the linen fibers used to make the thread from which the cloth was woven were twisted in an "*S*" fashion whereas a micrograph of the snippet used for the C-14 dating showed a "*Z*" twist . . . and of course, the church had picked an area that contained no blood.

Could the church have permitted them to take the sample from the very fabric that Godfrey Du Luc had woven into the Shroud to conceal what he had done? It seemed impossible but then . . . maybe not.

Dr. Goodenough, convinced that the Carbon-14 dating was in error, ordered C-14 dating of a very small segment of *her* sample, thought to be from the *original* fabric. This fell into Dr. Chin Won Chi's bailiwick.

A few fibrils from a spot that contained no blood stain were separated from the snippet. After careful preparation of the sample to remove all foreign matter, Dr. Chi's Molecular Physics Laboratory tests obtain a date of 10 AD to 125 AD with a 95% confidence factor.

Dr. Goodenough and her colleagues were elated.

The time frame was right.

This snippet might, indeed, be from the Shroud of Christ.

Natalie turned to Dr. Platinier, "Henri, everything seems to be moving much slower than any of us would have expected but we could have a breakthrough at any time and we must be ready when that happens."

She handed him a reprint of her paper from the *Journal of the Applied Genetics Society*, "Asexual Reproduction of Fruit Flies by DeoxyribonucleicAcid (DNA) Replication".

"I would like for you to review this paper which deals specifically with the cloning of fruit flies. In the appendix you will find a protocol for cloning any species. Please take this generalized protocol, extract pertinent parts applicable to *our* project, and give it specificity with respect to the cloning of a human being. What you prepare will be the Bible for this endeavor. I don't want to put you under too much pressure but this will be urgently needed soon. I don't know how soon . . . but soon. Please keep me informed as to your progress."

Dr. Platinier enthusiastically accepted the assignment. At least he would be doing *something* positive.

One thing about Natalie Goodenough had become clear to her entire team. Her name was a misnomer. A grade of 85 was not a passing grade *here*. There was no such thing as *good enough* in her vocabulary. Every thing was measured against a standard of perfection. Nothing short of that was acceptable.

CHAPTER ELEVEN

After much preliminary study and extensive laboratory tests, Dr. Goodenough and her colleagues felt certain that it was possible to clone a human being from DNA derived from a *good* blood sample from a *live* donor, . . . *but DNA from a sample that is nearly 2,000 years old?*

They were not as sure as they had once been.

The first question to be answered now was, "Are these 'blood stains' on the snippet really blood?"

The scientists and experts who investigated the Shroud in 1978 conducted a large battery of tests to determine if the stains on the Shroud were actually blood. In a sense, the tests amounted to overkill. But they wanted to be certain. They concluded that the stains were, in fact, blood by virtue of their microscopic and forensic appearance, by reflection spectrometry, by microspectrophotometry, by positive hemochromogen tests, by the presence of bile pigments and protein, by the presence of albumin, by the chemical generation of porphyrin fluorescence, positive protease and cyanmethemoglobin tests, and by X-ray fluorescence detection of slightly higher levels of iron in blood image areas. The preponderance of this evidence pointed irrefutably to the stains being blood.

They even typed the blood. It was type AB.

But what about the stains on Dr. Goodenough's snippet?

There were nagging questions regarding the chain of custody of this sample and its authenticity as a piece of the Shroud was more a matter of faith than proven fact. Up until now everyone just assumed that the stains *were blood* but if they were *not*, a lot of time and money will have gone right down the drain.

Natalie castigated herself for not checking sooner. She called her first special staff meeting and placed the subject on the table for discussion.

It seemed pretty clear that this was a job for Forensic Hematology.

Dr. Manfred Höltmeyer readily accepted the assignment. Dr. Goodenough was concerned about the conservation of her precious resources. The snippet was not very large and the blood stains did not completely cover it.

"Manfred, how large a sample will you need to make a positive determination?" she asked, "Like the carbon dating, this is a destructive test and this snippet is all we have, but on the other hand, I don't want you to give you too small a sample and have to run the test over again. That would be counter productive."

Dr. Höltmeyer thought about it for a long time while everyone held their breath. Then he answered, "At the risk of boring those of you who may be familiar with this technique, I want to explain exactly what I need to do."

He walked to the chalk board and started sketching. "A major constituent of blood is hemoglobin. A crucial constituent of hemoglobin is heme porphyrin and at the center of the porphyrin molecule is an atom of iron."

He sketched the molecule and tapped the iron atom with his chalk for emphasis.

"I propose to chemically excise the iron atom from the heme porphyrin. Having done this, I shall expose the residue to ultraviolet light. If the sample is blood, the residue will fluoresce, that is, give off light of a specific but different wavelength from the light used to stimulate the fluorescence. For this, I will need a very small amount, around . . . 600 to 700 picograms, or so." Then he added, "The test will not take very long. You can all watch if you like."

No one was going to miss this. It was the very essence of The Project. Everything hung on the result.

They adjourned to the Forensics Laboratory and waited nervously for Dr. Höltmeyer to set up the test.

When ready, the snippet was carefully placed under the microscope. Dr. Höltmeyer slowly manipulated the snippet until he found a fibril with a relatively large globule of blood (if it was *indeed* blood) on the tip. He invited Dr. Goodenough to look.

"That one," he said, "should do just fine."

Natalie sat back and nodded.

Dr. Höltmeyer carefully removed the specimen from the fibril. It weighed out at 650 picograms. The rest of the team marveled at his skill in estimating such small weights . . . but of course, that is why he was on the team. Such skills are not developed overnight but only through year of experience in one's craft. They all had equal skills in *their* areas of expertise.

Manfred moved his sample to a laboratory table where he had set up the test and the team gathered around. He placed the sample in a Petrie dish and then, like a medieval alchemist, added hydrazine, then formic acid. It was pure theater. A dense cloud of fumes rose from the dish. The rest of the team was not expecting it and jumped back with surprise.

"It does that *every* time," he said, with a twinkle in his eye. Under his stern exterior, Manfred had a sense of humor after all.

He asked for the light to be turned off, waited a few moments for their eyes to adjust to the dark and flicked on the ultraviolet lamp.

At first there was stunned silence, then "Ooohs" and "Ahhhhs", then a spontaneous outburst of applause. The red fluorescence was visible to the naked eye. The elation sent chills through the entire team. It *IS* blood.

"How much confidence do you have in this conclusion, Manfred?"asked Natalie.

"I would say 99.9999% confident."

"But not 100%?"

"Oh, *it's* blood. The heme porphyrin fluorescence test is quite definitive. There are, of course, several other tests for identification of blood. Each of them is very accurate and, like this test, each of them is accepted in a court of law as proof of the presence of blood. For example, I could test for hemochromogen, or for cyanomethemeoblobin, those are bile pigments, or I could take some of the serum crystals from the edge of the stain and do a microspectrophotomet scan of them. Positive results from any of these would be accepted in the courts. All of them together would be irrefutable but we have a very small sample to begin with and we don't want to waste any of it . . . and this test *was* exciting, Yes? Believe me, it's blood."

The team returned to the conference room.

Natalie asked,"Any questions?"

Dr. Brüer raised his hand and Natalie nodded toward him.

"It seems to me that if *I* were going to fake something like the Shroud, I would want it to be as realistic as possible . . . so I would use real blood but not necessarily human blood. Did this test prove that it is *human* blood? Could it be the blood of a goat, for example? How can we tell?"

Manfred, a quick study, had read the professional backgrounds of the other members of the team and was familiar with all of their capabilities. Dr. Richard Mansic was the only MD on the team consisting otherwise of Ph.Ds. One of his specialties was immunology.

Manfred replied, "I could answer that but should yield to Dr. Mansic."

Natalie said, "Dr. Mansic?"

Dr. Mansic rose but spoke from his place at the conference table,"This is an area in which Dr. Höltmeyer and I overlap, but if he wants me to pick it up at this point, I shall."

Mansic took off his glasses, breathed on them and wiped of a spot with the end of his tie. "It may seem strange to you that we can find the answer to that using immunological techniques . . . You are probably wondering what immunology could possibly have to do with this. Well, it has everything to do with it.

I should start with a brief refresher on antibodies. Antibodies are protein molecules that the immune system manufactures to deal with any foreign bodies like bacteria, viruses, or protein from another species, and neutralize them. Every protein has a unique three dimensional shape and is soluble in blood. An antibody is manufactured to fight a specific invader. It precisely fits the shape of the foreign protein and bonds tightly with it. The protein and attached antibody have an altogether different shape from the original soluble protein. This new shape is totally alien to the host body and is insoluble in the host's blood so it precipitates. Are you still with me? . . . Good."

Dr. Mansic paused for a sip of water.

"OK, what we will have to do is this. We will inject some human serum albumin, . . . any volunteers to be the donor? . . . into a laboratory animal which will immediately produce antibodies to cope with this foreign protein. Then, we draw some blood from the laboratory animal, centrifuge out the blood cells, leaving only the serum which now contains anti-human albumin antibodies. I won't go into the details, but we will then attach a fluorescent tag to the antibodies."

Lisa Hampton, the Archivist-Librarian, raised her hand. The idea of being an active participant in the technical aspects of the project excited her. "I volunteer to give a blood sample,"she said.

Dr Mansic acknowledged her offer with a nod in her direction.

He pauses again for another sip. It is a ploy he uses to collect his thoughts before continuing, "Now that we know that the stain on the snippet is blood, we will remove a very small sample of serum crystals from the light area around the perimeter of the blood stain and put it in solution. Some of this will then be added to the serum from the laboratory animal. If this is *human* blood, the antibodies will attach themselves to the protein and, voilà, we will get a reaction, specifically a fluorescent precipitate. It will not be quite as exciting as Dr. Höltmeyer's test but the answer will be just an important, will it not?

Another sip of water. "For this, we can also set up some control tests. I will need samples of blood from other mammals . . . perhaps one of our laboratory rats, blood from a pig, cow, sheep . . . anything. The original serum containing anti-human albumin antibodies should not react to any of these. The control tests will not require any of the serum obtained from the snippet."

A final sip. "We will not be able to perform these tests today, even tomorrow will be too soon. Lets say the day after tomorrow, first thing in the morning?"

The following day, the members of the team reported to their offices and tried to make some progress toward their own goals but none of them could keep their minds on their work. Most of them were of a single thought. *"Damn that Brüer. Just when everything seemed right, he throws in his damned monkey wrench."*

But, more than anything, It bugged *all* of them that in their elation over the success of the porphyrin fluorescence test none of *them* had thought to ask it.

The day was, of course, too short for Dr. Mansic and his assistants. Getting blood samples from pigs and cows turned out to be a lot more difficult than it seemed. Ultimately, they had to settle for dogs and cats which were just as good, but just not what they were sent after.

Finally, morning of the second day arrived and everything was ready. The entire team came in an hour early, anxious to find out for sure. They assembled in the conference room.

Dr. Mansic had been up half the night preparing the test. He gave them a brief summary of the tests they would see and the team moved to his laboratory.

Mansic moved efficiently through the steps he had described earlier. When he put the solution containing the dissolved crystals of serum from the snippet into the serum containing the anti-human protein antibodies. The fluorescence tagged antibodies attacked the human protein, attached themselves to it and the molecules to which they had attached themselves precipitated out of the solution. The precipitation took a while but as the insoluble molecules piled up in the bottom of the test tube, the ultraviolet light revealed the unmistakable fluorescent glow.

The stain on the Shroud snippet was *human* blood.

The control test with blood from non-human mammals was anti-climax. There was no reaction. None was expected. Not getting something, when that is what you expect, is not very exciting . . . but it was certainly comforting.

Cloning was not the simple matter that the Networks' science editors made it out to be. The replication of the complex dual helix of DNA was an extremely difficult operation. The DOE's Human Genome initiative was bogged down in bureaucratic quicksand. There was heavy interdepartmental politics as the heads of each of the Directorates jockeyed to get the biggest slice of the funding pie and the available personnel. There is never enough money or personnel to suit any government agency and the DOE was no exception. This was frustrating but there was nothing Dr. Goodenough's team could do about it.

At the next regular staff meeting, Dr. Lennart Jurgensen, Director, Genome Development and Evaluation gave a very discouraging report. He could not conceal his frustration. All of the DOE Genome Project Directors had their staffs writing operating manuals and departmental procedures, typical bureaucratic "gobbledygook, none of which had any direct bearing on their *raison de être*, genome mapping. They had not even fired up any of their Cray computers. "Dr. Genome" as his associates were beginning to call him (because his full name and title were a mouthful) was obviously dismayed.

The reports from her own Directors were similarly negative. There had been no real progress in any department . . . except one.

The only encouraging report was given by Dr. Mansic.

"Good morning. I have one bit of news that is both positive and puzzling. I have typed the blood on the snippet."

Dr. Mansic poured a glass of water from the decanter, made them wait while he took his usual dramatic-emphasis sip and paused a bit longer to get their full attention.

"While we are now sure that the stain on the snippet is really blood and human blood, at that, there is still the open question as to whether this snippet actually came from the

Shroud of Turin. I won't keep you in suspense any longer. The stain on our snippet *is* type AB, the same type as the 1978 Scientific investigators found on the Shroud."

Dr. Goodenough interjected, "This *is* good news. It further corroborates our assumptions and greatly increases the probability that our snippet actually came from the Shroud."

This blood type, however, was indeed puzzling to some of the team.

Dr. Fenton raised his hand.

Natalie nodded acknowledgment, "Dr. Fenton?"

Dr. Edward Fenton, Director, Genetics, said,"When the 1978 study found the blood on the Shroud to be type AB, I must admit that I was baffled. Intuitively, I suppose, I would have expected it to be type O, universal donor. I know it is not good science to anticipate an outcome. That often tends to cloud the results, but I just had a visceral feeling about type O. The virgin birth conjures up visions of a clone, but Christ could not possibly be a clone of Mary. She was a female and He was a male. But what about the Immaculate Conception? And the notion that Christ and God were one. This is a heady concept. Could Christ have been a *clone* of God implanted in Mary to fulfill the prophesy?"

A clone of God?

After collecting his thoughts, Fenton continued,"Could *God* be type AB?"

He paused again . With a humorous tone and poorly disguised pride, said, "*I* am type AB."

That obviously made him feel special.

God . . . type AB? . . . And Fenton? It boggled the mind.

Clearly, they could reach no meaningful conclusion so the discussion ended and the meeting was adjourned.

By this time each of the Directors and some of their staff members had donated blood so there was plenty of it for the many tests and procedures on the teams list of objectives but one procedure after another led to a dead end . . . and this was with blood from *live* donors.

THE SHROUD

As Natalie pondered the prospects of cloning from a sample from a *deceased* person her discouragement was visible.

———————————————

At the next staff meeting, Natalie decided that a pep talk was in order, not just for her team, but for herself.

"Good morning, people, before we run your progress reports I have a few thoughts to throw on the table.

We are running into a lot of dead ends but there is something we can do to prepare ourselves for the moment when all of the pieces finally fall into place.

We are a team, not a sports team, the stakes are much higher than that, but a team none the less. In most team sports there are strategies for success.

Not all of you are familiar with the American game of football. I like to watch it but I will be the first to admit that I do not understand all of the nuances of the game. However, it is, I believe, a sport that is different from all other sports in one important respect. It is an intermittent game. Much like our work, there is a lot of stop and go. In this game, a play is run and after the play, both sides regroup and another play is run. The thing that is unique to this sport is the 'play'. There are a few exceptions, . . . plays designed to advance the ball only a short distance in order to retain possession of the ball, . . . but, in general, plays, if perfectly executed, are designed to produce a score.

To this end, the coach spends many hours a week diagraming the plays on the blackboard and explaining each individual's role in each play. Then the team goes to the practice field and runs through the plays over and over again until each player executes his assignment faultlessly on every play.

The practice field is one thing; the game field is quite another. The game field is 'real life'. On the game field things go wrong, . . . all sorts of things . . . the weather, . . . injuries, . . . momentary attention lapses, . . . all sorts of miscues, . . . and Murphy's Law is always lurking in the shadows . . . any or all of these can thwart the perfect execution of a play.

But when a superbly coached team, in the peak of condition and preparation, takes the field, plays will be executed to perfection often enough in every game to propel the team past all obstacles to whatever goal the team has set for itself . . . perhaps a National Championship.

It will be the same with our team."

Dr. Goodenough was not quite sure how many had followed this analogy up to this point but she continued, "You may recall that several weeks ago I asked Dr. Platinier to study the general protocol that I developed for cloning any species and modify it to specifically address the cloning of a human being. Dr. Platinier has done that. I have reviewed his work and modified it only to assign specific tasks to each of you."

"Here it is."

Natalie held up a rather imposing spiral bound document.

"This is our 'play book'. It has only *one* play in it, a play designed to reach the goal we have set for ourselves, a viable human clone. Note that your copy has your name on it. Every step assigned to *you* is highlighted."

She turned to Lisa Hampton, Archivist and Librarian,"Would you please pass these out."

While the documents were being passed out, Natalie resumed, "We will not have the luxury of running our play dozens of times. Our resources are very limited . . . so we are going to do what a good football team does, we are going to practice . . . practice . . . practice . . . until what we do in the Eugenics Lab becomes second nature to each of us."

"Take this protocol back to your office and study it thoroughly. Beginning tomorrow, we will start having what coaches call 'skull sessions'. Be prepared to explain any part of the protocol with particular emphasis on your specific role. We never know when the breakthrough will occur, or in whose area, but when it happens we will be prepared to spring into action on a moments notice with no lost motions.

We will also have unannounced practice sessions, 'fire drills' if you will. To make these practices as realistic as possible, we will fertilize real human ova in vitro and assume that the resultant zygotes are clones. Our play book was prepared to optimize our chances of producing a viable fetus from a zygote. We will then care for the fetus as though it were our clone. When satisfied that all has been properly done, we will *terminate* the experiment and get back to our preparations for the real thing."

Thereafter, there were "fire drills" at irregular intervals. Sometimes the results of a *practice* session were interesting enough, from the standpoint of either success or failure, to preserve the specimen but, in every case, the "fire drills" were carefully documented.

Natalie was pleased at the growing proficiency of her team and her confidence in their ability to deal with the real thing solidified.

CHAPTER TWELVE

Everything was still moving slowly . . . too slowly. Natalie could detect the disappointment in the eyes of her entire team. While gloomily considering their lack of progress at the regular staff meeting, Sarah Buckley had one of those once in a lifetime moments of inspired insight.

She said, "I would like to propose a test. The test will not prove that it *is* possible to clone a human being from ancient DNA but if it is *not* possible, the test will clearly and unambiguously show *that*."

Sarah explained the test to them. It was a lengthy and complicated test with many steps but after she had described it and answered all of their questions, the Directors all agreed that the test was valid . . . But it had such an aura of *finality* about it.

Natalie put it into perspective, "If it can't be done, it would be better to find out now, and not spin our wheels any longer on a lost cause."

The team really didn't want to get such potentially fatal news concerning The Project but they had gone through this before, once to determine whether it was *really* blood, then to determine if the blood was *human*. A negative finding on any of those tests would have killed the project, too. Even a finding that the blood type on the snippet was anything other than type AB would have been a major, if not fatal, setback. Natalie asked for a show of hands and the team unanimously decided to go for broke and conduct the test using a microscopic sample from the Shroud snippet.

The wait was grating on all of their nerves. They were divided on the prospect of a favorable result but at least, they would know.

It was planned that when the time came, the actual cloning would take place in Dr. Henri Platinier's, Eugenics Laboratory. The Eugenics Laboratory was the most tightly controlled area in the Project Building. This laboratory was placed out of the mainstream of department activities in the least accessible part of the Project complex. Natalie did not want *anyone* to inadvertently blunder into *this* area. It could only be reached through Dr. Platinier's office. Other than Dr. Platinier's immediate staff, and the other Project Directors no one was permitted access. Only Dr. Platinier's personal key could be used to gain access to his office and to the Eugenics Laboratory. No one could enter without being accompanied by Platinier and he was instructed to stay with any visitor at all times. No exceptions. This included Dr. Goodenough.

Sarah had no lab of her own and while this was not intended as an actual cloning attempt, Sarah's test had many of the attributes of the real thing so the Eugenics lab was the logical locale for her test.

The test was a complicated one. Dr. Platinier presided over the experiment and Dr. Buckley assisted. At one point a microscopic fluid sample was pipetted onto a culturing medium in a Petrie dish and set aside for future use.

The entire team focused on the main experiment and while their attention was directed elsewhere, a remarkable thing was happening in the Petrie dish. A strand of DNA started unwinding and then began to replicate itself. Cell mitosis occurred and there was soon a cluster of cells clinging to one another replicating at an exponential rate. A zygote had developed and was now almost large enough to be visible to the naked eye. The next step involved the contents of the Petrie dish.

Sarah reached for it and her sharp eye caught sight of the zygote. Her first reaction was that the culture had somehow become contaminated. If so, the experiment would have to be terminated and begun anew.

"Damn," she thought, *"What did we do to cause this?"*

"Oh," said Sarah as she carried the Petrie dish to a microscope. "We may have a little hitch here."

She placed the dish under the objective lens of the microscope, illuminated it and peered into the eyepiece. What she saw puzzled her. It was so unexpected that she mentally ran through a catalog of other possibilities but kept coming back to her initial reaction. She gasped and then spoke with a formality that she had not used for years, "Dr. Goodenough, you had better look at this."

Natalie moved to the microscope, "What is it?"

"You will have to see for yourself."

Natalie sat at the microscope, adjusted the focus, and pondered what she was seeing.

"Oh, My God, How is this possible?"

The others, completely in the dark as to what was happening, crowded around the microscope. Natalie got up and one by one they took turns looking into the dual eyepieces.

There was shocked silence as the reality of their observations struck home. When they had all seen it, Natalie took one more long look, followed by Sarah.

She looked around the room.

There was ecstatic disbelief on the face of each member of the team.

There was a question on every mind, *"How?"*

Finally, someone vocalized the question.

Natalie replied,"I have no idea. It defies explanation but . . . how can we explain the Virgin Birth of Christ? You have all followed the experiment. How do *you* explain it?"

They took turns again looking into the microscope. There was no doubt about it, the zygote had grown substantially since their first look.

"OK, people, we have things to do, NOW. The protocol for care of the zygote after the initial cloning should be deeply implanted in your minds. We have rehearsed it many times. This time it is *not* a drill. We appear to have a human clone in this dish and all of our activities must now be directed toward insuring its survival."

CHAPTER THIRTEEN

Sarah and Dr. Platinier were discussing the astounding result of her experiment when a slight movement caught her eye."My God! It's alive !" Sarah spoke the words she didn't think would ever be spoken by anyone as the small form in the laboratory tank turned its head to look at her and blinked.

When they had begun The Project several years ago, neither she nor her superior, Dr. Natalie Goodenough, had really believed they would be so successful so quickly. Cloning mammals from DNA had been developed by the Irish in the now famous "sheep from nowhere" experiments in early 1989 but human testing, much less cloning experimentation, had immediately been outlawed by every nation on earth. Yet, here they stood, observing what they had done.

The fetus had developed from a zygote cloned from a single strand of DNA but seemed doomed to failure. It looked like a normal human fetus but, up until this moment, there had been no sign of life from the inert form in the tank.

"Quick!" Sarah blurted out, "call Dr. Goodenough, She has got to see this."

A simple test to prove that ancient DNA could *not* be used to clone a subject had, in a sense, backfired. No one would have dared to predict that a rapid burst of replication might occur as a consequence of the test, but here they were, looking at a living exact replica of the DNA donor. The test did not find that it could *not* be done. Quite the contrary, they had not only cloned a human, perhaps the first, but they had done it using 2,000 year old DNA.

When Natalie arrived, they all just stood there staring in wonder. *Could this really be a clone of the Savior, Jesus Christ?*

The rapid development of the fetus would have surprised the team were it not for the reports of accelerated development of the sheep clones. In only nine weeks or so, the fetus had reached what appeared to be full term. There was much to be done and quickly, The fetus was suspended in the amniotic tank, a glass tank filled with artificial amniotic fluid. It was connected by its umbilicus to a machine that superficially resembled a dialysis machine. It was a mechanical placenta which not only cleansed, oxygenated and circulated the fetus' blood but injected nutrients into the bloodstream.

This was the moment of truth when their training and rehearsals would pay off. Everyone donned masks, sterile gowns, and surgical gloves. The amniotic tank was drained and the fetus was carefully dried off and lifted onto a blanket on the small preparation table attached to the tank. Dr. Mansic, the only MD on the team directed the clamping and cutting of the umbilical cord. The entire procedure only took seconds. He then lifted the baby by it feet, gave it a healthy whack on the back and was rewarded with a loud cry.

The tiny plugs were removed from the nostrils, the eyes were carefully washed out and the baby was quickly checked to make certain that everything was there and in the right place but they already knew the answers to those questions. His fingers and toes had been counted many times as he developed in the amniotic tank.

A nursery area had been prepared in the Eugenics Lab. The baby was diapered, wrapped in warm blankets and taken to his new quarters in the nursery.

The team wanted to cheer but they didn't for fear of frightening the baby.

Natalie gently picked up the baby and held it up for all to see.

"We did it. We really did it. I am so proud of all of you."

She placed the baby back in its crib.

Then, as an afterthought, "He is a Jew, you know. He should be circumcised in accordance with Jewish tradition. Does anyone know who should do it, when it has to be done, and whether a religious ceremony must be observed?"

They all shrugged and shook their heads.

Lisa Hampton volunteered. "I'll find out what has to be done."

Lisa contacted the Rabbi of a Reformed Temple. He was curious about the lack of living parents or relatives but one of the consequences of the Holocaust of World War II was that many Jewish families had been decimated and survivors were scattered to the winds. It was a common thing for relatively small groups of relatives to attend a briss. While this did not apply in any way to *this* event, the Rabbi accepted the contrived explanation for the missing relatives although they were not sure that he really believed the story.

The Rabbi explained the circumcision should occur on the eighth day after the child's birth. There must be a religious ceremony. He could handle that.

He also explained that the briss could be performed by either a mohel or a doctor.

The fewer people involved the better. The mohel was out. Dr. Mansic would handle that end of it.

On the eighth day, the clone's crib was transferred to Dr. Mansic's Microbiology Laboratory where he was circumcised by Dr. Mansic. The only others present were Natalie and the Rabbi. The Rabbi must have thought it strange that the baby's size and general appearance was that of a one month old child.

The clone's physical development progressed at a rapid rate, like the sheep clones, roughly four times the normal growth rate of a human baby, but his intellectual development took place much faster.

As Natalie proceeded with her project, the mirrored lives of the two Irish sheep began to show subtle changes. Small things at first. The donor was passive, docile, but the clone was mean and aggressive. Natalie believed that this was only the result of the less than perfect controls of the testing areas. "*That surely wouldn't happen to this experiment*", she thought.

Of course, no one would ever know. They *couldn't* know, because *this* experiment could never be revealed to the public or even to the scientific world. What they had done must remain a secret, forever. This was something she had not considered before. *How could they bring this project to a close?*

They couldn't terminate it in the usual sense. If the experiment turned out as everyone hoped, the new Christ would just have to be cut loose to bring love and harmony to a troubled world. After all, there was a period of relative obscurity in Jesus Christ's life after which he burst forth with his message of peace and good will to all. They hoped that history would repeat itself.

Back in Ireland, however, the sheep cloning experiment has had a tremendous setback. The cloned sheep has become the antithesis of the docile donor sheep. It killed the donor sheep while it slept . . . and attacked all who tried to capture it with flying hooves and bared teeth.

The cloned sheep was subjected to extensive tests. The scientists could find no reason why this might have happened. The clone was healthy in every respect and an autopsy on the donor sheep found no trace of any disease or other abnormality. There was much speculation as to the cause of the attacks. Some of the possibilities put forth were, to say the least, bizarre, but in the end the scientists settled for sibling rivalry, exacerbated by the fact that the clone's jealousy of the donor was extraordinary due to its genetic closeness to the donor.

In the usual cases of sibling rivalry, it is the *older* sibling that is jealous of the younger arrival. No one could come up with a good reason for it but maybe in this case it was the other way around. They were uncomfortable with the theory it but it was all they had.

The outward manifestations might be the same and it is understandable that confusion might result if similar aberrant behavior is ever observed in a human clone. The possibility of a similar human clone problem poses other questions. In this specific case, there is no living donor to be the target of such behavior. Also, while they cannot prove it, Dr.

Goodenough and some of her colleagues have begun to suspect, privately, that if DNA is derived from a dead person, it might no longer carry the essence of a soul. In this case the clone would have no sense of right and wrong. It would be an amoral creature. What would a clone of Christ be like if he had no moral values? And what if the growing view of geneticists that all clones might have, for whatever reason, the opposite personalities of the donors applied to *their* clone? Is it possible that *their* clone might exhibit aggressive behavior akin to that of the sheep clones . . . or even worse? What would Christ's opposite personality be like?

For now, however, the question was academic and was pushed into the backs of their minds. Their clone had not exhibited any aggressive behavior and was, in fact, almost too good to be true.

The clone was hungry now and he indicated this fact to the lab assistant assigned to take care of his needs.

The lab assistant said,"That kid cries louder than anything I've ever heard!"

The team took turns monitoring, around the clock, the remarkable event that had taken place in the Eugenics Laboratory. Sarah Buckley had the morning shift again, which meant that there would be feedings every hour. This baby had already put on five pounds and was less than a month old! At this rate it would be full grown by the age of five !

Back in the library, Natalie was reviewing the files she had downloaded from the internet concerning the sheep in Ireland. The information concerning the growth rate intrigued her and she compared Andrew's growth rate to the early period of the sheep's growth. This accelerated growth rate was another aberration of the developing body of knowledge regarding cloning. There was no logical explanation for it but there it was. What other surprises lay in wait for the experimenters?

They had named him Andrew after the professor Robert K. Andrew of the University of California, Berkeley where she and Sarah had first met and had begun their studies of the science of cloning. Professor Andrew had been their mentor and had guided both of them through their doctoral studies. He had also monitored, with pride, their research projects. Professor Andrew had passed away in 1988. What would he think if he were here today?

Since he needed a last name, and they opted not to use either of their own, they chose Kreist after the "Otto B. Kreist Trust for Genetic Experimentation". Kreist was an eccentric billionaire who put his money into all sorts of projects that many characterized as "off the wall" but without this building and the funds to pursue their theories that the Kreist Trust provided, there would never have been an Andrew

Natalie secretly suspected that Otto was way ahead of Doktor-Professor Helmut Grünter and was not as altruistic as he appeared in funding this project. Otto was funding his own immortality through cloning. She was sure of it, but he had never ever suggested it, so this was another gift horse's mouth she was willing, at least for now, to ignore.

Andrew went through the "terrible twos" in a matter of three months but during that time he severely taxed the patience of everyone with whom he came in contact, since he, in a manner of speaking, compressed a whole year of bad behavior into this short period. the team seriously considered the reported aberrant behavior of the sheep clones to be a universal aspect of cloning but when he passed through that phase and exhibited more normal behavior, they gave a collective sigh of relief.

Andrew decided to sit up and stretch. He weighed almost forty pounds now and had been walking around the room exploring when no one else was around. Somehow he instinctively knew that it wasn't time for anyone to know his true capabilities, *yet*. His understanding of language was getting better, too. Even though he couldn't form the words with his tongue yet, he could hear and understand most of what was said in his presence.

Andrew would not have been able to read at all were it not for the lab assistant reading to him while giving him his bottle. There were no children's books available so she read to him from whatever was available, usually technical books. That seemed to keep him quiet and indeed it did. The lab assistant scanned the lines with her finger as she read. He followed her finger movement and soon caught on to the meaning of the characters on the page.

He tried to read some books on his own when no one was in the room in it but his reading was at best rudimentary.

It was November 1, 1991. As he looked across the hallway, he saw Sarah and Natalie coming to his room with something that had one lit candle on it.

Natalie had all the data now. The complete files from the Irish and Scottish experiments had arrived at the Project Complex yesterday and she had spent most of the night reading and re-reading all the information. She hoped she would find an error. Perhaps, some information had been misinterpreted and had caused the disastrous final results reported in the scientific journals. But there was no mistake. Like its Irish counterpart the cloned Scottish sheep's behavior had grown more and more different from its DNA donor until finally it had attacked one of the handlers and driven its hooves through the girl's head. The clone had to be destroyed. The autopsy on the clone showed no illness or disease that would have caused this reaction. It just seemed that the cloned sheep had become the exact opposite of its donor. The animals were identical in every other way. Their size, strength, and abilities were the same but the docile donor had cloned a savage beast.

The cloning teams in Sweden, Germany, Italy, and France reported similar disturbing observations. Their clones had all become vicious and attacked their donors and handlers as well. This was a most unnerving development for the entire genetic community.

A consensus grew among genetic experts that clones seem, for unknown reasons, to assume the *dark* side of the personality of their donors. And this seemed to be an inexorable outcome of all cloning experiments. The notion was rapidly spreading that *all* cloning experiments should be terminated until more is learned about this phenomenon.

Natalie was discouraged but not convinced that the other experts were on the right track. She did not want to believe what she feared and grasped at straws for some other explanation. She knew who the donor of Andy's DNA was and feared that a reversal of *that* temperament would be a horror that mankind could not withstand.

But there might be a way out. What if they took a sample of Andrew's blood? They had drawn blood many times before for tests. Why hadn't she thought of it sooner? If a clone takes on the opposite personality of the donor, what would happen if they made a clone from a clone. Would that make a second reversal that would make things right again? It was worth a shot if all else failed. Natalie extracted a test tube full of his blood and froze it for that contingency.

Andrew's physical development continued at the phenomenal rate observed during his first year, and tracked closely with the high rate of growth of the sheep clones. Every aspect of his development was monitored, tested and retested. There seemed to be no explanation for it. The team took some comfort from the fact that the sheep's growth rate slowed down as it approached the physical capabilities of the donor.

But what about Andrew? There was no *living* donor. Would he level off when his physical characteristics approached those of Christ when he was crucified? He was approaching two years of age but had the physical and mental characteristics of an eight year old. At this rate, he would reach Christ's age at crucifixion in roughly six more calendar years.

Andrew got a bike for his next birthday. Sarah bought it even though Natalie was opposed to the idea. At two years old, Natalie felt that Andy was too young. Yes, he had the frame of an eight year old, but she thought he was not mentally ready. If Natalie had known how far wrong she was, she may have ended the experiment at that moment. Sarah had not thought much about it one way or the other. There was no place for Andrew to ride his new bike. The lab that had become his home was big, but not *that* big.

Well, a boy needs a bike, even if he has no place to ride it right now. Maybe someday we will find a safe place for him to ride it, away from prying eyes.

Andrew *was* ready for, but not particularly interested in, the bike. He was more interested in reading. He had read every book in the study area and had even begun reading the one the cleaning lady had left behind.

This one was so thick, it must have more in it than the others. As Andy read the book, he got an eerie feeling. He had read about this feeling in one of the other books. It was called "déjà vu". He wondered why he should feel as if he had read this book before, but it was late and Andy was tired. He put the Bible down and went to sleep.

When food was taken to Andrew, he consumed it with gusto. Soon there was no more but he was still hungry . . . only scraps of food left . . . he looked at the plate and wishes for more food . . . the plate, once again, was full to overflowing.

Andrew realized that this was a power to be exploited when the time is right, but he dared not use it in the lab except to get a second helping now and then. He now knew that he no longer needed Sarah or the assistants assigned to care for him, but must not give it away so he continued the subterfuge.

Andrew kept his intellectual development to himself. He read everything he could get his hands on, contemplated the meaning of what he had read and gained insights into areas beyond the comprehension of most.

CHAPTER FOURTEEN

Natalie and the other scientists working on the experiment were much too preoccupied with the project to think about *teaching* Andrew anything. Besides, he always seemed to just know what they expected a child of his physical maturity to know.

It did not even occur to them that a clone of Christ would have to be *taught* moral values, or anything else for that matter. He was so young and while his rapid physical development and occasionally precocious behavior should have cued them to start some kind of formal education they were just too busy so he was left to his own devices.

While he did read the Bible left behind by the cleaning lady, it was just one of hundreds of documents he devoured in the laboratory and in their offices after hours. Not being an *inherently* moral creature, he viewed the Bible as a quaintly worded history of events that occurred long ago and did not view it as a significant guide for his personal conduct.

After all, in the Bible, much more was written about sin than about moral behavior. And why was it written in such an obscure way, lending itself to different interpretations by the reader? To him it seemed to be a relatively neutral document and he derived no moral insight whatsoever from it. He developed as an amoral person. He was yet to discover the facets of life that would excite his interests and, when he did, it would be his prurient interests that would be titillated.

Time seemed to rush by as Andrew's physical development brought him quickly through puberty during which he underwent battery after battery of tests, The team, while still baffled by his accelerated growth rate were pleased that his development appeared to be happening in a perfectly normal way for his *apparent* age. Though his calendar age was just a little over three, he went through all of the changes that occur when testosterone surges through a young male body. The rapidity of these changes made this a very stressful time for him He became angry for no apparent reason, sometimes going into rages and throwing chairs about in his quarters. He was rude to everyone and frequently went into surly moods that the staff just had to wait out. He went through the usual siege of pimples and zits but they were soon behind him, too. This was all written off as normal for a young man going through puberty.

The staff gave him intelligence tests. These tests probably had little validity where Andrew was concerned. It is not really possible to devise an intelligence test that is not, to a large degree, based upon experience and Andrew's experience was far from normal. It was, in fact, extremely limited. There were huge gaps in experience relative to any normal teenager. Yet, he scored well enough on the tests that he rated well above average in intelligence. The staff should have wondered at this but missed the cues altogether. His pubescent behavior was studied and judged to be normal for his apparent age although the mood swings were much greater than expected and the staff was hard put to cope with his tantrums at times.

Andrew rode out puberty and then went through a period in which he knew more about *everything* than any one else. There was nothing unusual about that. *All* teenagers know more about everything than anyone else. These were difficult times for those charged with his upbringing but they were looking forward to the time in 1997 when his apparent age would be approaching 32. Would his development slow down to a normal rate at that time? They hoped so. That would indicate an age comparable to Christ when he was crucified.

The prospect of that happening was exciting to all of the team. It would be further evidence as to the authenticity of the Shroud.

They should have been concerned with more troubling aspects of Andrew's development but they were all so absorbed in his exterior development that they were oblivious to his incredible mental capabilities.

A major part of the human brain is devoted to speech. It takes a large amount of cerebral activity to vocalize ones thoughts because so many muscles must be controlled by neural impulses from the brain to make intelligible sounds. This activity is electrical in nature.

Andrew soon found that he knew what people in the room with him were about to say before they said it. He was picking up the electrical emissions from the brains of the speakers. At first, he interpreted this as having already heard what the speaker is saying. Indeed, he had, but only milliseconds before, during the burst of electrical activity that occurs in the period of translation from thought to manipulation of the muscles of the lips and tongue and vocal cords to articulate the words.

Speech produces much more powerful electrical activity than simply thinking about something and the electrical impulses generated by those who are talking override the signals generated by those who are merely thinking. There are many more signals permeating the environment from those who are thinking but these are so numerous and so weak that Andrew is aware of them only as background noise.

Eventually, however, Andrew developed the ability to receive and understand the weaker "thinking" signal from those nearby in the laboratory environment. He soon discovered that people do not always say what they think. He found that lying is an art and that some are more proficient at it than others. He was intrigued by this and began to study the duplicitous behavior of the scientists working on this project, whatever "this project" was. He enjoyed duplicity and made a game of concealing what he knew and what he was able to do.

Andrew sharpened this skill and was soon able to filter the thoughts of specific individuals out of the cacophony of noise from all of the other thinkers in his vicinity and he was able to tune in on the thoughts of specific individuals, even over considerable distances. He became finely tuned to Dr. Goodenough and listened to her most private thoughts.

An extrasensory voyeur, he often eavesdropped on her dreams.

The sexual neutrality of the laboratory and sterile nature of the work repressed Natalie's sensuality. However, once she dropped off to sleep, the barriers all came down and she had passionate experiences in her dreams that Andrew did not understand at first, but they excited him and filled him with urges and desires that had to be fulfilled. Andrew found that he could participate in her erotic dreams by projecting his thoughts onto her dream screen and experienced orgasmic unions with her. Thereafter, when he saw her in the laboratory, he saw her in an entirely new light and while he was certain that she did not know of his involvement in her dreams, she shyly diverted her eyes when she saw him looking at her and a blush came to her cheeks. "Yes," he thought, "She feels it but she doesn't know what."

Almost psychically, Andrew realized that he was part of some important experiment, something that involved terms that he didn't understand but which caused excited thought among these scientists and he wanted to know what it was.

One day, he was alone at a laboratory table and decided to scan through a book that one of the technicians left across the table from him but before he could reach for it, it moved. Just a few jerky random moves at first, but then it slid purposefully toward him and stopped right at his finger tips.

He had discovered his psycho kinetic powers. He wished for the pencil and notepad at the other end of the table and they also moved to him. Then he willed them back to their original places. He practiced this newfound skill at every opportunity when he was alone in his quarters in the laboratory. He discovered that he could speed up and slow down the laboratory clock, even stop it, at will. He had fun with this, sometimes speeding up the clock in the afternoon hours and causing the workers to leave for home early.

One evening, Natalie was driving home and glanced at her watch. She was puzzled, turned around. and drove back to the laboratory. Meanwhile, Andrew had reset the laboratory clock to the correct time. Natalie was thoroughly confused because *all* of the lab personnel had gone home early. Had they all hallucinated about the time? That did not seem possible. Natalie's return made Andrew realize that fooling around with the clock was a dangerous prank. It could have resulted in Dr. Goodenough returning to catch him at something that would give him away. He would have to be more careful in the future.

At the regular staff meeting, Dr. Fenton brought up the question of Andrew's appearance. "I have been thinking about Andrew and the Shroud image. He is approaching manhood and should, by now, be very close to his adult appearance. The image on the Shroud does not look very much like him, but the long hair, the beard, the bruises, the wounds, the image aberrations resulting from the flash photolysis and the mirror image all obscure the underlying face. It is possible, however, to use computer enhancement to remove the hair and correct for the other aberrations and develop a pretty good picture of the person portrayed on the Shroud."

Natalie interrupted,"Couldn't we do this ourselves and avoid involving outsiders in this?"

"I have such an image enhancement program on my computer but I think that we should contract out the job of enhancing the Shroud image to an outside firm. I am concerned that if we do this ourselves our own preconceptions might alter the final product. I propose that we go to a firm specializing in forensic enhancement of skulls and other deteriorated images. They don't have to know *why* we want this study done."

The study was commissioned.

In a matter of days, Dr. Fenton asked for a special staff meeting to view the results. The consultant had brought a video tape to help him. He took his place beside the video projection screen with a laser pointer.

THE SHROUD

The room was darkened and on the screen was displayed the full length image of the Shroud.

"This is one of the most interesting assignments I have ever undertaken. This image has many aberrations that must be corrected for. For example, This is a mirror image of the subject so the first thing we did was digitize the image and reverse it. We then had to consider the mechanism by which this image was formed. This caused a narrowing of parts of the image giving his face, arms, legs, and hands an unnaturally long and narrow appearance.

I had to develop an algorithm for dealing with this problem. After application of the algorithm, the image looks like this."

The consultant advanced the tape.

"Note that the face, limbs, and body no longer have the gaunt skeletal appearance of the initial image. It has filled out quite a bit and the cheekbone structure is not so prominent. This is obviously a more robust man than any of us might have assumed."

The tape was advanced again.

"Some cosmetic things were now done to remove blemishes of several types. A smoothing algorithm was applied to the raised bruise on the cheek. It is now more symmetrical with respect to the other cheek. None of us has perfect facial symmetry so this is just a guess but probably a good guess."

The consultant used his laser pointer to indicate the many puncture wounds caused by the crown of thorns.

"These present a slightly different but easily solvable problem. Notice that the blood stains are quite dark. Here the solution was to manually tackle each stain, pixel by pixel, converting each pixel to the same shade of grey as the unstained skin next to it. If the skin was a different shade of grey on either side of the stain, we worked from both sides and, to avoid a seam where the grey sections merged. we made a smooth transition from the lighter to the darker grey. This was a tedious manual exercise but ultimately worth the effort."

"Now lets see what is under all of that hair."

The consultant rolled the tape again. Slowly, the long hair disappeared and was replaced by a modern hair cut.

The Directors started whispering to one another.

The tape continued to roll, the beard dissolved, and the face beneath it began to emerge. The team was of one thought, "*My God. It is Andrew. There is no doubt about it.*"

There was an audible gasp from the entire audience.

The consultant was puzzled by the simultaneous reaction.

"What?"

Even though the consultant was not finished, Natalie seized the initiative, "Thank you very much. That was a most enlightening presentation."

"Are there any questions?" The consultant was confused at being cut off short in his presentation.

"No, thank you. That was most enlightening," Natalie repeated herself just wanting to get rid of the consultant before someone blurted out something that the consultant should not hear. "May we keep the tape?"

"Of course. You paid for it."

"Dr. Fenton, will you please see our guest to his car."

Fenton rose and escorted the consultant out of the conference room.

If they ever needed sufficient proof as to the authenticity of the snippet, this was it. All doubts vanished. They felt certain before, but now they *know*. Andrew *is* a clone of the person portrayed on the Shroud.

Andrew tired of the simple games he was playing with his psycho kinetic skills and moved on to more difficult activities. Soon he was able to manipulate the pins and tumblers of the locks on the door to the quarters into which he was locked every evening.

At night, he started exploring outside his quarters. At first, he merely explored Dr. Platinier's office and the corridors but could not contain his curiosity about the offices of Dr. Goodenough and her associates. He explored them and devoured the knowledge found in their libraries, often reading several books in an hour or two. They were all interesting but narrowly focused.

He wondered why the books and papers concentrated on such subjects as mitosis, amino acids, blood typing, chromosomes, ribonucleic acid (RNA), deoxyribonucleic acid (DNA), alleles, electrophoresis, chromatography, genome projects, C- A- T- G, replication, genetic engineering . . . and cloning.

He read reports on artificial insemination experiments in which a sperm cell from an anonymous donor was injected via a micro-pipette into an egg cell from another anonymous donor and the fertilized egg had undergone many cycles of mitosis, in vitro, and had developed into a recognizable human fetus. Then, when the objectives of the experiment had been met, the living fetus was killed with formaldehyde and pickled in a laboratory jar (neatly labeled and dated), and placed on a shelf with other specimens) or, if there was nothing noteworthy about the experiment, it was flushed down the drain like so much garbage.

Andrew noted with detached interest that over a period of time, one experiment after another had been *terminated*. He quickly grasped the fact that *termination* did not mean just the end of the experiment, it meant the demise of the object of the experiment. These were living creatures, but they were *terminated* coldly, clinically, without remorse.

If Andrew drew any conclusion at all from this, it was that life of any kind has no intrinsic value. When it has served its purpose it can be *terminated*. Andrew made no judgments about this. He was a soulless individual, amoral, unable to make ethical judgments. It was plain enough to him. *One does what one has to do . . .* and that became his credo.

––––––––––––––––––––––

He understood all that he read as though he had always known these things. His problem was why Dr. Goodenough and her associates saw it as such a difficult thing to understand . . . and why they picked such strange words and phrases to describe such simple concepts. It was their scientific terms that, for a while, stood in the way of his assimilation of the knowledge collected in their books and papers. Then, in Dr. Jurgensen's office, he ran across a glossary of terms relating to the Human Genome Project. He read it from beginning to end in less than an hour and quickly absorbed the contents. Now he no longer had to stop and puzzle over the meaning of the terms he encountered in the various books and scientific papers.

There were numerous papers on cloning studies documenting attempts that had failed but many in which lower animals, like newts, had been successfully cloned.

Struggling with the scientific language, he almost missed the essence of what they were doing here until he digested the glossary. Then it hit him.

This was a study of enormous import and *he* was at the center of it.

They were cloning something, . . . some creature, some*body* very special.

It was him!

HE was a clone!

This angered him. No mother? No father? Only a tiny double spiral of matter from the blood of some unknown (at least to him) donor?

Andrew was alone in his quarters in the Eugenics Laboratory when Dr. Platinier came in to check on him. Platinier had a clipboard under his arm. He sat down with Andrew and started making some notes. Andrew had discovered a new skill. He could freeze Platinier in mid-thought, mid-speech, or mid-action. He could, in effect, stop Platinier's cerebral time. During the time freeze, Andrew could move about completely unnoticed by the good doctor. At first, he froze him for only short periods of time but gradually extended the periods causing Platinier to have "missing time" episodes (the mental equivalent of psycho kinetically stopping the laboratory clock and then starting it up again). Andrew started having fun with this new found capability and was soon causing confusion among the lab assistants and cleaning people.

No one guessed what was going on and Andrew obtained his daily chuckles watching the consternation on the faces of people who took what they thought was a 10 minute restroom break only to be gone for an hour and be reprimanded by coworkers by abusing their break privileges.

It was Dr. Goodenough's staff meeting. Everyone was in place but Henri Platinier. Natalie impatiently tapped on her wrist watch as the time stretched to 10 . . . 20 . . . 30 minutes. She had started the meeting on time, without him, and it had gone smoothly but she was such a stickler for order and Henri had not given his report in the proper point in the rotation.

"Where can he be?" The question was not just on Natalie's mind. It was on everyone's.

The conference room door opened and in strolled Platinier. He thought it a bit strange that everyone else was already seated. It was his habit to get there well ahead of the scheduled meeting time, but *somebody* had to be last so he gave it no more thought.

"Your alarm clock malfunction?" It took him a moment before Henri realized that the question was directed at him but when he saw Natalie's stern expression, he was at a loss for an answer.

"No, I arrived early, went to the lab to do the regular morning check of Andrew and then came directly here."

"And how long did it take to check out Andrew?"

"Ten minutes, . . . max."

Natalie directed her gaze toward the conference room clock and Henri followed it.

It hit him like a bucket of ice water in the face. By *that* clock he was nearly 45 minutes late. In disbelief, he quickly glanced at his wrist watch. It showed the same time as the conference room clock. Dr. Platinier was *non plussed.*

How is this possible?

"I . . . I . . . I . . . I can't explain it."

"Well, we are behind schedule so please give your report."

Henri gave his report, hesitatingly, frequently distracted by his inability to account for the missing time.

Andrew was tuned in to the thoughts of the people in the conference room and quietly chortling to himself.

Before John, Natalie was so enmeshed in every aspect of her scientific endeavors that she did not realize how out of balance her life was. John provided a much needed emotional stability. He was an attentive caring lover. Their affair was a continuous courtship, but the "M" word was never brought up by either of them. Natalie's professional drive brought on an unusually early menopause which she sailed right through without the usual side effects. Children were, therefore, out of the question. John provided sufficient affection to compensate for this void. Their lovemaking was conventional but always exciting and climactic, and of course, there was Andrew, . . . not quite the same as a child of her own, but he provided an outlet for her lingering maternal instincts.

August 1995, "Today in Science" magazine reported that "microscopic organic materials may have interfered with the dating results, making the Shroud appear much younger than it actually is." Two prominent scientists of the University of Heidelberg Health Science Center had subjected small residual samples of the Shroud to mass spectroscopic and infra red analysis. They found the samples to be coated with bacteria, fungi, and biogenic varnishes that would materially affect the Carbon-14 dating results, making the Shroud appear to be much younger than it is. This was, of course, old news to Natalie, but getting confirmation from another source bolstered Natalie's belief that her snippet *had* come from the Shroud and Andrew was indeed cloned from the blood of Christ.

Andrew had realized from the outset that he was very special. Dr. Goodenough and the others did not have his grasp of the way things are. They clearly did not have his ability to read one another's thoughts and none of them could manipulate objects without touching them the way he could. He was indeed special but who had they cloned him from and why?

————————

At night they all left the laboratory complex.
Where did they go?
What did they do?
What was there outside the sterile environment of this laboratory?
Andrew's nightly forays carried him further and further afield until one night he reached the door to the outside world. He stood looking out the window of the heavy door and his curiosity could not be contained.

He looked at the lock, concentrated on it and heard the pins and tumblers click into place. The handle slowly turned, the bolt made a loud clunk as it slid clear of the striker plate, and the massive door swung open.

Andrew stepped out into a world quite different from the only world he had known up to this moment.

————————

CHAPTER FIFTEEN

Guided by the glow in the sky, Andrew wandered into the heart of the city. He was astonished at the flashing neon. After the cold white sterility of the laboratories and the Doctors' offices, he wanted to see more. He covered his ears to block out the raucous sounds of the city. He had no idea what it all was. Automobiles frightened him . . . and their horns. The blare of music and voices from a thousand loudspeakers all enticing him to come in and enjoy the exotic pleasures offered inside. What pleasures? He could not read the minds of tape recordings. When he tried to enter some of those glittering palaces, he was repulsed because he had no money. Money? What was that? He would have to find out . . . and get some of it. Money seemed to be very important in this world.

A young man on a street corner sized him up and approached. He asked Andrew if he was looking for a good time. Andrew indicated that he was and the young man took him by the hand and lead him down a dark alley. Andrew was still preoccupied with the idea of money. He asked the young man if he had any money. The man, thinking that Andrew wanted to be paid for sexual favors, said "yes." He took a fifty dollar bill out of his wallet and said, "Will this cover it?" Andrew was reading his mind but really didn't comprehend what the man was thinking. He took the fifty and turned to walk away.

"Hey! Wait a minute. I paid you. If you are not going to do anything, give me my money back." He tried to grab the money out of Andrew's hand. Andrew turned and grabbed the man by his throat and squeezed . . . hard. Something was crushed. He could feel it. The man went limp and fell to the ground. Andrew had no idea that he had done anything wrong. Remembering the man's wallet, he took it, put the fifty back in it and left. When he got back out into the light he took out one of the bills and examined it. It was just *paper*. How could it possibly have any value?

He shrugged and walked slowly down the light drenched street.

A hustler urged him to come into a theater where a porno movie was showing. They wanted money before they would let him in. He took out one of the bills, a ten dollar bill, and gave it to the woman in the glass box. She gave him some money back.

There were several bills in his change and he puzzled over the transaction.

"She wanted money; I gave her one money; and she gave me back several monies?"

That suited him just fine. He didn't understand the transaction but, if every time he gave someone money, they gave him back more monies than he gave them, he would never run out of it.

He took a seat in the back of the theater and watched the screen. He felt an excitement that he did not understand but as he watched, he thought about Natalie Goodenough's dreams and this somehow related. As he watched, he took mental notes, "She has never done *that* in her dreams. I will think about *that* the next time I involve *myself* in one of her dreams. I know she will like it."

He just sat there but soon realized that he had already seen it, . . . twice. He had no idea how those images of people got up there on the screen but wondered why they started all over again and did and said the same things as before.

"Is that all those people know how to do?"

He left the theater and drifted back out along the street. Eventually, he wandered into a bar and sat on one of the stools.

"What'll ya have to drink, buddy?"

Andrew shrugged.

"Scotch OK?"

Andrew shrugged again. He hadn't a clue as to what the bar keep was talking about.

"Neat?"

"What?"

"Neat."

Andrew shrugged again and the bar keep set a shot glass in front of him and poured a shot of straight scotch. Andrew was thirsty. The man hadn't given him very much. He looked at it then tossed it straight down.

It tasted awful. He turned to leave and the bar keep yelled,"Wait a minute, buddy. You didn't pay for that."

"What?"

"Money, buddy, . . . money."

"Oh."

Andrew took a five dollar bill out of the wallet and handed it to the bar keep. The bar keep put it in the register and closed the drawer.

"Don't you give *me* some money, now?"

"Are you kidding? A shot of scotch is five dollars in this joint."

Andrew is now really confused. The stuff tasted bad and he had been given so little of it and then the man had kept his money and not given him any in return. He obviously did not know everything he should know about this paper stuff they call money.

Despite its awful taste, the scotch *did* make him feel warm inside. It was, paradoxically, unpleasant and pleasant at the same time. Andrew decided to try it again. He entered the next bar, sat on a stool and ordered a scotch, neat. He was quite pleased with himself. He tossed it down. It still tasted bad, . . . but not nearly as bad as the first one. He pulled out a ten dollar bill and handed it to the bar keep. To his surprise, he got back five ones.

The bartender obviously wanted to make sure he had small enough bills to leave a tip. Andrew, of course, knew nothing of tipping but made a mental note to come *back* to this place because they gave him back more of these money things than he gave them.

A few more stops and the lights of the city were spinning, but pleasantly so. Soon, he was thoroughly confused and he noticed that he had no more money. How could that be?

He discarded the wallet and, despite the haze, found his way back to the Project building and back into his laboratory quarters. He used his psycho- kinetic powers to lock himself in but neglected to lock the main entrance door.

Soon he was sound asleep and no one noticed his disheveled appearance or tried to awaken him.

———————————

His foray into the outside world did not go completely unnoticed, however.

Dr. Goodenough was the first to arrive that morning and was startled to find that the front entrance was unlocked. After checking to make sure no one else was in yet, she immediately put a message on everyone's voice-mail calling for a special staff meeting at 9:00 AM *sharp*.

"OK troops," Dr. Goodenough began, "Yesterday evening, all of you left at about the same time. To the best of my knowledge, I was the last to leave. Did any of you come back later last night?"

They all shook their heads, "no", almost in unison.

"Are all of your keys accounted for?"

Each checked and answered affirmatively as she took roll call around the conference table.

Dr. Goodenough said sternly,"I am certain that I locked the door when I left last night, but it was unlocked when I arrived this morning. Is there any evidence of unauthorized entrance into your areas?"

She went around the conference table again. Each Director indicated that while there was no direct evidence of unauthorized entry, sometimes books and other objects seemed to have been moved about in their offices and labs during the night. Even more disturbing, however, was the report of several Directors that while nothing was missing, the contents of their office safes appeared to have been rearranged. This was a chilling revelation because the safes had lock systems that permitted each Director to pick his own combination and to change them at will.

THE SHROUD

Dr. Goodenough knew the weakness of *this* system. People tended to write their combinations, passwords, and the like in insecure places like in an unencrypted computer file or even on slips of paper taped to the underside of desk drawers. She had insisted from the outset that they commit their combinations to memory and not record them anywhere. However, there is a downside to that, too. Nobody wants to forget their combination so they tend to use something like their phone number. A smart intruder would have no trouble finding or working out most combinations in a few minutes. In the front of Natalie's mind was the suspicion that the office safes were the least secure items in the facility.

"It appears that we have a serious security problem. Tomorrow I will have the locks all changed and issue you new keys. I am not sure what has happened here but I am confident in the security of this kind of lock. In addition, all safes will be replaced. Entry will require both the insertion of your personal key and the entry of a combination which will consist of a part chosen by you and a part chosen by me. I won't know your part of the combination and you won't know mine. My part will be entered electronically from my office, by me. All three will be required to gain entry to your safe. I don't know what is going on here but I mean to end it *now*. We dare not risk compromising what we are doing. I have considered putting on security guards but the more people there are on the premises, the poorer our security will ultimately be, so I do not plan to add security guards at this time. Meanwhile, stay alert."

Andrew awakened while the meeting was in progress. He tuned in on Natalie Goodenough's thought patterns and realized that he had made some serious mistakes while browsing around in the offices and while outside the building. The new pick-proof locks will be no problem for him. These are designed to thwart manipulation from *outside* the locks, but he manipulated the pins and tumblers, in effect, from *inside* the lock. He looked forward to the challenge.

THE SHROUD

*In the future, however, he will have to be careful to put
everything back exactly as he found it when he exits any of
the offices.*

After the staff meeting, Natalie invited Sarah into her
office.

"What do you think?'

"There is something very strange here. Too many things
just don't make sense."

"How about lunch? 12:30?"

"OK, We can talk about it. See you then."

Sarah stoppped by Natalie's office at 12:30.

"I've made reservations at Café de Georgio".

This was Natalie's favorite restaurant, a little pricey but
quiet. The maitre de knew her and had reserved a table in a
secluded niche where their conversation could not be
overheard.

After ordering cocktails, they dawdled over them for
two or three minutes before either spoke.

Sarah broke the ice, "I don't know what to make of this.
Someone left the front door unlocked. It *might* have been one
of the team, but that leaves it open to two possibilities. Is
there someone on the team who is not what they purport to
be and if so what are they up to? The second possibility is
that one of the team carelessly left it unlocked and is too
embarrassed to admit it . . . I would like to think that *this*
is the answer, but if so, what were they doing here after we
had all ostensibly gone home?"

Natalie replied, "No. We have a more serious problem
than entry through the front door. Someone appears to have
gotten into several individual offices despite the unique keys
required to do so . . . and an altogether different kind of
problem . . . access to the contents of their safes . . . Is
this some new kind of hacker who can defeat any sort of lock
system?"

Sarah considered this for a few moments.

"That is a really scary thought. It is well known that computer hackers have broken into some of the most secure electronic systems ever devised. . . . bank systems, the IRS, even the computers of the North American Air Defense Command and the Pentagon. That was one of the reasons why Natalie had chosen a purely mechanical security system in the first place. But, now, how successful would she be in trying to hold <u>this</u> kind of hacker at bay?"

"Maybe this guy is just a mechanical whiz. It does not seem likely that he would also be a clever computer hacker, too. As you said, we probably should consider a hybrid system having the best features of mechanical locks and electronic security systems, too. Also, there are some security measures that are very hard to defeat. Maybe we should consider devices that check against an archived voice print, thumb print, hand print, or retinal scan."

"I considered those initially, but they did not live up to their press releases. They work perfectly every time in 'spy' movies, but they are *not* fully invented yet. When the actual systems were demonstrated, they were subject to more frequent identification errors than we would find acceptable. Actually, I would consider *one* error unacceptable but the best systems available made a lot more than that. Thanks for your input but I think we need to go at this one step at the time. Today, we will change the locks. Then we'll see what happens."

When she returned from lunch, Dr. Goodenough called John, at his office at MAXXX Security Systems, asked him to come by her office because she didn't want to discuss the subject over the phone. He arrived at 2:00 PM and Natalie went over the problem with him in great detail. Flabbergasted is too mild an expression to describe Pearsons' reaction.

"Impossible! No, I'm sorry, obviously not impossible. But, are you sure of all of the incidents?"

"Yes, I am."

"But for the system to be compromised in so many places at once . . . the common areas locks, . . . the personal areas locks, . . . not just one, but all of them and the safe locks, as well. It is incomprehensible. You don't know this, but the main entrance lock, while it is operated by the common areas key, is a new design. It uses the same key but it operates on a completely different principle from the rest of the common area locks. We consider it to be more pick proof than any of the others and no one has ever picked one of *those*. As you know MAXXX has a standing offer of $1,000,000 to anyone who can pick *any* of our locks. We have had no takers."

"That may be, but the facts speak for themselves."

"I know and I can't explain it."

"Maybe someone thinks that something we have in here is worth more than a million dollars, making it more profitable to break into our facilities than to collect on your challenge."

"Possibly. Do you?"

"That's the strangest part of all of this. I don't know, but someone *might* think so."

"OK, I suggest we change all of the key-operated locks to our new design and install our latest and most secure safe-lock system. You recall that we discussed our hybrid safe-lock system when we bid this project, initially. I recommend that you go to that. We can finish the key-lock exchange today and complete the installation of our hybrid safe-lock system by this time tomorrow. You were concerned about discussing this on the phone. I assume you worried about telephone security. Your phones *might* be bugged but it is conceivable that your *office* could be bugged, too. Accordingly, we will sweep your phone system and your office for bugs. I will hand deliver to you, tomorrow, a set of personal and serial numbered manuals explaining the safe-lock system and I recommend that after each of your key people has read his copy, he shreds it and burns the shreds."

At that moment, Natalie regretted that she had said so much about the new safe-lock system at the staff meeting but what's done is done.

Pearsons' question about the financial value of their work troubled her greatly. The stories about the wealthiest people of the world setting up their own laboratories to clone themselves for body parts was very plausible. Maybe this *was* a case of "industrial espionage". There were obviously those who would pay heavily for immortality. If word got out about Andrew, the Project records would indeed be worth a king's ransom.

The electronics security specialists swept the phone systems, all of the offices, and all of the common areas. No bugs were found. In a sense, Natalie was more disturbed by this than she might have been if they had found something. Of course, a bug would not explain *everything* but it would, at least, have been a start. Now, she still had nothing.

After the locks and safes were changed, Andrew decided to wait for a few days to let the storm abate. He was becoming more and more restless and found an outlet only in his ability to inject himself into Natalie Goodenough dreams. He projected, onto her dream screen, the lurid activities he had seen on the screen in the porno movie house. Both enjoyed incredible orgasmic releases. Natalie moaned passionately and cried out to John. She could not see the face of her dream lover. It had to be John but he had never made love to her like this.

"Natalie?"

She felt John's gentle touch on her shoulder.

"Natalie? You were dreaming."

"Oh. John . . . ", Natalie turned toward him, groping. Their lips met and they merged in an urgent passionate sexual explosion.

Afterward, all John could say was,"Wow!"

Andrew was now becoming fully aware of his own sensuality and his sexuality. He did not understand them but they were there, and were powerful stimuli. After only two days of self imposed confinement, waiting for the flap over his explorations to die down, he had urges that could not be ignored and could not be fully satisfied in either *his* dreams or Natalie's. He needed to get out *now* and the wait until closing time and the departure of the Dr. Goodenough seemed interminable. He could not wait any longer.

CHAPTER SIXTEEN

As soon as the last person was out of the building, he started working on the Eugenics Laboratory lock. It took him a bit longer than the original lock but he quickly figured it out and found himself in Dr Platinier's office. He did not tarry there but moved on to the main entrance.

In the windowless environment of The Project complex, there was no way to tell what conditions existed in the outside world. Was it Hot? Cold? Night? Day? Wet? Dry?

It came as something of a surprise that it was still daylight when he reached the front door. Andrew weighed the risks. He *had* to get out. He mentally manipulated the lock and it opened for him for the second time.

Andrew now knew the way and went directly to the honky tonk part of the city.

He *loved* it. There was an air of excitement here that was impossible to describe. It generated a heady feeling just being here.

As darkness descended, the street lights and neon signs started winking on up and down the strip. The loudspeakers started salaciously hawking appeals to the lusts of the passersby . . . peep shows, . . . slot machines, . . . crap tables, . . . adult book stores, . . . XXX-rated movies, . . . topless bars, . . . adult video tapes, . . . pimps and hookers . . . massage parlors . . . The entire gamut of vice and debauchery reaches out to Andrew, beckons to him, invites him to partake and he is receptive. He is more than receptive. He is eager.

He is now more focused in his needs than he was the first time. The money thing was a problem. He has none, but he had none the first time, either. That was a bridge to be crossed when he got there but, at least, he had figured out how money worked. Andrew wandered up and down the strip until well into the night.

He watched three prostitutes working the opposite street corner. Two of them made deals and climbed into cars that sped away. The remaining hooker flaunted her wares in a gaudy red top, tight miniskirt, and high white boots sprinkled with glitter. She waved down car after car without making a sale. Then she spotted Andrew watching her.

She strutted, wiggled, and gyrated across the street to where he was standing.

She was very street wise and knew how to avoid entrapment.

"Hi, baby, are you a badge?"

Best to lay it right on the line.

"What?"

"Come on. You know what I mean. Are you vice? What?"

"No, I don't know what you mean."

"Don't try to snow me, baby. Are you the police?"

Andrew does not respond.

"OK. I will take that as a 'no'. It is fifty dollars either way, . . . seventy five for the whole package. Take it or leave it."

Andrew finally figured out what she was selling and it was precisely what he wanted. He wasn't sure what it meant but answered,"OK, the whole package."

The hooker motioned to a tawdry hotel where she and the other two hookers shared a pad. When they reached the room, they stepped inside, closed the door and she said."Lets get this straight . . . nothin' until I see the cash."

"The cash?"

"The money, baby, the money." She rubbed her thumb and curled fingers under his nose.

Andrew grabbed her, threw her on the bed, and ripped off her clothing.

She screamed and Andrew lashed out with his fist and broke her jaw. She still tried to call for help. Andrew punched her in the face and continued to pummel her, blackening both eyes and raising large welts on face. Her cheekbone was shattered and she cowered, whimpering, in the fetal position.

Andrew brutally raped her several times and when he was finished, he beat her to death and did something else, too, something horrible.

The hooker's pimp had cleaned her out just an hour ago so she had only the payment from her last John in her purse. Andrew got only fifty dollars. It would have to do.

He took in another porno movie where he observed acts that were different from those in the previously seen movie, and then went from bar to bar until the fifty dollars was gone. When he arrived back at the Project complex, he was very careful to lock the door at the main entrance. Similarly, he quickly made his way through Dr. Platinier's office and into the Eugenics Lab carefully locking the doors behind him.

He went to his washbasin and scrubbed the dried blood off his hands. When he washed his arms and face the stinging sensation alerted him to the scratches. He would have to make up an explanation. He faked a fall in which a broken dish could be blamed for the abrasions and contusions. The cuts and bruises on his knuckles made his explanation less credible. If they had been the least bit suspicious they probably wouldn't have bought it, but they did.

The following night, Andrew once again invaded Natalie's dreams but this time he had actual experiences to guide him and the porno movie had given him some ideas to pursue. This time, he was not just a detached voyeur. He injected himself into her dream but controlled her dream in such a way that he was a faceless lover. They undressed one another. She yielded willingly to his caresses. He made passionate love to her . . . ravished her, . . . and the climax of her dream was spectacular for both of them.

In the Eugenics Laboratory, Andrew looked at Natalie in such a knowing way. It was like he was accessing her most intimate thoughts. His piercing eyes caused galvanic sensations along the nape of her neck that were extremely unnerving and she felt more and more ill at ease in his presence. She tried to suppress the stirrings inside her but couldn't.

Natalie crossed her arms over her breasts to conceal the involuntary hardening of her nipples, made an excuse for leaving, and hurried back to her office. She shut the door and sat at her desk flushed and gasping for breath. She had no control over this phenomenon. Even her reveries about her most intimate times with John did not cause such a reaction.

What is going on here?

And why?

For a person who was always in control this was unacceptable . . . absolutely unacceptable. Andrew was reading her thoughts and willed another involuntary action. She teased her fingers around her hard tender nipples and felt a powerful surge of release. Andrew knew and smiled.

"My God", she thought, *"What is happening to me?"*

The problem became worse over the next few weeks. Whenever she was around Andrew, she could not keep her mind on her work. Her sensuality was running rampant and her mind was filled with lewd and lascivious ideas, far beyond anything she and John had ever done. More and more often she found herself rushing back to her office to relieve her yearnings.

Sarah, being a woman, was more perceptive than the other members of the team. It was clear to her that something decidedly *female* was going on here and she asked Natalie to join her at lunch.

Sarah made a reservation at Café de Georgio, Natalie's favorite eatery. Both were quiet during the ride over. The maitre de seated them in the same secluded niche as the last time. Natalie selected a Pouilly-Fuissé. After the wine steward served them, the waiter took their orders and disappeared. They finally had a few moments to themselves.

"You've noticed haven't you?" Natalie stared vacantly into her wine.

"Yes. Something is bothering you. Does it have to do with Andrew?"

Natalie was startled by Sarah's insight. "Why do you say that?"

"You are not at ease when you are in the same room with him."

"It is worse than that. I can't explain it but my mind is preoccupied all day and night with the most erotic thoughts imaginable. I've tried to force myself to ignore them but that seems to trigger even more intense sexual arousal. I have always had my emotions under control. You know that . . . but now, I just can't. It is driving me up the wall."

"Do you think Andrew has anything to do with it?"

"How could he?"

"I don't know."

"Neither do I."

But it wasn't just a consequence of her affair with John. This went way beyond that.

That ended the conversation. Their food had arrived anyway.

On the way back to the Project Building, both silently mulled over their conversation. This was most baffling and disconcerting.

The Directors of the departments were not all confident that the new security measures had solved the problem. Several decided independently that they would attempt to detect any invasion of their areas.

Before Dr. Mansic left each day, he placed books and documents at precisely measured locations on his desk and reading table. The next morning, nothing appeared, to the eye, to have been disturbed. But when he got out his scale and measured the reading table he found that the book he had left on the table was 1 cm closer to the front edge and ½ cm further from the left edge of the table than he had left it.

Dr. Fenton took a different path. He thoroughly cleaned and waxed his desk and table top removing all traces of fingerprints. When he returned the next morning, he sprinkled talcum powder on the surfaces and then blew it off.

There, all over both surfaces were distinct palm and fingerprints . . . lots of them. There was no mistake. Someone *had* been in his office overnight.

Suspicious that it might be a team member, each privately disclosed his findings to Dr. Goodenough. That was a mistake. Andrew was sharply tuned in to Natalie and knew instantly what was going on. He would have to stay out of the offices. He had obviously underestimated Natalie's colleagues.

He no longer needed whatever he might find in their offices. Now, he was interested only in the outside world and fingerprints would not be a problem. He used his psycho kinetic abilities to manipulate the locks so no fingerprints would be left behind.

At the next staff meeting, Natalie announced that she was planning to put a security guard station at the front door. She did not elaborate on this but she was obviously disturbed by the reports by Doctors Mansic and Fenton.

This was a new challenge for Andrew. He had been thinking about it anyway. Now it would be put to the test. To him it seemed simple. He would impose his thoughts on those of the guard and walk right past him without being seen. He decided to try it out. He strolled right past Dr. Platinier and then back into the Eugenics Laboratory without being seen but it required intense mental effort, more than he had anticipated. He did not think that he could do this with two people simultaneously. Well, there was going to be only *one* guard and he could handle that.

Andrew was content to stay in his quarters in the Eugenics Laboratory for the next few days. At night he continued to amuse himself by projecting his thoughts onto Natalie's dream screen and having erotic adventures with her. The variety of activities increased as he drew on the library of erotica that he had stored during his visits to the porno movie houses. Suppressed inside Natalie's outer shell was a sensual sexual vixen that was turned loose in her dreams and what she did in her dreams heighten her sexual intensity with John.

It was exhausting but John was enjoying it too much to think about what might be triggering it.

Andrew enjoyed this virtual sex, but it stimulated his urge for more of the real thing.

He could not wait any longer.

Dr. Goodenough and her team had all gone home for the night. The security guard desk had been put into place and the guard was seated there alert and ready for any contingency.

He subconsciously ran over a mental checklist, touching each of the items as he ticked them off: *badge, ID card on his lapel, flashlight, handcuffs, mace, . . . gun . . .* he fondly caressed the butt of his Glock. The Glock was a splendid weapon, lightweight polymer frame, . . . 9 mm, . . . 17 rounds, . . . fast and accurate, . . . He had never had to use it, except on the pistol range, where he was expert, but it made him feel powerful. As he fondled his automatic, he fantasized about the voluptuous females on "Babes on the Beach", his favorite TV program.

Andrew read the security guard's thoughts.

"This will be easier than I imagined."

Andrew projected a situation onto the guard's fantasy screen in which the guard was a participant. As the guard reveled in the ocean of bosoms, Andrew unlatched the front door and confidently walked out into the night.

It was not quite as easy as Andrew had imagined. He had to keep the guard's fantasy going while concentrating on the lock. That required a level of concentration that he had not reached before but he was up to the challenge and headed for the Strip .

"I am invincible," he thought as he stepped up the pace and strutted toward the Strip.

Andrew looked up and down the gaudy, raucous Strip and had a feeling of belonging. This was his kind of place. Not just his kind of place, *his* place. He owned it. With his new-found ability to affect the thoughts of others, he was no longer impaired by the money thing. Everything here was his for the taking.

He sauntered into a bar and ordered a scotch, neat. The bartender poured him one and said, "That'll be five dollars." Andrew made the bartender think that he had been given a bill. Without realizing it, Andrew had visualized a *ten* dollar bill. The bartender went to the cash register, went through the motions of putting the *virtual* bill into the cash drawer and returned with a *real* five dollar bill, Andrew's change.

Andrew went from bar to bar. He was a bit too tipsy to balance on one of those high bar stools so he sat at a table. He had collected several monies in his pocket and didn't know what to do with them. Then he noticed the well endowed waitress. As she bent over to serve the table next to his, her miniskirt hiked up in the back.

The men at the table she was serving did not get the view that Andrew got, but her skimpy bra revealed much of her full frontal plentitude to them. Andrew had noticed that from time to time a customer would tuck one of those money papers into her bra, while taking a liberty or two with his hands.

After she finished with the adjacent table, she turned to Andrew. When she leaned over to take his order, he tucked a bill in between her breasts and gently squeezed them. Andrew observed that she was much more receptive to his caresses than she had been at the next table, . . . and why not? He had made it so.

When she returned with his drink, Andrew simultaneously tucked a couple of monies between her breasts and slid his hand up under her skirt.

As he touched her secret place he whispered in her ear, "Don't you get off right now? We can go to your place."

The waitress said something to one of the other waitresses, nodded toward Andrew and returned to the table. Andrew made his face a blur in the mind of the second waitress.

She took him to her apartment in her car.

———————————

It was a long walk back to the Project Building. On the way, it started to rain, gently at first but then a downpour, a rare occurrence in LA. It was nearly dawn. Andrew contemplated finding shelter and waiting out the storm but the rain kept coming down harder by the minute. There was a freshly seeded place in front of the Project Building and Andrew took a shortcut across it. Again he was confronted with the problem of simultaneously confusing the guard and unlocking the door. It was doubly difficult in his partially drunken state but he managed.

Concentrating, as he was, on the task at hand, he failed to notice that he left a trail of muddy footprints across the lobby floor, past the guard desk and down the corridor toward the Project office complex. Luckily, the prints faded out as he made his way back toward the Eugenics Laboratory. Despite his foggy state, he remembered to lock all of the doors behind him. He got out of his soaked clothing and hung everything up in his closet, hoping no one would notice, dried himself off and climbed into bed.

When Andrew returns each night he assumes the identity that he knows Dr. Goodenough has come to expect. He thoroughly enjoys this kind of lying in which he lets them believe what they want to believe and does nothing to disabuse them.

Natalie was the first to arrive. She drove in early in order to get a head start on traffic. It always got tied up during rush hour on days like this. If she had arrived ten minutes earlier, she would have seen Andrew returning. However, she did arrive in time to see the still wet footprints.

The guard said, "Good morning, Doctor Goodenough, Nasty out, huh?"

Natalie shook the water off her umbrella and replied. "Looks like someone else is an early bird, too. Who arrived before me?"

"Nobody. You're the first."

"I can't be. What about these?" Natalie pointed to the muddy trail of footprints. "*Somebody* came in ahead of me."

The security guard stared in bewilderment at the prints. Obviously, he didn't have a clue.

"Well, can you explain this . . . and it had better be good."

The guard just stared and said nothing.

"The tracks are still wet. Whoever it was may still be here. Lets check."

The guard unsnapped the safety strap on his Glock and nervously felt the handle. It was comforting to know he had this much firepower if he needed it . . . But he hoped he wouldn't need it.

When the guard came on duty, he was not given a key. He was locked in. He was provided with a private line to Dr. Goodenough's home and an alarm button to summon police or firefighters but he could not unlock the main entrance and could not access any of the common areas.

The only room he could enter on his own was the public restroom next to the lobby. He thought about that. He did have to relieve himself once during his shift but that was early in the evening. If the intruder had come in then, the tracks would be dry by now but they were wet . . . *fresh.*

They followed the tracks until they ran out. Natalie used her key to open the doors to all of the common areas but, of course, could not open the doors to any of the offices, labs, or other areas requiring a private key for access.

They found nothing. Natalie and the security guard returned to the guard desk.

`   "Wait here", she said.

Natalie went to her office and placed a call to John Pearsons at MAXXX Security Systems. She half expected to have to leave a voice-mail message but Pearsons answered the phone himself.

"John, this is Natalie Goodenough. We have a major problem. Tell me about the security guard we had on duty last night."

"Why? Did he do anything wrong? He is my most reliable man. Worked for me for years with nothing but good reports."

"That may be, but last night I think he fell asleep on the job."

CHAPTER SEVENTEEN

"Tell you what. Send the guard home. I will be over in twenty minutes . . . half hour tops. I have a compact self-contained video camera. It takes one picture per second and runs unattended for a week and has several features like recording the date and time on each frame. I can install it behind one of the ceiling tiles in the lobby where it can see the front door and the guard station. There is something really strange going on here and I want to get to the bottom of it as much as you do."

True to his word, John Pearsons arrived with the camera and it took him only about ten minutes to install it. No one arrived during the installation so only Natalie and John knew about it but, best of all, Andrew was sleeping off his bout of drinking and debauchery so he was completely unaware of what had taken place.

Pearsons had one final word, "I would suggest that you not tell *anyone* about this."

Natalie nodded agreement and Pearsons left.

At this point, Natalie did not know who to trust.

In line with the old adage *"If three people know, it is no longer a secret,"* She did not even tell Sarah.

The next night, when the waitress failed to show up for work and did not answer messages left on her machine, one of her co-workers went to check.

When the police arrived the co-worker met them at the door and vomited in the hall outside the waitress' apartment. There were bloody shoe prints and drops of blood leading down the corridor away from the victim's apartment. The police who answered the 911 call were homicide detectives who had seen many gruesome crime scenes in their careers but nothing like this.

The woman's breasts had been sliced off with a razor sharp 12 inch butcher knife and nailed to the wall over the head of the bed. Long wide slices of her skin had been similarly nailed to the wall, along with her genitals which had been carved from her body with the same knife. The bed and floor were soaked with sticky drying blood.

The officers assumed she had been raped but there was no way to tell. That would have to wait for the autopsy.

"God, this guy is insane. The MO is different but it's got to be the same guy, the one who raped that hooker the other night and beat her to death. This is just uncontrolled viciousness. The perp's hands and feet had to be covered with blood but if he left during that downpour, all traces will be washed away. Damn that rain. I want this guy BAD!"

The other detective said, "Don't forget that fairy we found in the alley. That was a completely different MO, too, but there *is* a common thread, the eyes. Also, all of the victims either worked, or were found, within a couple of blocks of one another. I know we are looking for just one guy for all of them but there is nothing consistent about him, except the eyes, nothing else I can put my finger on. Just a really strong gut feeling."

When Sarah arrived the next day, she stuck her head into Natalie's office, "Did you catch the 11 o'clock news?"

"No. Why?'

"There is some crazy out there killing people on the other side of town. So far, it is hookers and waitresses but who knows when he will set his sights higher. Be careful when you go home."

"You, too."

After Andrew sobered up, he checked out the clothing he had hung up in the closet. They were still damp and there were splatters of blood all around the cuffs of his trousers, he quickly took them off the hangers, went into his bathroom and scrubbed the legs of his trousers in the wash basin. It took a long time. Even though the trousers were still damp the blood stains stubbornly refused to yield to his efforts and it took him the better part of an hour to get them to the point where the stains would not be noticed unless, of course, someone was looking for them. Then they jumped right out at you.

Andrew showered, and put on fresh clothing. After that it was a normal day of routine tests, and he did not do anything to arouse suspicion.

CHAPTER EIGHTEEN

Midweek, Andrew was again overwhelmed by his urges.

This time it was a little easier to get past the guard and out into his world of lascivious pleasures.

Once again, he walked down the Strip looking for his special kind of excitement and wandered into a massage parlor. That was a new experience for him and when the masseuse offered a little something extra he accepted and when she offered something *really* special he took her up on that, too. When she was finished, he killed her. Later that night he went to a house of ill repute and, after satisfying himself, killed the whore and left.

He did not butcher these two victims but in both cases he did as he had done in all of the previous murders. He ripped out the eyeballs. In all instances, except the fairy, they were found in the toilet bowls. In his case they were found on the ground in the alley.

The *eyes*, the one commonality connecting all of the victims, were never reported to the press by the police. They wanted to head off an outbreak of copycat killings and, except for the eyes, the murders were so different that a potential copycat had nothing to copy. There were the rapes, of course, but the fairy wasn't raped, it is pretty hard to tell if a hooker or whore has been raped and, anyway, rape killings were a dime a dozen . . . there was nothing to inspire a copy cat. Homicide hoped to keep it that way. The team of detectives assigned to the "eyeball killer" already had a full platter.

There was nothing mystical or mysterious about Andrew's obsession with the eyes. He had dispatched all of his victims face to face. A completely amoral creature, he had no compunctions about either the killings or the mutilations, but those eyes, filled with terror, staring straight into his, were disquieting, so much so that he ripped them out before he finished his *experiments*.

And these were *all* experiments. When an experiment was over, he *terminated* it, . . . not always the same way, but he terminated it. That is what was done in *their* world and that is what he does in *his* world.

Andrew has become a feral beast. He has no knowledge of right or wrong but only that he has ever increasing carnal appetites that must be satisfied.

CHAPTER NINETEEN

The video camera had been in place for nearly a week. It was about to run out of tape.

John called Natalie at home.

"Hi, this is John. Since it is the weekend, can I assume that no one is working at the Project Complex? I would like to come over, pick up the tape, and change the batteries."

Natalie replied, "Good. I am anxious to see if you caught anything. When do you want me to let you in? I'll have to get dressed first. How about in an hour? . . . Ok, I'll meet you in the parking lot. Take Sarah Buckley's spot. It is right next to mine."

They arrived almost simultaneously.

"Good timing," commented Pearsons, "When we get to the lobby, can you distract the guard long enough for me to make the swap? Ask him to check out the rest rooms? Anything. I will only need about a minute."

"No problem."

"He will probably wonder why I am there, but we can make it look like a routine meeting."

Everything went off as planned. As they strolled back to the parking lot, John brandished the tape. "I will check this as soon as I get back to my office. Even though this was recorded at only one frame per second, I have a machine that I can use to fast forward to check it out quickly. Will you be up for a couple of hours?" Natalie nodded affirmatively. "OK, If I find anything I will call you."

Natalie was immersed in a review of her Directors' status reports when the phone rang. It was John. "Are you still dressed? You'd better come over and see this."

"What did you get?"

"Maybe you can tell me?"

"I'll be right over."

When Natalie arrived, John escorted her straight to his conference room.

Without a word, he started the tape player. "Nothing out of the ordinary here. Note, the guard is very alert and attentive to his job".

He fast forwarded and then resumed the one frame per second rate. "Here, the guard takes a rest room break. He is not away from his station any longer than necessary. Back at his station now and still alert. We can fast forward again."

John has notes that he took during his first viewing. He is watching the date-time display in the lower right hand corner of the picture and slows down the machine then stops it.

John inches the tape forward, frame by frame. "Watch closely now."

The guard is, without a doubt, awake and alert. A man walks slowly past him toward the door. The guard doesn't so much as twitch.

"My God, it is Andrew."

Pearsons caught the flicker of recognition in Natalie's eyes.

"Do you know him? He came out of the corridor leading to the Project Complex."

Natalie was flustered. "No."

Pearsons persisted, "He had to have come from the Project Complex, but we have no pictures of him entering that area. Take another look."

Natalie stared at the picture. There was no doubt in her mind. It was Andrew, *"But how . . . ?"*

"No, I don't know him."

Pearsons inched the tape forward again,"Watch *this.* You won't believe it."

"What did I miss?"

"Watch the door handle. It is only five or six frames. I will take it real slow."

Natalie could not believe her eyes. The handle clearly turned downward without him touching it and the door slowly opened. It closed behind Andrew and he disappeared into the dark.

"Wait, I want to show you something else,"John backed up the tape player and played the same sequence again. "Watch the security guard. He is wide awake and alert yet that man walked right past him as though invisible. I have never seen anything like it."

"Nor I."

John fast forwarded again. "Look at the time. It was nearly dawn when this sequence was recorded." The sequence showed a disheveled Andrew returning, unlocking the door without touching it, walking within two or three feet of the security guard and vanishing down the Project Complex corridor.

"Anything really strange about that to you?" asked Pearsons.

"Everything . . . All of it."

"Think about it. That man didn't break *in*. He broke *out*."

Natalie thought *hard* about it. *"Clearly it is Andrew, and clearly he has powers that we never dreamed possible. What do we have on our hands. My God, what have we done."*

"Are you *sure* you don't know him? He disappears into your area, is there during daylight hours, and then goes out at night."

Natalie just sat there shaking her head in disbelief.

"Ok, here we are a little later. Here are all of your people coming in. Notice the security guard checking them off as they come in. None of them resembles this guy."

Pearsons fast forwarded and then slowed down, "Here are some of your people going to lunch, moving the tape forward, and here they are returning, fast forwarding again, and here are your people leaving for the day." Pearsons narrating the events as people came and went until he ran through the entire tape.

When he got to the end of the tape Pearsons said, "That man did not arrive or leave with any of the staff and the security guard checked off each of them. The guy must still be in the building. Do you want to see the two segments again?"

"No."

Pearsons is thinking, *"Who in Hell can it be?"*

Natalie *knew*.

CHAPTER TWENTY

John Pearsons had another gadget in his bag of tricks that he wanted to try out and this gave him a perfect opportunity.

He unlocked a cabinet in his office and removed a small device. It had an antenna just a few inches in diameter. It nested in the device but could be pulled up and unfolded like a fan to make a shiny dish that pivoted to permit it to be aimed in any direction. It was a miniature television transmitter.

John said,"I would like for you to distract the guard again while I connect this to the hidden camera. Without the burden of the recorder, the camera battery has a greatly extended life and the transmitter has its own extremely long life battery. I will be able to monitor what goes on in the lobby and also record the activities right here in my office on my own machine."

When they arrived back at the Project building, Natalie opened the front door. She and John signed in and they both went to her office. Natalie returned to the guard's station and after a few innocuous pleasantries, asked him to make the rounds of all the common areas with her to check out the security.

She used her key to open them and then went through the motions of checking things out.

Meanwhile Pearsons had ample time to disable the tape recorder, connect the transmitter, switch it on and aim the dish in the general direction of his office building. He had a tiny portable television receiver in his coat pocket. He flipped it on, determined that the transmitter was functioning properly, and returned to Natalie's office.

When Natalie returned to the office John said, "Now we shall see what we shall see. Are you free for dinner tonight, . . . my treat? There are some troublesome aspects of this case that I would like to discuss."

"I think so. What time?"

"Can I pick you up around eight?"

"Eight will be fine."

Unlike many of her female associates who felt that it was fashionable to keep an escort waiting, Natalie was punctual in every aspect of her daily life and was ready well ahead of time. John was the punctual type, too, and appreciated the fact that she never made him cool his heels whether the appointment was business or social.

Once in his car, John said,"I hope you don't mind a little ride out into the Valley. I made a reservation at a place I think you will really like and I'll bet you have never been there."

It took nearly an hour to get there. They occupied themselves with small talk but Natalie sensed that something was really bothering Pearsons.

She *had* never been there, but as advertised, the dinner was superb . . . Champignons a la Greque, Château Brion for two . . . very rare . . . a splendid Château Lafite-Rothschild, and for dessert, a Mousse Chocolat. John certainly was a gourmet and so was she . . . but she was anxious to get to the real reason for the meeting.

As they sipped on a delicious Château d'Yquem, John finally got around to it.

Pearsons paused, "Natalie, do you recall exactly when you found the front door unlocked?"

"The time?"

"No, the date."

"I'm pretty sure it was the 26th of last month."

"How about the date on which you found the muddy footprints in the lobby?"

"Oh, that was the 5th. I sure of that."

"I am, too. My office records confirm it. That was the date of your call."

John continued, "Now, we have your mystery man on tape, going out on the night of the 17th and returning on the morning of the 18th. Have any bells gone off?"

"No, not yet."

"Lets assume he went out on the nights *before* you found the front door unlocked and discovered the muddy foot prints. He would have gone out on the 4th and returned on the morning of the 5th, right?"

"I guess so."

John took an envelope from his inside jacket pocket, removed the newspaper clippings from it, and spread them on the table in front of Natalie.

She gasped.

The dates of the hideous murders coincided with the dates on which Andrew had apparently gotten out of the building.

After noting that Natalie had grasped the significance of the stories, Pearsons continued, "This is all just circumstantial, of course. But, . . . "

John gathered up the clippings, put them back into the envelope, an deposited the envelope back in his inside jacket pocket.

"I don't feel well. Could we leave, please?"

John signaled for the check, paid with his credit card, and they left.

They did not speak on the way home but Natalie's head was spinning with thoughts of the sheep cloning experiment that had gone sour, with the cryptic comment by Dr. Brüer that the image on the Shroud is the *opposite* of Christ in *every possible way*, her own nagging suspicion that the blood of a dead donor had lost the essence of its soul, and the evidence presented to her by John Pearsons.

How could she have missed so much of what was going on? It was all too much to digest at one time.

There was a three day conference in the Century Plaza on the Possibility of Cloning Humans. Natalie took time out of her busy schedule to attend, hoping against hope that someone would have found an explanation for and a "fix" for the *dark side syndrome*.

At the conference on cloning, paper after paper arrived at the same conclusion. The *dark side syndrome* was something they did not understand and therefore had no remedy for. The consensus of all of the experts at the convention was that until they fully understood this phenomenon, all cloning activities should be terminated immediately.

Natalie finally accepted what had happened. She did not discuss *her* experiment with any of the scientists attending the conference but discussed the negative aspects of the other clones with their scientific teams. There was no question, Andy had become the exact opposite of the donor . . . or worse.

———————————

CHAPTER TWENTY-ONE

Early the next morning, Natalie made several phone calls from home, one to Sarah, one to her secretary, and one to the Braley Conference and Convention Center about 100 miles north of the Project Building.

She picked up Sarah and headed for the Conference Center, "I've booked a conference room where we can talk without any interfering phone calls. My secretary will take all of my calls today. We need a few private hours for this."

Sarah sensed the seriousness of the matter and decided not to press Natalie for an explanation. She will get to it when she is ready.

They stopped for a light breakfast. Sarah's curiosity was at the bursting point but Natalie still said nothing.

When they arrived at the conference center, Natalie checked in. She ordered a pot each of decaf and the hard stuff and a tray of assorted sandwiches to be delivered to her conference room. After freshening up she and Sarah strolled to the conference room.

Ordinarily Natalie came to meetings with her briefcase or at least a file folder but this time she carried nothing. This puzzled Sarah.

"Let's wait for the coffee", Natalie hardly knew where to start and needed a little more time to collect her thoughts.

A steward arrived with the coffee and poured them each a cup.

Finally Natalie opened up, "Can you imagine what it is like to be in the eye of a tornado? It is dead calm, but all around you there is total chaos. The storm is weaving and the sense of security conveyed by the calm is nothing but an illusion. The terrifying wall of the funnel cloud is just a few feet away and will, at any moment, sweep everything away, destroying you and everything you hold dear."

"No . . . I can't imagine it. I guess you just have to be there."

"My dear Sarah, you *are* there and the storm is even more terrifying than you can possibly imagine."

Natalie paused for a sip of coffee, "We have created a monster, . . . an unimaginable horror."

"Andrew?"

"Yes. I don't want to accept it, but the evidence is irrefutable, and he seems to have powers beyond my comprehension. The more I think about it, the more I find things that I should have seen but ignored."

"Like?"

"Like telepathy. I think he knows everything we are thinking and is often one jump ahead of us."

"Why?"

"I don't know. It is just a feeling."

"A feeling is not much to go on."

"It is more than that, much more. Like my dreams. I think he has some kind of reverse telepathy and can project his thoughts into my mind or even affect *my* thinking. I think he is responsible for my recent extraordinary sensual and sexual phantasies."

"Do you know how paranoid this sounds?"

"Yes, that's why I'm telling *you*. I know *you* won't think I am crazy."

"Is that it?"

"No. He also has psycho-kinetic capabilities. I don't mean simple stuff like moving pencils across a table. I mean incredible things like opening our pick-proof locks and moving about the laboratories with impunity, . . . even making excursions outside of the building."

"That is pretty hard to believe."

"We have proof."

Natalie then laid it all out for Sarah, the unlocked front door, the muddy tracks, the video tape, everything.

"Sarah, I'm frightened. It is much worse than you could imagine. Every time Andrew has been out, awful things have happened . . . really horrible things."

Natalie then reviewed her meeting with John and the revelation of the news stories on the murders.

"It could be coincidence."

"Perhaps, but John is now able to record and monitor our front entrance directly from his office. Another incident will be more than coincidence."

"My God!" said Sarah, "I wonder what his range is, his telepathic range, I mean. You don't suppose he could be listening in on us right now, do you?"

"He's a hundred miles away. Do you think he could really do that?"

That thought brought the conversation to an end but the fact was, a hundred miles was *well* within Andrew's ever expanding range.

CHAPTER TWENTY-TWO

Luckily, Andrew was preoccupied, teasing the guard at the front entrance. Once again the guard was fantasizing about his favorite TV program "Babes on the Beach" and Andrew was leading the guard into one of the watch towers alone with several of the pultritudinous lifeguards where his wildest desires were being realized. The guard had to dash into the men's room to avoid an embarrassing ejaculation behind the guard desk.

Natalie did not take the rest of the department heads into her confidence. She did, however discuss the sheep cloning disasters with them. She was concerned that there was a generic problem attendant to all cloning that caused the unexplained behavior of the sheep clones and that it might also affect *their* clone.

Many alternatives were considered, one of them being that in the cloning process, the clone was, by some unknown mechanism, given the donors *dark* side. There was no way prove this. Nothing in their experience could be used to validate it so they kept coming back to intense sibling rivalry as the only reasonable explanation.

Well, that did not explain Andrew's behavior. He had no identifiable sibling. Natalie tried to find something to hang her hopes on but it just wasn't there. The more she thought about it, the more she kept coming back to Dr. Brüer's chilling comment about the image on the Shroud,"The image is, therefore, not only a *negative* image, in the photographic sense, it is also a *mirror* image of Christ. Everything about the image is *backwards*. The image on the Shroud is the *opposite* of Christ in every possible way."

Andrew was the opposite of Christ in the worst possible sense. Andrew had been cloned from the blood of a cadaver, blood that no longer carried the essence of a soul.

Andrew had no soul.

As this stark reality finally soaked in, it sent chills through Natalie. . . . *"The opposite of Christ in every possible way."*

May God have mercy on us. We have created the Antichrist.

Natalie was raised from a deep and erotic sleep by the incessant ringing of her telephone. It was John.

She answered it with a groggy, "Hello?"

Natalie glanced at her clock. It was midnight.

"Natalie"?

"Yes?"

"This is John. Sorry to bother you at this hour but there is something you ought to know. I just got home from a late meeting and decided to check out the tape."

He paused for a moment.

"He, whoever *he* is, is out again."

"But . . . "

"That's not all. When I saw this, I immediately turned on my police scanner. There has been another terrible murder . . . a teenage girl . . . raped . . . horribly mutilated . . . and the police say it is the same perp. He left his signature."

"What's that?"

"I don't know, but it sounds really bad."

"Oh, my God! I don't want to know."

"I will bring my gun. Please meet me at my office as soon as possible. We will drive over together. Maybe we can get him when he returns."

Natalie immediately called Henri Platinier.

"Henri, this is Natalie. I didn't wake you up did I?"

"No, I was watching a movie on TV."

"Sorry to bother you at this hour but I have a feeling that all is not well with Andrew. Would you mind meeting me at your office ASAP so we can look in on him. It is just a feeling."

"OK, I'll be right there. Meet you in the lobby."

It took only fifteen minutes for them to get there.

"Lets just check the Eugenics Lab and see if he is OK."

They checked in with the guard and went directly to Platinier's office.

Just seconds behind them was Andrew. He mentally manipulated the lock, walked right past the guard, and hurried to the Eugenics Lab. He wasn't expecting to find anyone there. Platinier was starting to unlock the lab when Andrew froze their cerebral clocks. He mentally unlocked the lab, squeezed past them, went into his quarters, cleaned up, climbed into his bed and waited for his heart to stop pounding. When he was under control again he feigned sleep and released Natalie and Henri from their time freeze.

They looked in on him and all seemed well.

As they went back to their cars, Natalie made a feeble excuse for her conduct, "I don't usually pay much attention to dreams but this one was so real and it concerned Andrew's well being. Sorry about the false alarm."

Natalie then drove straight to John's office.

He met her with, "You've had a busy night. Huh?"

"Damn, I forgot all about the camera." Natalie made up a lame excuse for what John obviously saw on his monitor but she knew he wasn't buying it. She could not lie believably anyway, but especially not to John. They had spent too many intimate moments together since the start of the project.

"Well, there is no way to catch him tonight. He entered the lab directly behind you and is probably well hidden in there somewhere. That was a crazy thing you did. He might have killed you. It was very close. You might have encountered him."

"You are right. I won't do anything like that again."

The next night John called again, "I know it is two AM, but he is out again. Can you meet me in the Project Complex parking lot?

"I'll have to dress. Be about twenty minutes."

"I'm going now. I'll be there when you get there."

Andrew was sharpening up a new skill. He imposed his thoughts on the mind screens of individuals and made then think that they had been paid. Sometimes he even got change. It wasn't necessary to *terminate* any of the people with whom he had encounters so he was able to return to the Laboratory Complex earlier than usual.

Natalie got dressed but dragged her feet a bit, praying that Andrew would get back before they could get there.

John drove to the executive parking lot and parked in a spot where they could see the front door.

In a few minutes, Natalie arrived. She got into John's car, "Anything happen yet?"

"No. We'll wait."

They waited.

Dawn came and the other members of the team started arriving for work.

Finally, John grunted, "Damn, he probably got back while we on the way over here. I'll take you back home and will check the tape to be sure."

After freshening up, Natalie was leaving and was just closing the door when the phone rang . It was John again.

"Natalie?"

"Yes."

"He's back. I checked the tape. He got back before we got there. The guard never noticed. Who the hell could it be and how does he do it? . . . and where could he hide so no one knows he is in there during the daytime?"

Natalie did not answer any of his questions. Instead she proposed a weekend meeting at a different conference center, this time, one that was in Chicago more than a thousand miles away.

At the meeting, John suggested that they lay a trap for him.

Natalie stalled, *"My God, it will all come out . . . not just that we have cloned a human, but the whole story . . . the world's reaction to our arrogance . . . our presumptuousness, our unmitigated audacity. . . . trying to clone Christ "*

What could she do? Again grasping at straws, "It could all be just another coincidence."

But she knew in her heart that it was not.

"We have searched everywhere. There is no trace of the person on the tape."

"You obviously haven't searched *everywhere* because he *is* there. The tape evidence is irrefutable . . . and everything considered, . . . I am not sure that you really *want* to find this monster yourself."

John knew that *she* knew more than she was telling.

Natalie could see it in his eyes.

Back home again, Natalie wondered if the thousand miles she had placed between Andrew and their meeting was enough. What *was* his range? She had the uneasy feeling that Andrew knew all about the meeting. She had good reason for concern. A thousand miles was *well* within Andrew's ever increasing range but, once again, Andrew was preoccupied with more local mischief and had not picked up on her thoughts. He could have. He just hadn't put his mind to it.

Andrew was not to be kept in the dark forever.

The next time he went out into the city, Pearsons was watching his monitor as Andrew clouded the mind of the security guard and mentally manipulated the pins and tumblers of the lock of the main entrance door. The handle turned down without Andrew touching it and he was quickly out the door.

Pearsons was baffled again."How does he *do* that?" he muttered to himself.

He had Natalie's number on his speed dialer. He called it up and she answered on the first ring.

"He has done it again. He is out. Can you come over to my office."

When Natalie arrived, he had a large pot of coffee brewing.

"This might be a long night. How do you like yours?"

"Black."

John poured two cups and they both sat on the couch in front of his monitor.

John cut in a second recorder so they wouldn't lose anything, rewound the first to a time that he had entered into its memory, and hit the start button.

He put his arm around her shoulder and pulled her close to him.

Natalie needed his comforting touch at this moment.

"OK, Just like before, the guard is sitting there . . . awake . . . nothing unusual . . . Look, here he comes. . . . . The guard is oblivious to him. . . . He unlocks the door without touching it. . . . He's out . . . The door locks behind him."

The guard got up once to relieve himself.

After that it was pretty boring fare.

John spoke. "That guard is going to wear out the grip on his Glock if he keeps fondling it like that."

It wasn't really funny but Natalie managed a feeble laugh.

"Before I found that security was a safer and much more profitable business, I was a cop. I enjoyed stakeouts and I guess I had my share of cold coffee and stale donuts. This is an infinitely better way of doing it and I don't miss the donuts."

Natalie had nothing to contribute to the conversation so it ended right there.

John's police scanner came alive. There had been another murder, as horrendous as the rest had been.

The police were still keeping quiet about the eyes to discourage copycat killers, but they referred to it in their radio traffic as "the signature". The homicide detectives, en route to the crime scene, asked about the signature and got an affirmative response.

John said, "It's him."

THE SHROUD

The police were looking for him in earnest. The flashing lights and blaring sirens, up one street and down the other, caused Andrew to take a tortuous path back to the Project building. He ducked into alleyways, cut across back yards, hid behind dumpsters, hedges, trees . . . anything that gave him some degree of cover. Then he was home. He was so excited and pumped up from the chase that he had to pause to collect himself before he could attack the dual problem of the guard and the lock.

John said,"Look! There he is. You can just make him out through the door. The handle is turning . . . Damn, the guard doesn't have a clue."

Andrew was gasping for breath as he rushed past the guard and disappeared into the bowels of the building.

"And you are *sure* you don't know him?"

"I'm sure." It was not Natalie's nature to lie about anything and the few times she tried during her life, she *knew* that she hadn't gotten away with it and she knew now that she was not fooling John Pearsons.

"We can't let this continue any longer. I have *got* to devise a way to trap him." Pearsons' determination was passionately stated.

"And I can't let you. It will ruin everything. I have to find a way to resolve this myself."

CHAPTER TWENTY-THREE

"Sarah, I would like for you to join me in a weekend retreat to discuss and resolve some of the major issues concerning The Project. I have booked a lodge in Canada and plane tickets. We need some quiet time to hash things out. We can leave Dr. Platinier in charge of things while we are away, . . . and we could both use some fresh air."

On the flight to Calgary they watched the in-flight movie. This was the first recreation for either of them for months and even though the movie was mediocre, they thoroughly enjoyed it.

Long plane flights are seldom considered restful but their recent months had been so stressful that both arrived at the lodge regenerated and ready to take on the world.

After a deep sleep they had a light breakfast.

It was time to get down to business. Natalie had difficulty deciding where to start but it didn't much matter, she had to lay it *all* out sometime during their retreat.

Natalie went through everything in painful detail, the problems with the cloned sheep in Ireland and Scotland, the pig in Sweden, the dog in Germany, the chicken in Italy and the duck in France. She discussed the possibility that these might all have been due to sibling rivalry but added the consensus of geneticists everywhere that clones seemed to assume the *mirror image,* the *bad* or *dark* side, of their donors and were recommending cessation of all cloning programs.

Not much of this was news to Sarah. Most of it had been covered at one time or another in the staff meetings.

Her concerns that Andrew had extraordinary mental powers were then discussed. Sarah was already familiar with his apparent invasion of Natalie's dreams and she had been stunned to hear of his excursions into all of the offices of the Project Directors.

Psychokinesis was the domain of many charlatans and magicians who *bent* spoons and iron bars but those were all tricks of legerdemain. Andrew was endowed with the *real thing*. He could manipulate the mechanisms of unpickable locks and safes and who knew what else.

It was a beautiful crisp day and Natalie suggested that they take a stroll in the woods and continue the discussions out there.

Natalie made a thermos of coffee. They went outside, strolled briskly through the woods and down to the lake where they paused to catch their breath and have another cup of Java.

This seemed like as good a time as any to tell her. As they sat on a log savoring the warm brew Natalie said, "He has been *outside again*."

Sarah was stunned. She watched the steam spiral up from her cup,"Are you *sure*?"

"Like before, we have it on video tape . . . and that's not all, it seems certain that he has other mental powers like the ability to impose *his* thoughts on others. He makes himself invisible to the security guard and walks right past him. We must assume that he has used this ability on members of the team although I can't prove it . . . and I think that it is a given that he has extraordinary telepathic powers. We must assume that he can read all of our thoughts, but I have no direct evidence."

Natalie gave Sarah time to digest this and continued,"I have already told you some but not the worst of it."

The worst of it was much worse than Sarah had steeled herself for and Natalie did not spare her any of the gory details. Sarah became physically ill.

When she recovered her composure, she asked,"Can they prove any of this? Couldn't it just be an incredible string of coincidences?"

"Perhaps, but the odds in favor of me winning the lottery are better . . . and I don't even have a ticket. I didn't mean to make light of this. It's bad, really bad. Every time he is outside something horrible happens."

"Do you suppose it is due to the unexplained *dark side* factor the other geneticists are leaning toward?"

"Frankly, no! I think it is due to an altogether different cause."

"What?"

"Andrew was not cloned from living blood; he was cloned from blood taken from the Shroud of Turin. I think that Christ's soul had departed his mortal body and the blood on the Shroud no longer contained the essence of his soul."

Natalie found it hard to *say*, "Andrew *has* no soul."

"That would not necessarily make him *immoral* but perhaps *amoral*."

"A possibility, but we failed to consider this during his early development. With 20/20 hindsight we probably could have tipped the scales by giving him a thorough grounding in morals and ethics but we taught him nothing. We just left him to his own devices and he took the wrong road. It is too late to try to salvage him. He has done too much harm and he now has an appetite for awful things."

Sarah had put too much into this to give up. "With his incredible powers, think what a marvelous force for good he could become. We can't give up. We must try to turn him around."

"It is too late, Sarah, He is beyond redemption. I just have to figure how to deal with this."

They had exhausted the subject.

They spent the rest of the day exploring the woods and then went home early.

———————————————

CHAPTER TWENTY-FOUR

The first day back on the job, Natalie called John. She spoke in veiled terms as she inquired about the "problem".

John, unaware of her suspicions about Andrew's ESP, spoke more openly,"While you were away, he came out again. There was another event in which he left his signature. This one was exceptionally brutal and - - Can we meet somewhere? I prefer not to discuss this on the phone."

"My office?"

Natalie would have preferred someplace a half a continent away but time was short. She didn't want John to take any precipitous action while she was working out a solution to the problem.

John met her in the parking lot and escorted her into his conference room.

There were no formalities. He played the latest tape for her.

"There is nothing *new* here. He walks right by the guard again. Within three hours, the police radio had a flurry of traffic about the latest murder. Here, I made an audio tape of the stuff on the police radio."

John let the video run and played the audio, too. The perpetrator evaded all of the traps set by the police. When it was clear that he had eluded them again, the frustration of the police was evident.

"Here he is returning to the Project complex and, again, he somehow befuddles the guard and enters undetected."

"John, I know how important this is, and I don't want to put you on hold, but I have an urgent conference in Paris later this week. It has been on my schedule for months and may have a bearing on our 'problem'."

"Do you want to talk about it now? . . . The problem, I mean."

"No, but . . . "

Natalie slumped in her chair, "The whole thing is so incredible, I don't know where to start."

"Why not start at the beginning."

What was the beginning? The crucifixion? The first recorded viewing of the Shroud by Robert Di Clari in 1203? The fire in Chambréy Castle in 1532? The theft of the snippet by the weaver Godfrey du Luc? Gaining possession of the snippet through Godfrey's descendant, Richard Halpern? The surprise turn of events in Sarah's experiment?

That all seemed so long ago.

Natalie decided to tell him *almost* everything.

"John, we had the best of intentions. We thought that what we were attempting would, if successful, benefit all mankind."

Natalie sobbed and had difficulty getting out the words, "From the time I was a teenager, my dream was to clone a human being. Through an incredible sequence of events I came into possession of a marvelous artifact, a snippet from the Shroud of Turin containing a bloodstain, . . . DNA from our Savior Jesus Christ. Imagine the challenge . . . to bring another Christ into a world that sorely needs as much help as it can get."

Natalie paused a moment. "Do you suppose I might have a glass of water?"

"Sure you don't want something stronger?"

"No thank you. Water will do just fine."

John retrieved a bottle of Perrier from the conference room refrigerator and gave it to Natalie along with a chilled glass.

He unlocked the liquor cabinet and poured himself a double shot of Glen Livet. He was sure that he would need it.

Natalie then backed up a bit, "There were several successful clonings of sheep and other mammals. There were some setbacks and a few aberrations like accelerated growth rate but nothing ominous at first. In the meantime, we created a clone from the 2000 year old DNA on our snippet from the Shroud."

This was going to be hard. Natalie steeled herself and continued, "It was an accident. There had been setbacks. We were discouraged but did not want to face the possibility that we had undertaken an impossible task. If we were just spinning our wheels it would be better to know now and not waste any more time on a hopeless pursuit. My Assistant Project Director, Sarah Buckley, proposed a test that, if successful, would have proven it could *not* be done. We prayed for the test to fail."

"It not only failed, it actually produced a viable clone. His name is Andrew."

"Imagine our elation . . . a clone of *Christ*."

Natalie let that sink in for a moment.

"Then things started to unravel. All of the mammals cloned by others, the two sheep, the pig, the dog . . . they seemed to have the opposite temperament and personalities of the DNA donors. Geneticists have started calling it the *dark side syndrome*, for want of a better term.

At a conference on cloning, paper after paper arrived at the same conclusion. The *dark side syndrome* was something they did not understand and therefore had no remedy for. The consensus of all of the experts at the conference was that until they fully understood this phenomenon, all cloning activities should be terminated immediately.

I did not discuss *my* experiment with any of the scientists attending the conference but discussed the negative aspects of the other clones with their scientific teams. There was no question, Andrew had become the exact opposite of the donor . . . or worse.

I reluctantly accepted their conclusion."

"My God! How dark could the dark side of Christ be?" John thought about it for a moment and then answered his own question, "Darker than anyone could possibly imagine, the personification of evil. It could be the Antichrist!"

"In our case, it might even be worse than that. Andrew was cloned from 2,000 year old DNA which, we now suspect, did not contain the essence of His soul. Believe me, we have tried to find some other explanation but, so far, there is none. That is why it is so urgent that I attend this conference in Paris. The sharpest minds in this field have been addressing this problem and I hope against hope that there is another factor that we have all overlooked."

"You know what could happen while you are away. Can you take the responsibility for another tragedy?"

"I must."

"Who else knows about this?"

"Sarah Buckley knows most of it. The rest of the people on the project probably know a bit here and there but not enough to put it all together. I will call you the moment I get back from Paris."

It was inevitable.

Andrew, having nothing more interesting to do at the moment, decided to tune in on Dr. Goodenough's thoughts.

He heard it all.

Survival, the most basic of all instincts, was now the driving force behind Andrew. As soon as the last of the department heads had departed for the night, Andrew mentally manipulated the locks and was quickly into Dr. Goodenough's office. He scrolled through her electronic Rolodex and found out who John Pearsons was and made a mental note of his home and business addresses.

Pearsons was his first priority.

Andrew went first to Pearsons' home. Pearsons was not there so he stood in the shadow of a large jacaranda tree and waited. After midnight he became restless and decided to check out Pearsons' office.

The lights were on at MAXXX Security Systems. There was a guard stationed inside the front door. This would be a piece of cake for Andrew. He imposed his thoughts on the guard, mentally manipulated the lock and strolled in like he owned the place. He checked out the directory in the lobby, and found Pearsons' office. In the laboratory that had been his home for his entire life, he had observed the operation of video tape machines and more complex electronic equipment, but there was so much he did not know. For example, the Project Complex was a single story structure. Andrew had, therefore, never encountered an elevator and had no idea how to operate one but he was clever enough to find his was around such challenges. He mentally unlocked the fire stair door and climbed the stairway to the 4th floor. He carefully unlocked the door and stepped into the corridor. Creeping stealthily along the hallway he moved from door to door until he found Pearsons' office. The door was unlocked.

Andrew opened it. "John?" he asked tentatively.

"Yes?"

John looked up and his eyes were suddenly filled with fear. Just as quickly, Andrew took over his thought patterns and a serene look spread across John's face. He faced the door calmly with no recollection of what he had just seen. Andrew checked out Pearsons' file cabinet and removed all files relating to the Project Complex. The video recorder was still running. Andrew ejected the cassette and put it in his pocket. Looking over the neatly ordered tape library, he found other tapes relating to the Project and collected them as well. He looked through Pearsons' desk drawers and found Pearsons' 357 Magnum in the center drawer.

Andrew turned to leave. When he reached the door, he turned back and pointed the pistol straight at John's heart. Then he unclouded his mind. John saw . . . and terror again filled his eyes for the brief moment before Andrew squeezed the trigger. The searing pain tore through John's chest as he took his last breath . . . but the fright in John's eyes had gotten to Andrew and he left his *signature* once more. He tore out those terror filled eyes and tossed them into the wash basin in John's private rest room.

Andrew smiled,"*Another experiment terminated*".

He descended the fire stair, befuddled the guard again and left MAXXX Security Systems for the first and last time.

On the way back to the Project Complex, Andrew tossed the gun, the files, and the tapes into a dumpster.

Once back inside the Project Complex, he went through the Directors' offices starting with Natalie's and collected all of the records concerning himself. It was a daunting task but he completed it before the Directors arrived for the day. He relocked all of the doors and hid the records under his mattress, in his closet, in the cabinet under his washbasin,   . . . wherever he could find a space large enough to hold anything.

Other than Natalie, Sarah was the first to know for sure that something must be done. She realized what a monster they had created and thought about Natalie, her long-time friend and colleague, and about the terrible decision she must now make.

It isn't fair. Natalie only wanted to do good, to bring back Jesus Christ our Savior and restore peace and order to the world.

Sarah did not want to do it but someone had to. She could not tell the world of the dangers that lay ahead. To do so would give away the work they had been doing, to reveal the terrible consequences, and disparage the entire life of her friend Natalie Goodenough.

Sarah made up her mind.

She would arrive early and on the pretext of drawing blood for a routine test, she would put Andrew to sleep forever, . . . and she would do it before Natalie returned from New York.

In her despair over the situation Sarah neglected to take into account Andrew's extraordinary mental capabilities.

Andrew, in Natalie's absence, had zeroed in on Sarah's thoughts.

He had planned to terminate her anyway. He would have to do it now.

As Sarah approached him with the hypodermic syringe, he used his ability to transmit and impose his thoughts on her. She could not resist his will. She injected the lethal needle into her own arm, walked out of the Project Complex to the cliff at the rear of the buildings, opened the gate and calmly strolled over it . . . Andrew knew . . . and was pleased.

Andrew waited until all of the Directors were in. He first clouded the mind of Dr. Platinier, Director of the Eugenics Laboratory where he had spent his entire life up to this point. He then piled all of the files, lab reports, books and other documents that he had collected on Platinier's reading table. He had never done this before but felt certain he could do it. He caused the pile to spontaneously ignite with a fierce burst of flame. He then ignited Dr. Platinier's desk and office furniture.

A smoke alarm went off.

As people rushed in to investigate, he froze them in their tracks. Andrew then went from office to office and laboratory to laboratory turning each into an inferno. He examined his handiwork and was once more pleased with what he had done.

Andrew made his way to the lobby, encountering and freezing the security guard along the way. He mentally manipulated the lock on the outside door, stepped out, and closed and locked it behind him. He watched from a discrete distance as the fire trucks arrived. By the time the firemen were able to smash in the nearly impervious front door the fire was completely out of control. The destruction was total. Andrew made certain of that.

The fire inspectors had never seen anything like it.

There was nothing left but grey ash, . . . nothing.

It is Wednesday, July 17, 1996, . . . decision time.

Back in her hotel room in New York, Natalie spent the whole morning going over alternatives, but it always came down to the same thing. The experiment would have to be *terminated.*

"Should I discuss my decision with Sarah or any of the others? No, This is all my responsibility. I will have to do it myself."

Andrew's ability to read her thoughts was a major problem. How could she do this without giving herself away to him?

The question laid heavily on her mind for the whole day. When her taxi arrived at the airport her resolve was steadfast.

It *must* be done, but she still had not come up with a workable plan.

Her taxi pulled up at the TWA terminal at JFK International Airport.

Natalie checked her bag at curbside check in. She was early so she walked to the Ambassador's Club to wait. She had to come up with a plan *now* and then, *if possible,* get it completely out of her mind before she got back to LA on Sunday.

Sunday would be too late. Andrew was reading her every thought as she sat in the assumed safety of a club more than two thousand miles from Los Angeles.

Andrew is well aware of the implications of the word *terminate*.

Natalie's plane is called for boarding . . . "TWA Flight 800 is ready for boarding at Gate 22."

Andrew started putting all of his energy into the most difficult psycho kinetic task he had ever undertaken.

The National Transportation Safety Board could find no valid reason for the flight to have crashed.

CHAPTER TWENTY-FIVE

John Pearsons was distraught.

He had utilized Natalie's absence to take care of several out-of-town business matters and had left his assistant and good friend John Wilson in charge during his absence. Driving back to his office he heard the news about TWA Flight 800. It was the flight on which Natalie was ticketed. The news was like a hard punch in the stomach. He made his way to his office and found John Wilson's body . . . A kick in the groin.

He saw what had been done to Wilson's eyes. When he called the police and told them what he had found, he heard the inspector say, "It's the *signature* killer again", and knew immediately that it was Andrew.

"My God! He must be after all of us!"

The homicide inspector was George Bennet, a long time friend, going all the way back to John's earlier days in the LA Police Department. They came out of the Police Academy in the same class, were partners, and had many hairy adventures together in their Black and White.

John had saved George's life in a wild shootout at a liquor store in Watts, a debt that George was sure he could never repay.

Now, George had been named to head up the special task force charged with the investigation of the *signature* killings.

"George, you owe me one. As soon as I figure this out, you will be the first to know. I promise. Can you keep this out of the media for a while and let this guy think he has killed *me*? I can't tell you how I know but I am sure it was me he was after and I need time. You owe me George, and I want to call in my marker."

"OK, John, I don't know why I am doing this. My ass is really on the line, Get the hell out of here . . . but keep me informed as to your whereabouts . . . and don't go too far."

"Thanks."

On the way back to his apartment, John's radio was still on and he heard the news stories about the conflagration at the lab and about the discovery of a woman's body at the bottom of the cliff behind the ruins of the lab.

The enormity of what had happened finally soaked in and John's eyes were swollen shut with tears by the time he got back home.

The phone was ringing as he entered his apartment.

He picked it up but was too choked up to speak immediately.

"John?"

"Huh?" John tried to compose himself.

"John, is that you? This is Natalie . . . John?"

He could not believe it, "Natalie?"

"Yes."

"But how . . . ?"

"I am all right, my love. Oh God, John, it is so good to hear your voice. I still can't believe it. I was right at the gate getting ready to board . . . and something told me not to . . . . I have been trying to get to you for hours. Oh God, John, it was awful what happened to those poor people on that plane."

"I think it was Andrew."

"What!"

"Andrew! . . . . Terrible things have happened here. The Project Complex was totally destroyed by fire. If there was any one in there they were all killed. Andrew went to my office and tried to kill me. My assistant John Wilson was taking care of things in my absence . . . in the wrong place at the wrong time . . . he left his *signature* again . . . too horrible to mention . . . "John poured it all out," . . . and I think he made your plane crash."

"But John . . . ", Natalie was devastated by all of this.

"Listen to me. He may think that he has killed everyone who knows about him . . . but we can't be certain. Don't tell me where you are over the phone. Do you have your laptop computer with you and do you still have your permanent e-mail address?"

"Yes, but . . . "

"No buts, Natalie, my love . . . I thought I had lost you. I don't want to lose you again."

John paused, "Hide somewhere, perhaps with a friend. Use your laptop, sign on with the local server and wait, I will come as soon as I can."

John hung up, took all of his *emergency* money out of his wall safe, packed a sports duffel with enough clothes for a couple of days, went straight to his car, and drove all night to San Francisco.

In Frisco, he went to a safe deposit box he kept there and removed all of the bearer bonds he had stashed in it. John believed in preparing for emergencies and now it was paying off. The bonds would be enough to provide them with a comfortable lifestyle for several years in Mexico or South America.

John called in another marker and obtained a new passport in the name of Marcel Dupree. The next day, he boarded a plane bound for Mexico City.

From there he e-mailed Natalie with instructions to go to Chicago, check into a hotel, and go on line with her laptop.

He then e-mailed her instructions to go to New Orleans, check into a hotel, and repeat the process. He then flew to New Orleans contacted her by e-mail with instructions to sit tight and wait. Eventually they made a date via e-mail and met at the Bourbon Street Inn.

He and Natalie had no way of knowing it, but these convoluted precautions were unnecessary. Andrew, convinced that he had obliterated all evidence and witnesses to his very existence, was concentrating on his new life in the outside world and soon put everything else behind him.

When they spotted one another, they embraced. Natalie burst into tears and as he held her quivering body tightly in his arms, John whispered, "When I heard about the plane, I died inside. I had no hope of ever seeing you again . . . and then when I heard your voice . . . Oh God, I had no idea how much I love you."

They savored the moment.

She was lost forever . . . and by a miracle, found again.

"It may be presumptuous of me, but I have registered us at my hotel as Mr. and Mrs. Marcel Dupree. That was the best I could come up with at the moment. That is the name on my new passport. I guess I didn't think about how it would sound. You can call me Marc, if you prefer. I have arranged for a forged passport for you. They will need a photo which we can have taken in the morning. Do you mind being Mrs. Dupree, tonight?"

"Not at all."

"You don't have to use Dupree as your last name on your passport if you don't want to, but it will simplify things, sleeping arrangements and the like, as we move about. Is that OK with you?'

"Yes, It does sort of *legitimize* our relationship doesn't it? I like it."

"You can pick any first name you like for your passport. Think about it."

"Can I keep Natalie?"

"Of course. I am very partial to it myself and would find it hard to break the habit of calling you that. OK, Natalie it is."

The waitress came to their table.

John asked, "Would you like a drink?"

"No I just want to go to our hotel."

John paid the waitress for his drink and they left, slowly walking arm in arm down Bourbon Street.

The did not bother to turn on the lights in their hotel room. They urgently stripped one another. They could see each other in the mirror in the surreal illumination of the flashing signs up and down the street in front of their hotel. The strobe-like effect reduced everything to a strange combination of slow motion and exaggerated speed like a Mack Sennet movie.

John . . . no, Marc . . . held her close against him in the flashing lights, caressed her breasts and kissed her. Their quivering tongues made contact and she returned his love, kissing him deeply, . . . passionately. They touched one another lovingly, all over, and when they reached each other's most intimate places, she felt the surge of blood into his erect manhood and pulled him urgently toward the bed.

It had never been like this before, not even when Andrew projected his most salacious images on her thought screen while she and John were climaxing together.

When it was over, John . . . no, Marc . . . (she would have to get used to that) held her tightly to him, remaining inside of her, and they both went to sleep in a warm embrace.

He remained tumescent even as they slept, and when they awoke, finding themselves still coupled, they resumed making love.

So this is what it will be like, playing the part of Mrs. Marcel Dupree. I like it.

They had room service bring them breakfast, and then made love one more time.

Later, they went into one of the dingier parts of town where, in the back of a tattoo parlor, the forger took her picture, used her own date of birth and other data needed for the passport. (He told her that the more her passport matched her real persona, the less likely she would be tripped up by a routine question at a border check point.) When he had all of the information he needed, he said the document would be ready the following day.

They spent the rest of the day exploring New Orleans and sampling the spicy Cajun cooking. Natalie was turned off by the crawdads but John . . . or, rather Marc, . . . loved them. One of their culinary stops had an oyster bar. Marc devoured two dozen on the half shell and ordered a third.

"That won't help, you know. It is a myth that just won't die, but they will not do anything for you, . . . not that you need any help." Natalie giggled.

"Well, It can't hurt."

Marc dug into the third dozen with lots of Tabasco and horseradish but Natalie did not care to try these either. They repulsed her even more than the crawdads.

As the evening wore on, they strolled up and down Bourbon Street past all of the famous jazz clubs listening to the sounds of Pete Fountain's clarinet, Al Hurt's trumpet, and the other jazz greats spilling out onto Bourbon Street. The performance of their dixieland masterpieces wrapped them in the sound of another time. It was almost enough to make them forget why they were there . . . *almost*.

Natalie squeezed his arm hard and began to cry. She was thinking about her colleagues who had been killed in the fire and about her closest friend Sarah.

By the time they got back to their hotel, she was emotionally drained and too exhausted for anything but sleep.

As she climbed into bed, she whispered, "Hope those oysters last 'til morning," and was asleep almost before her head touched the pillow.

Their hotel room had a very large shower. In the morning, they enjoyed it together, in ways that the shower manufacturer could only have imagined in his most lurid fantasies.

After another room service breakfast, they had one more passionate romp on the king sized bed, then got dressed, and went back to the tattoo parlor to pick up Natalie's passport.

They did not want to tarry any longer than necessary in the Big Easy. Marc, (it was getting easier to call him that) stopped at an airline counter in the hotel lobby and made arrangements for a flight to Cancun the following morning, . . . the best he could do.

They returned to their hotel for another round of incredible pleasures, got dressed and went to one of the city's classiest restaurant. Some places in New Orleans *outbrassed* the brassiest places anywhere else in the world but on the other side of the coin, there were classy restaurants that *outclassed* the best the world had to offer. Marc made dinner reservations at one of the latter, Antoine's. The meal was a gourmet's dream.

Dinner conversation centered on the new life they must make for themselves. They were so absorbed in the conversation that the next morning neither of them could remember what they ate or drank. Marc remembered the fact that the check was well into three digits and thought to himself, "*I hope we enjoyed it.*"

They boarded the plane to Cancun with some trepidation, wondering if Andrew knew . . . and if his evil powers could reach this far.

There was no need to worry, Andrew was thinking about other things.

The ride in from the airport was uneventful. It was a tropical paradise but Natalie did not notice. Her mind was filled by the terrible events of the past few days. Her closest friend Sarah . . . the entire team . . . the Project Complex . . . the passengers and crew of TWA Flight 800 . . . all gone. The guilt for her part in it was overwhelming. It would take a long time to ease the pain. Marc held her close and let her cry it out. There probably would be many such moments in the days and months to come.

Natalie felt very close to Sarah since she had no living relatives but the rest of her team were also family to her. They were all basically loners, tied together by the common bond of their work, but their friendships for one another had become much more than that. They had become truly *family* in the way they looked after and cared for one another. Just as she had lost her parents, her entire *real* family, in one tragic moment, now she had lost her entire *adopted* family in a event that was so devastating that she had difficulty in comprehending the depth of her loss.

THE SHROUD

Damn that Richard Halpern and his scrap of linen . . . NO . . . damn me for presuming that I could play God. There are some things better left alone.

They spent a week at a resort hotel, . . . tennis, swimming laps in the pool, basking in the sun, strolling on the beach, dining and dancing to the music of a steel band. There were long walks on the beach and every time they were alone Natalie sobbed uncontrollably. Her grief was overwhelming. The only thing that gave any relief from the pain was their lovemaking that just seemed to get better every time.

During their stay at the resort, Marc rented a convertible and they explored the countryside. On one of their excursions they found an out of the way place, a mountain top, where there were several villas for lease, They were widely separated from one another. All had marvelous views from sunrise to sunset. They afforded the privacy that both of them so badly needed.

After a brief consultation with one another, they found the manager and signed a six month lease. Their tourist cards were only good for 180 days. After that they would have to return to the US to obtain new cards and then return for another 180 days. Six months seemed like a long time. One step at the time. They did not feel that they could make meaningful plans any further ahead than that.

They could move in the following Monday so they made good use of their last two or three days enjoying the touristy pleasures of Cancun and shopping for everything they could think of that they might need on their isolated mountain top.

On Monday, they drove to their villa and spent the remainder of the day getting settled in. It was immediately apparent that they had overlooked many of the necessities of life when they were shopping in Cancun. Their new shopping list was long and growing by the minute.

Marc decided to drive to the closest village to pick up the more urgently needed items and invited Natalie to go with him. He just assumed that she would go and was surprised when she declined.

"I just need a few minutes alone. I'll be OK . . . but hurry back."

"I won't be long. Fix up that pretty face while I am gone."

It *did* need fixing. The frequent spells of grief had taken their toll. Her eyes were almost swollen shut. It was not an easy task. Every time she made a little headway, another outburst of tears undid all of her hard work . . . so she concentrated on her hair. It had been neglected, too. It took hundreds of brush strokes to get it back to some semblance of its usual appearance.

"Dear God, I thought I needed to be alone but . . . when will you be back? I miss you John . . . I mean Marc . . . (will I ever get used to his new name?) . . . so much. I need to hold on to you . . . I need for you to hold me and never let go . . . Oh John, please hurry, . . . I need you.

Natalie cried until there was not another tear left. She finally composed herself enough to complete her makeup. It wasn't perfect. She couldn't do much about the swollen eyes, but she was otherwise presentable and quite lovely despite the look of grief that could not be covered up.

Between the period of tears and guilt and self pity and loneliness (she had never felt so alone and did not want to ever feel so lonely again) and time at the dressing table trying to reconstruct herself, three hours had slipped by.

She was startled by the sound of pebbles skittering across the circular driveway and bouncing off the stone front steps. It was Marc, returning with the supplies.

She ran out onto the portico and met Marc at the top of the stairs with a fierce spinning embrace.

"I hope you remembered to get some tissues."

"Yes, they were not on the list but when I saw them in the market, I knew I'd better get some."

"Oh, John, don't ever leave me again . . . not even for a second," Natalie pressed her lips hard against his and then parted his lips with her tongue.

Marc swept her into his arms and carried her into the bed room. He gently undressed her and carried her to the bed. Natalie sat on the edge of the bed and removed his shirt, then loosened his belt. He kicked off his shoes as she lowered his zipper and slid his trousers down to the floor. He stepped out of them as she removed his briefs and fondled him. He picked her up and laid her gently on the bed.

They made love urgently. There was no air conditioning in the villa, only the warm tropical breeze flowing in through the open patio door and over their writhing hot naked bodies. Beads of perspiration glistened as they climaxed together.

All of her work of the last few hours was undone in a moment of wild lovemaking but Natalie didn't care. This moment was too precious to worry about such things.

They parted. Natalie kissed his sweaty chest and loved his salty taste. It was a moment that she had desperately needed. As the passion subsided, both fell into a deep restful sleep.

It was dark when Natalie woke up. She was confused for a moment, wondering where she was . . . the surroundings were so strange at first . . . but after getting her bearings, she once again sat at her dressing table repairing her makeup and in a few minutes was almost as good as new.

She looked at Marc's glistening naked body and there were warm pleasant stirrings between her legs.

"No. Not now, we can't spend our entire lives wrapped in one another's embrace."

But the prospect was certainly pleasant.

Natalie did not awaken Marc. She opened the trunk of the convertible and got out the supplies that Marc had purchased. The village market did not have the variety of items found in their neighborhood supermarket back in LA and many of the items on her list were missing. There was a box of cereal but no milk. Just as well, it would have spoiled by now, anyway, but Marc had found a variety of breads, a jar of peanut butter, and many attractive items from the produce section.

He had brought plenty of bananas, mangoes, passion fruit (*Sure, we really need those*), citrus fruit of all kinds and lettuce, celery, carrots . . . it looked like they would be eating a lot of salads from now on.

Natalie went out onto the rear terrace checked out the back of the villa. In the moon light, she could see that there was a large informal garden and several banana trees, all bearing fruit.

"And he bought bananas in the village", Natalie shook her head. *"Looks like we will be eating a lot of peanut butter and banana sandwiches . . . but not tonight."*

Natalie made a spectacular salad, with *no* bananas. set it aside, made a pot of tea, and waited for Marc to awaken.

She walked into the bedroom and admired his muscular form. She wanted to embrace him again but opted to let him sleep.

"I love him so," Natalie sipped her tea, *"I don't think I can get through this without him."*

Natalie fantasized about their most recent amorous adventure in the bedroom and released with a spectacular galvanic sensation.

She jumped up, frightened that, once again, Andrew might be affecting her thoughts, ran into the bedroom, shook Marc until he was wide awake and hugged him fiercely.

"Hasn't Mrs. Marcel Dupree had *enough* for one evening?"

"No, I could never have . . . but I . . . I was having some tea waiting for you to wake up. I started thinking about making love to you and had . . . an orgasm . . . just sitting there . . . thinking about you . . . It was so wonderful and, at the same time, frightening . . . do you suppose that Andrew . . . ?"

"No, I don't think so. It was just our . . . our magic."

But Marc wasn't too sure. They would have to be very careful.

"Come on and see what I have made for you."

"Let me at least get dressed."

"No. Come now, naked." Natalie rubbed her hands on his chest. "Ummm, you excite me so."

"Then you take off your clothes, too."

She did, and they enjoyed their first naked meal together.

"You didn't use any of the bananas."

"Don't worry, by the time we leave, you will not want to see another banana, . . . ever."

In the morning they strolled through the garden, picked two bunches of bananas to munch on for breakfast, and sat on the bench looking out over the blue-green Gulf and tried to forget about the recent events.

The mental images were too intense to ignore. Marc held her close as Natalie sobbed on his chest, the feelings of guilt tearing at her heart, "He is loose in LA . . . a monster . . . that I created . . . It is so painful to think about the terrible things he might be doing at this very moment."

"The LAPD will get him. George Bennet, my partner when I was on the force, is in charge of the case. George is the best, . . . tenacious as a bull dog. He won't rest until he nails him. I'm confident of that."

"Did you tell him about Andrew?"

"No time, but George will figure it out. You can be sure of that."

CHAPTER TWENTY-SIX

Andrew spent a lot of time on the Strip over the next few weeks. It was familiar territory and he had pretty much figured out how to use his incredible mental powers to take care of his physical needs. He even found that his sexual appetite could be satisfied without any *terminations*. He simply made the hookers *believe* that they had been paid for their services. He soon discovered that there were many young attractive ladies anxious for a night of pleasure and even if they did not have the hookers' repertoires of skills they were much more pleasant to be with and they cared for him, even in one night stands, whereas, with the hookers, it was strictly business.

The police were baffled. There had been such a flurry of vicious killings, obviously done by the same perpetrator and now they had stopped as abruptly as they had started. *What kind of person could do these things? What did he look like? What triggered this guy on and off? When would he strike again?*

And where?

Police officers in major cities in the US and Canada were on special alert. Interpol checked and rechecked the reports on all of the murders attributed to this killer, watching for him to emerge in Europe.

LAPD did not have much to go on. The variety of MOs astounded them as did the variety of his victims who seemed to have very little in common. The only solid thing they had to go on was his *signature*.

There were hundreds of fingerprints collected at the many crime scenes, and some prints were found at more than one scene, but that was to be expected, at least in the cases of the women. Hookers and masseuses probably had many repeat customers. Some of the prints found were those of known felons but pursuit of those clues only led the police into one dead end after another. Overlooked in their zeal to wrap this up quickly and pin it on a known felon were many fingerprints, including Andrew's prints, that were not on file *anywhere*.

After the fire that obliterated the Project Complex, the police found Sarah Buckley's body at the base of the cliff behind the site of the lab. The autopsy revealed the lethal injection but Andrew had not killed her himself and there was no *signature.* Her death was not connected to those attributed to the *signature* killer and despite the close proximity of her body to the site of the fire, the police could make no direct connection with the fire either. They could not ignore the possibility of suicide but something just didn't feel right about that so Sarah soon joined a growing list of unsolved deaths.

Nevertheless, Sarah still had living relatives and friends in other states. She did not keep in close touch . . . just holidays . . . and not all of those . . . It did not surprise anyone that they had not heard from her recently. Her new job was apparently very demanding. In time however, people will become concerned and eventually start looking for answers. Meanwhile, she was just another Jane Doe.

Andrew was concerned about this loose end but in the long run it benefitted him. It made him ever so careful about loose ends thereafter.

Andrew had no pangs of guilt about the killings. He had absolutely no concept of right or wrong, but he closely followed the news reports about the *signature* killer and was puzzled. Other people had confusing ideas about what he had done. In the laboratory, fetuses were *terminated* without remorse yet the community outside of the laboratory seemed to find *his* terminations to be abhorrent. He did not see any difference and quickly dismissed the subject.

It was becoming clear to him that he could get along nicely outside of the restrictions of the laboratory environment and if the people out here did not like *his* terminations he would just stop . . . for now.

In a crowd Andrew could go virtually unnoticed. He was not a virile macho type. He had soft hands and soft features, almost effeminate. His eyes, however, were quite remarkable, a very powerful weapon for him. His gaze could pin one to the wall like a butterfly specimen. For that reason, he tended to avoid direct eye contact until it suited his purpose.

As the days stretched into weeks, and the weeks into months, Andrew became completely comfortable in his new environment.

The chill of winter was in the air. This was a new experience for him. He needed warmer clothing and a light jacket but it had now become second nature to buy things and make the salespersons believe that they had been paid in cash. He was oblivious to the trail of hookers beaten up by their pimps for holding out on them, and sales people having their paychecks docked, or even being fired, for shortages when their registers were zeroed out at the end of the day.

He was a quick study and, just by observing, soon mastered what most people had learned gradually throughout their longer lives and took for granted.

He got into elevators with other people and watched how they selected their floors.

He took many cab rides, in the course of which, he observed how the drivers operated their cabs and was, in a sense, competent to drive a car long before he ever got behind the wheel of one.

Not *everything* was going as he would have wished, however. From time to time he would be asked to show some form of identification. His problem was that he had none. He didn't exist. There was no record of his birth, no medical records, no school or college records, no driver's license, no bank accounts, insurance records, no home address, no marriage certificate, and . . . an increasing concern . . . no passport.

The recent actions of the European Union to remove travel restrictions and abolish check points at national borders had made it as easy to move from country to country as it is to move from state to state . . . but he could not leave the United States to go to England or the mainland of Europe without a passport. It was not a good idea to go to

Mexico or Canada either without proper credentials. If for some reason, his US citizenship was challenged at a border while trying to return to the US, and he had no passport, . . . well, he just didn't want to risk that.

The eastern block countries still had checkpoints at all borders and travel was as severely restricted as it had been before the fall of the Berlin wall and the breakup of the Soviet Union. Old habits die hard. Passports, visas, travel documents . . . these all required identification but Andrew found that a judiciously offered bribe here and there to relatively low level bureaucrats enabled him to establish a document base giving him an identity. He also discovered that there was a thriving business in forged documents at any level. He took advantage of this to provide himself with an increasingly broader base of identification. He was confident that he could pass any but the most rigorous background check.

Andrew didn't mind using forged background documents like his birth certificate to establish his existence but he drew the line at his driver's license and his passport. For the future that he was planning for himself, these must be the real thing. And he needed a well established and documented cover identity.

He chose to be "himself".

He kept the name given to him by Natalie and Sarah and bit by bit he emerged as a bonafide human being, Andrew Kreist.

Some of these identification documents required finger printing . . . sometimes a full set of prints, sometimes just a thumb or index finger. The latter usually went on the driver's license or similar ID card, just for verification of identity, but the full sets went into data banks where they might someday be compared to other prints in police files.

That concerned Andrew because he had undoubtedly left prints at the scenes of some of his early *terminations*, before he learned about fingerprint identification. He managed to smudge or slightly smear the full sets but not so much that he might be called back to take them again.

He had become very careful since his early mistakes in leaving prints and it was Andrew's good luck that police had concentrated their investigations on the known felons whose prints had been found at the crime scenes. It had been just too much bother for them to try to run down a person whose prints were not on file anywhere and who had no criminal record.

Andrew did not mind being photographed for identification purposes. After all, he *was* Andrew Kreist and his picture would help set that in concrete.

It took a while but eventually, Andrew established a broad enough background to obtain a driver's license and passport.

By December he owned a Mercedes Benz limo, was living in the finest hotels, and eating in the most elegant restaurants . . . And, all the while, he was leaving behind a trail of broken lives, . . . people accused of theft or embezzlement, or worse.

In conversation with some recently acquired associates, Andrew found out about Las Vegas. It sounded like his kind of place so he decided to check it out.

He drove there himself, his Mercedes becoming a comfortable cocoon, providing protection from the searing heat of the desert. The road was so straight and the traffic so sparse that he managed to drive at well over 100 miles per hour for most of the trip.

When he arrived in Vegas, he checked into the Hilton, took a hot shower and got a good night's sleep. On the following morning, he drove up and down the strip checking out the marquees, stopped in a couple of the casinos, and played the slots. After a light lunch, he returned to his hotel and rested. Tonight he would really check out the casinos, . . . but it was clear. This *was* his kind of place.

CHAPTER TWENTY-SEVEN

George Bennet's *signature* killer task force was not making any progress.

George was a tenacious cop. He bothered and picked at every tiny thread until a case finally unraveled. He had patience and time. There was not nearly as much pressure on him now that the killings had stopped . . . but on the other hand, every day that passed, the trail grew colder. The case was now in the phase where an informer or similar break was usually needed for a solution.

How long would it take LAPD to put it all together?

There was a growing body of evidence connecting Andrew to the *signature* killings and other crimes. But the police were unaware of most of it.

There *were* the prints. Andrew had left fingerprints at the scenes of the early murders but at that time there was no record of his existence anywhere. Known felons had also frequented the abodes of the hookers and masseuses and the police had been thrown off the trail by directing their attention toward the known felons, running into one dead end after another.

Some day, they might run out of leads and take another look at those John Doe 7863 prints. However, Andrew was not the only John Doe in town. A lot of respectable business men from all over the world, with no prior records, frequented those places or solicited the services of hookers when they were in town and left prints, not expecting that they would ever be lifted by the police. LAPD had John Doe prints on file from crime scenes all over LA. But there was nothing unusual about Andrew's so they rested quietly in the files alongside all of the other John Does.

Andrew had to establish an identity and his efforts to do so required the taking of prints for drivers licenses and other documents. He had no way of knowing, of course, but when the police had found absolutely no proof of his existence, they put his prints back into the files and forgot about them.

No one ever compared the *new* prints of Andrew Kreist, after the fact, to the crime scene prints.

Similarly, the computer consultant who reconstructed the face on the Shroud, an accurate representation of Andrew's face, wondered, for a brief moment after the fire at the Project Complex, if the face that he had reconstructed had any connection to the fire. It seemed like such a stretch that he put it out of his mind, copied the reconstruction from his hard drive onto a floppy disk, carefully labeled it and filed it in the vault in which his company kept such records . . . and he made a copy for himself. It had been his most interesting assignment, and because of that, the consultant would take the disk out every few months and look at it. He knew that his starting point was a picture of the Shroud of Turin. Why was that so important to all of those scientists? He had no way of knowing it, but he was one of the few outsiders who had ever been with all of them at once. Who *were* they? Had they *all* died in the fire? The news accounts of the fire did not list any victims, but nagging questions popped up every time he looked at the image on his computer screen.

While Natalie had her briefcase with her when she opted not to board TWA Flight 800, her luggage *did* get on the flight. Her ticket had already been lifted when she changed her mind about boarding so the record showed that she was aboard the flight. Of course, her body was never found so she was listed as missing and presumed dead. However, one of her suitcases floated to the surface. It was never claimed because she had no living relatives and she was too terrified that Andrew might find out that she survived to try to recover the luggage herself. It was stored in the unclaimed property locker set up for items recovered from the crash. In the suitcase, was Natalie's diary, . . . damp, moldy, and getting moldier by the day.

Natalie had been very circumspect when putting her thoughts into her diary. She knew well, from the experiences of some of her high school friends, that the contents of a diary might not remain secret forever. All references to the cloning of Andrew were carefully couched in phrases that might not be readily understood by a casual reader. However, if all of it was taken together, and thoughtfully analyzed, the truth was there to be found and exposed. The contents of her diary would be frightening to anyone, but represented a *real* threat to Andrew if they should ever become public.

There was also the stuff that Andrew had tossed into the dumpsters after killing John Wilson.

There is nothing secret about trash. Andrew had not reckoned on the "dumpsters miners". They operate on the principal that one man's garbage is another man's treasure.

Dumpsters miners, an army of grubby night people, dig through the contents of dumpsters and garbage cans every night hoping for a bonanza. One of these dumpsters miners found some items that were interesting. The 357 Magnum automatic obviously had some cash value and maybe the video tapes and folders full of records. The time of finding complete documents in the trash was long into the past. Today, everything of any value goes through a shredder but here they were. Someone obviously wanted to get rid of this stuff in such a hurry that they hadn't taken time to shred or incinerate it. Why? Maybe it is worth something to *somebody*. The miner took the pistol and the rest of the stuff back to his shack to go through at a later time.

He thought about the pistol. It was brand new, in perfect working order. Why would anyone throw it away? He smelled it. It had been recently fired. It had to be "hot" so he would hide it for a while to let it cool off . Then he might get the word out on the street and sell it.

He had no way to view the tapes but he never threw away *anything* so he squirreled them away, along with the documents, for another day.

Altogether, the fingerprints, the gun, the tapes, the digital image on a floppy disk, the project files, and Natalie's diary told a most remarkable story about who Andrew *really* was. Would anyone ever piece it all together? At the moment it did not seem that there was any hope of that ever happening. And if they did would anyone ever believe it? It was so bizarre.

There was another time bomb ticking as well. The other members of Natalie's team who perished in the fire were a big question mark as far as Andrew was concerned. Surely friends and relatives were becoming concerned about them. Andrew was oblivious to the fact that one of the attributes of Natalie's team was that they were all basically loners. None were married now although Dr. Mansic had been for a short time, many years ago. All were so absorbed in their work that they had all pretty much alienated their parents and siblings long before they started work on the Project.

Generally, they had not even mentioned their moves to Los Angeles so most relatives thought they were located in their last cities of residence *before* LA.

If any of their relatives or friends bothered to write or phone, their mail was returned "Address Unknown" or "No Forwarding Address", and they got a "not listed" response to phone inquiries. This did not set off any alarms. It had happened many times before and there was nothing to do but wait. Eventually they would get around to making contact again . . . *but don't hold your breath*. That was just the way things were.

Sarah did not fit into the *signature* pattern so her death was not assigned to George Bennet's task force. For the moment, it was on some other cop's plate and he was not getting anywhere either, . . . except for the hypodermic syringe. It had become dislodged from Sarah's arm as her body tumbled down the cliff. It was far up the cliff from the point where Sarah's body finally came to rest. The police had not found it in their crime scene investigation but six months later, some kids scrambling around on the steep slope spotted it and luckily did what they had been taught, The turned it in to the police. They handled it, of course, but the police were able to lift some prints from it. However, they belonged to the kids and Sarah, known to the police only as Jane Doe. Andrew had not touched the syringe so the police would get no help there but they were able to trace the syringe back to the manufacturer and a trail of invoices led to the laboratory that had been destroyed in the fire.

So, . . . she *was* connected in some way to the fire. Maybe she worked there.

Again, since she had no prior record there was little to go on but she must have had prints on file somewhere, prints that might, at least, give this Jane Doe a name. Dogged police work might turn up something from this meager clue but this was the kind of work that took a lot of time and effort. What the LAPD needed was a big break and there did not seem to be one on the horizon.

There was something very strange about the fire. It seemed to have started all over the building at the same moment. That suggested arson, so the LAPD's best arson squad was assigned to the case. The aspect of the fire that puzzled them the most was the fact that there was not a trace of any known accelerant.

The destruction was total. There was absolutely no trace of a body anywhere, but there was no trace of anything else either . . . no furniture, no books, no documents, no machinery or equipment of any kind, no carpet or tile, no plumbing, no toilets, no glass, . . . nothing. Just a homogeneous grey ash.

The arson squad sifted through the grey ash and found no clues whatsoever.

What about the people? Surely someone worked here. If they were here when it happened, why can't we find some trace of the bodies . . . And if they were not here, where are they? . . . why haven't they come forward?

It was most perplexing. The best they could do was collect samples of the grey ash. The entire area was marked off in a grid pattern and samples of the ash were collected from each square in the grid, bagged in ziplock bags, and carefully labeled as to the grid square of origin.

Hundreds of samples were collected and sent to the LAPD Forensics Laboratory for analysis. What would they look for? It would be hard to decide where to start.

It rained the next night and the ash turned to sticky gooey mud. It all ran together and much of it washed over the cliff into the gully below. Hopefully anything that might be used for evidence had been collected. If not . . . further collection would be useless.

Forensics was a thankless job. No one, from the top down, appreciated how much effort had to be expended for so little tangible work product. Everyone wanted answers *right now*. Well, it just didn't work that way. Forensic work ran into a lot of dead ends but nothing like this. This investigation was nothing *but* dead ends.

———————————

CHAPTER TWENTY-EIGHT

In Las Vegas, Andrew found the money tree. It took him several nights of observation to figure out the best way to do it. The slot machines first caught his eye. The mechanical machines were a snap. He could mentally control the spinning cylinders and won heavily, at least in terms of the sizes of slot machine jackpots but this was chicken feed compared to the money changing hands elsewhere in the casinos. One slot machine, however, represented a bonanza. It was the huge machine at the entrance of one of the casinos. It had a ten million dollar payout. His greedy heart yearned for that jackpot but he quickly realized that a winner on *that* machine would set off whistles and bells. There would be a big to do and photos would be taken. That was something he chose to avoid at all costs.

Andrew looked around the casinos and made mental notes. *"The crap tables would be easy except for two things. A long string of straight passes would defy the laws of probability and arouse suspicion. Well, even if they become suspicious, they are **their** dice and they won't find that they are loaded. But those surveillance cameras are another matter. They can slow down the video tapes and quickly detect that last little flip as the dice come up the way I want them to. Better look elsewhere."*

The blackjack tables had a similar surveillance problem. *"The house is especially wary of the possibility that a dealer might give good cards to an accomplice and the house does not like to be taken by their own employees. Also, there are too many eyes watching the play from all angles and distances to chance mentally manipulating the cards on the table."*

The baccarat tables were even worse. There were those damned surveillance cameras again . . . and no chance to mentally manipulate the cards in the shoe.

Eventually, Andrew arrived at the roulette tables. The surveillance cameras kept a close watch on the croupiers and the players but he didn't have to touch anything but his chips. And the way that ball bounced around on the wheel . . . .

It was a simple feat to stop that little ball on any number he wanted. By this time he had become astute enough to quit after modest winnings which, in these casinos, could still be substantial because he was rubbing elbows with some high rolling jet setters. *Win a few; lose a few; but always win more than you lose.* Every night was a good night for Andrew and what started out as a small stake soon grew into an appreciable fortune. He became a familiar face at the roulette tables at all of the casinos, his bets gradually increased, and the house soon became comfortable with him being there.

One night after a very good streak at the roulette table, Andrew was leaving for the night. He left an especially generous tip for the croupier and worked his way toward the door. As he passed the giant slot machine at the entrance, his mischievous nature took control. There was a beautiful statuesque blonde dropping tokens in the machine. Andrew guessed that she was a show girl who had a sugar daddy nearby. He could not resist the temptation. He concentrated on the rotating drums. One by one the images of gold bullion bars clicked into place. The blonde screamed with delight as bar after bar lined up. Then the last one stopped on the same icon. There they were. Eight gold bar icons across the board. Her shriek could be heard all over the casino. Andrew smiled because, as he had surmised, strobe lights started flashing, a klaxon bonked raucously, the tune "I've Got Plenty of Money" blared out of the loudspeakers, and bells were ringing all over the casino.

Andrew turned his back on the turmoil and gave the valet the ticket for his Mercedes. As he relaxed into the soft leather seat, he thought, *"Now, she won't have to sleep with anyone anymore . . . unless she wants to."*

Andrew saw something special in her . . . and he had plans for her.

Soon, he started arriving at the casino with the blonde in tow. It was a life style that suited his ever increasing appetite for power. And after the gambling, they had dinner together . . . and after the dinner, ...back to their hotel suite for an orgy of depravity and incredible sex. She had urgent sexual needs that were almost as strong as his. She was a handful . . . two handsful . . . almost more than he could handle . . . almost. She certainly satisfied all of his lusts to the extent that his eyes never strayed. But this wasn't all she provided.

After the first time they had sex, she said, "I know who you are but I don't think I told you my name. I'm Madeline Belvoire."

Classy name, . . . and a classy broad, too.

It turned out that she was, indeed, a *classy broad*. She was the only daughter of an upper crust New England family, the product of education in expensive and exclusive private schools, debute at a cotillion, one year at Sarah Lawrence and then a falling out with her family. She was a free spirit, not about to be reined in by a controlling mother who had already chosen an *appropriate* mate for her. They had cut her off without a cent but she had managed to get by on her wits . . . and other attributes.

She had more than tasted the good life and was hungry for even more of it. Her demeanor rubbed off on Andrew and she gave him a polished and aristocratic air that helped him fit in with the moneyed class.

Andrew and Madeline insinuated themselves into the lives of the high rollers and they were frequently invited to parties at Marina Del Rey on yachts as big as battle cruisers. The incredible blonde was constantly at his side.

It was good to have money, . . . lots of it. Money meant power and power brought everything. It was *all* about *power* and these people had it. They were the shakers and movers and Andrew resolved to be one of them . . . more than just one of them . . . the top dog.

Zepp Grinkov went to the baccarat table and whispered in the ear of his boss Gregor Vuchkovitch.

"Where?"

Zepp nodded toward the nearest roulette table.

"Which one?"

"The Tux . . . with the blonde eyeful."

"OK, Wait until I pass the shoe."

Eventually, Gregor rose from the table. He and Zepp strolled over toward the roulette table but stopped a discrete distance away.

Gregor scrutinized the man in the tuxedo.

"What have you been able to find out about him?"

"Not very much. Looks like he just materialized out of nowhere, . . . but he has the Midas touch. I have tailed him as he makes the rounds of the casinos. Only plays roulette but *always* leaves the table a winner . . . and I mean *always*.

"How do you think he does it?"

"I don't know. It is uncanny. He just seems to have incredible luck."

"Nobody is *that* lucky. He must have some kind of gimmick."

"I don't think so. He doesn't touch anything but his chips. Beats me how he does it. He just intuitively knows where to put his chips. When he is playing, he is kind of out of it, like he is hypnotized by the wheel. He just stares at it.

He moves on to another casino as soon as he is well ahead. I don't think the house in any of the casinos has a clue as to how much he is taking them for."

"Invite him up to my suite for cocktails tomorrow. Lets see if we can loosen him up. Maybe he will let us in on his secret."

Andrew's telepathic skills enabled him to monitor the entire conversation.

Well, if these guys want to play, lets see who plays with who.

The next evening, Andrew arrived at Vuchkovitch's penthouse suite with Madeline on his arm. Zepp Grinkov greeted them at the door. "Mr. Vuchkovitch is very pleased that you accepted his invitation."

Madeline was draped in an ermine stole that dragged on the floor.

Zepp reached for the stole, "May I take this? It will be on the bed in the master bedroom when you are ready to leave."

Andrew waited at the door for Zepp's return.

"Come in, let me introduce you to your host."

Zepp escorted them across the room and out onto the terrace overlooking Las Vegas. Gregor Vuchkovitch was in animated conversation with another man but when he saw Andrew, he gave a slight wave of the hand, summarily dismissing the man who quickly went back inside.

"Mr. Vuchkovitch, may I present Mr. Andrew Kreist and his lady . . . ?" Zepp looks questioningly at Andrew.

"Madeline Belvoire," the blonde interjected.

"More like Ima Strumpet, if I am any judge", thought Zepp.

"Zepp, would you get Miss Belvoire a drink and introduce her around. I would like a moment with Mr. Kreist."

Gregor guided Andrew to the bar, "What's your poison?"

Andrew had gotten over his initial dislike for Scotch and it was now his libation of choice, "Johnny . . . Black . . . neat."

The bartender gave him a very generous shot and Gregor nodded for Andrew to follow him.

They walked out onto the terrace. It wrapped around three sides of Gregor's suite and had a breathtaking view of Las Vegas.

"Let's drop the formalities. I'm Gregor."

"And I am Andrew."

"These people are pretty genteel considering their reputations for ruthlessness."

Andrew had already done some research himself and was well aware of the hard ball played by the Russian Mafia.

Meanwhile, Zepp introduced Madeline to some of his cronies and signaled that they should keep her busy for a few minutes. He then made his way to the master bedroom, checked out the label in the ermine stole, and made a phone call.

When he emerged from the bedroom he caught Gregor's eye.

Gregor said, "Please excuse me for a moment."

He walked over to Zepp.

"It's the real thing."

"I thought it would be."

"He paid for it himself and it cost a bundle."

"Thought that, too. "

"And he paid *cash*."

"Hmmmm," Gregor rejoined Andrew on the terrace.

"Andrew, it looks like your drink needs to be freshened."

"That's all right, I'm OK for now."

"You can't buy a better view of Vegas than this . . . at any price."

Gregor paused and they both surveyed the vista in silence for a moment.

"Tell me, Andrew, what do you do for a living?"

"*Ah, the game begins*." Andrew sipped his drink. "I make money."

"I assumed *that* but, how?"

"Would you like for me to ask *you* that?"

Gregor paused.

"Ah, we understand each other . . . suffice it to say, 'I have wide-spread interests and keep a low profile.'"

After a brief pause, Gregor continued,"Zepp tells me that you are very lucky in the casinos."

"I hadn't noticed. Do you have an interest in any of them?"

"Not directly."

"Oh?"

"Lets just say, "If *they* make money, *I* make money."

"Then we should both do what we can to keep them solvent," Andrew held out his glass in a toast and they clinked glasses.

This guy is skimming the take at all of the casinos. They have apparently elbowed out the Italian Mafia. It takes a lot of muscle to do that . . . and he is not too happy about me getting my share first.

Andrew made some more small talk and then said, "Madeline and I have tickets for a show and will have to hurry to make it. Nice meeting you and thanks for inviting me up here. It is great to see the view from the top of the world."

"Then we will have to do it again . . . and soon," Gregor oozed charm.

He, or Zepp, would cut my throat in a second. He won't though. He is too curious about how I do it. He won't try it . . . at least for now.

"Zepp, he knows you now so get one of your men to follow him around. Give him a small stake . . . say a grand. Tell him he can keep his winnings but he has to tell us how he does. Have him play the same numbers that Kreist plays and see how he makes out. I want to know how much he is taking us for."

Andrew shook his head in disbelief. Gregor, Zepp, and the higher ups in the Russian Mafia all wore the finest Italian silk suits but the underlings wore ill-fitting Russian suits having heavily padded shoulders, wide lapels, and heavy chalk stripes, right off the rack at GUM, Moscow's huge department store. These goons were reminiscent of the gangster movies of the '30s . . . and they all smoked big cheap cigars. Andrew had never seen a gangster movie, of course, but these clowns would stand out anywhere . . . (they didn't know that this was the case because they had no fashion consciousness and, back in Moscow, they blended in perfectly).

The underling was going over his instructions in his head. Unfortunately, he was thinking in Russian and Andrew could not understand a word but he had a pretty good idea what he was up to when he started duplicating Andrew's bets.

"I think I will give him a little ride."

Andrew placed another bet and the goon bet on the same number but not nearly as much as Andrew. The number came up a winner and the goon smiled.

The next number also came up a winner, but from that point on, Andrew made no effort to control the outcome and both he and the goon lost heavily. The goon soon blew his entire stake and retired from the fray to report to Zepp. As soon as he was gone, Andrew placed one more bet that was more than enough to make up for his earlier losses and left the casino.

When the underling reported the results to Zepp he could not believe it.

"Maybe he just has lucky streaks," Zepp reported to Gregor, "He didn't win *all* of the time when I was watching him . . . but in the long run he came out ahead. I'm sure of that."

"Who did you give this job to?"

"Ilyev."

"Kosinko? Why him? He is as dense as a rock. Send someone with some brains and try again."

It didn't really matter who they sent. Andrew had acquired a sense of what was proper dress for any occasion and as long as they came wearing those stupid Al Capone era gangster outfits, Andrew could spot them a mile away, and, one way or another, he kept them from getting the information they were after.

Some of Andrew's cultivated acquaintances were heavily into the stock market. He had, very early on, intuitively concurred with the old adage that it is better to keep your mouth shut and be thought a fool than to open it and remove all doubt . . . so he listened most of the time, . . . and made mental notes.

Andrew developed a different view of the stock market from that of his new associates. They viewed their shares of stock as investments to be traded. Buy low; sell high. That was all it meant to them, but to Andrew, a share of stock represented *ownership*. True, one share did not represent a lot of ownership but many shares represented ownership of a substantial part of a company and enough shares gave you control of the company's destiny. A lot of shares represented *real* power and Andrew was developing an insatiable appetite for *that*. He set a personal goal of ownership, *ownership of not one but many of the largest companies in the world.*

Taking control of a single major company was a long way down stream for Andrew, but for now, he had a near term objective, to get rid of Zepp who was becoming a major annoyance by constantly checking up on him. It occurred to Andrew that he might achieve two objectives at once . . . dispose of Zepp and grab his job as Gregor Vuchkovitch's top lieutenant.

Andrew imposed his thoughts on Gregor from time to time and gradually brought him around to the point of offering him a job in the organization. Zepp was suspicious of Andrew. He got Gregor off in a corner where he proposed a test of Andrew's trustworthiness. Have Andrew do the collections for a week or two.

Zepp was certain that Andrew would skim some of the take so he proposed that Gregor plan in advance exactly how much each casino would turn over to him.

Then, when he came up short, Gregor would finally understand what Zepp had been trying to tell him all along.

Andrew eavesdropped using his telepathic skills. Here was his chance. A bit at the time, he planted seeds, nourished them, and let them develop and flourish in Gregor's suspicious mind.

Gregor liked the idea of the test but wanted time to think it over. If Andrew did have as larcenous a heart as Zepp intimated, he would be nailed . . . and eliminated.

It did not take Andrew long to formulate a strategy. Before Gregor could put the test into action Andrew made a preemptive strike while Zepp was still designated to make the collections. Andrew imposed his thoughts on Gregor.

Somebody is cutting in on the take from the casinos. Zepp makes the collections for me. Why should I take Zepp's word for it that Andrew's winnings are responsible? He has not provided any proof. Maybe Zepp has his hand in the till.

At every opportunity, Andrew reinforced this idea but never said anything aloud to Gregor.

Gregor seethed at the idea of his most trusted lieutenant betraying him in this manner. Didn't he pay Zepp enough? Yes, . . . probably more than he deserved.

Andrew kept inserting the blade of suspicion deeper and twisting it.

He now even inserted these doubts into Gregor's dreams. *It is time.*

Andrew determined that Gregor and Zepp were having a drink together in Gregor's suite.

Perfect.

He took a large amount of cash from his box in the hotel safe, placed it in a cardboard box and took it to Zepp's hotel room. The box contained more money than Zepp could possibly explain. Andrew viewed it as an investment.

The hotel used "credit card" type door keys, but behind the magnetic reader was just a very ordinary lock. Andrew had no trouble with it. After using his psycho kinetic powers to unlock Zepp's door, he entered, placed the box under Zepp's bed, and departed.

That night, after Gregor went to sleep, Andrew projected a very intense image onto Gregor's dream screen as he slept. Gregor awoke with a start. It was so real. Zepp had taken a lot of money from the large briefcase that he carried when he made the collections. Zepp had then put it in a cardboard box and slipped it under his bed. At first Gregor tried to pass it off as just a wild dream but it seemed so real.

He had to know. Gregor dressed, put a silencer on an unlicenced pistol, and went to Zepp's room.

Zepp answered the door groggily.

"It must be important to wake me up at this hour."

He invited Gregor in. Gregor walked right past the nearest chair and sat down on the edge of Zepp's bed. Pretending to tie his shoe, Gregor leaned over and spotted the box under the bed, right where it had been in his dream.

"How could you do it, Zepp?"

"Do what? I don't know what you mean."

Gregor reached under the bed, pulled out the box, and dumped its incriminating contents on the bed.

Zepp was dumbfounded."I . . . I . . . I don't . . . "

Zepp never finished the sentence. Gregor's fury was unleashed as he fired eight bullets into the astonished Zepp. His body jerked backward as each slug slammed into his body. Gregor was certain that no one heard the silenced shots.

He quickly put the cash back into the box and returned to his suite where he put the cash in his wall safe.

His ties to Zepp were well known and the police would be asking a lot of questions so, before dawn the next morning, Gregor drove out into the desert, disposed of the gun and silencer, returned to his room, and went back to sleep, confident that he had solved his problem.

The housekeeper found the body while making her rounds later that morning.

The Las Vegas police could not overlook the obvious link between Zepp and Gregor and, as expected, they were at Gregor's door within minutes of the discovery of the body. Gregor seemed genuinely surprised and shocked at the news of Zepp's murder.

"He was here last night", Gregor volunteered, "We had a few drinks. He left around midnight."

"You didn't see him after that?"

"No."

"Do you own a handgun?"

"Yes. It is registered," Gregor removed his 9mm Walther PK automatic from his shoulder holster and handed it to the detective. "I'm licensed to carry. I'm sure you know why."

"We will want to run a ballistics test on it", The detective bagged the pistol. "And we would like for you to come down to the station with us for a paraffin test."

"I can tell you before we go, I will test positive."

The detective raised his eyebrows questioningly.

"My guys and I frequently go out in the desert to an arroyo, set up cans for targets and shoot into the sand bank on the other side." The detective did not seem to be buying it.

"Look, it's stupid to carry and not know how to shoot the damn thing, . . . wouldn't you say?"

The detective grunted and made notes.

"You should check out all of my guys. They shoot out there, too. We will probably all check out positive."

"When was the last time you were out there shooting."

"Yesterday, . . . yesterday afternoon."

"Anybody with you?"

"No."

"Where is this arroyo?"

"I can have one of my guys show you."

It all checked out. There were ammo boxes . . . 9mm mostly, hundreds of shell casings, bullet riddled cans, bullets embedded in the bank of the arroyo and much other evidence that a *lot* of ammo had been expended there. Gregor's pistol as well as those carried by his underlings all sailed thru the ballistics tests.

Gregor and several henchmen tested positive on the paraffin test but after the evidence found at the arroyo this proved nothing other than that they had all recently fired guns and they all admitted to that.

The police viewed Zepp's killing as a mob hit, but it was more vicious and bloody than most. Usually, small caliber bullets ricocheting around inside the skull from two tiny neat entry wounds behind the ear was sufficient for the job and much neater than the bloody machine gun slayings of the gang wars of the 60's and 70's.

Someone was apparently sending a message here that was not meant to be ignored.

There was a spectacular funeral for Zepp, rivaling those of the Chicago gangsters during the prohibition wars. Gregor Vuchkovitch was a high profile mourner and appeared to be in deep grief over the loss of his lieutenant. The police took pictures of both the mourners and the crowds at the funeral. Andrew was there, giving comfort and support to Gregor. The police had photographed these things before but no one paid particular attention to the new face at Gregor's right shoulder. The photos went into the files for future reference.

The photographer for one of the Los Angeles papers took essentially the same shot. The story and picture appeared on the first page of the Metro section.

The police speculated that this might be the opening gun of a new war among the various factions of the Russian Mafia. Gregor welcomed this. It took the attention away from himself and put police pressure on his rivals.

"A new gang war?" Gregor was amused at the idea.

He *certainly* did not intend to take any "retaliatory" action against anyone.

A new gang war? . . .

"Huh, Wishful thinking."

Gregor put Zepp's test into action and Andrew came through with flying colors.

Eventually, he was trusted with other important organizational matters and given a say in organization meetings. Andrew played it straight and soon earned the full confidence of Gregor Vuchkovitch. He became Gregor's strong right arm . . . a big mistake on Gregor's part.

CHAPTER TWENTY-NINE

Press Report, Turin, April 12, 1997

April 12, 1997. Sacred Relic, The Shroud of Turin, believed to be the burial shroud of Jesus Christ, was unharmed in a fire that severely damaged the Cathedral in Turin.

The fire badly damaged the dome of the chapel in which the Shroud resided. The Shroud was encased, for display, in a polycarbonate bullet proof vault to protect it from vandals.

Debris from the dome rained down on the vault and it was feared that the entire dome might collapse on the Shroud.

The vault was too heavy to move. One of the firemen, Mario Trematore, attacked the "bullet proof" glass with a sledge hammer and in a feat of superhuman strength shattered the polycarbonate case. A team of firemen then plucked the Shroud from the case and carried it to safety. Trematore, praised as a hero, said that God gave him the strength to save the Shroud.

In their zeal to save both the Shroud and themselves from the danger of a possible collapse of the dome, the firemen did not feel or otherwise notice the fact that part of the Shroud snagged on the shattered polycarbonate and a small piece was torn off and remained caught in a crack in the case.

More than two hundred firemen battled the blaze before it was finally brought under control.

After the fire a team of structural experts examined the dome and determined that it was not in immediate danger of collapse. But there was a monumental cleanup job facing the crew charged with that chore.

The Shroud was stored for safekeeping elsewhere and was closely examined for signs of damage by experts who discovered the fact that a small piece of it was missing and presumed to be somewhere in the chapel. Crews searched through all of the debris in an attempt to find it but to no avail.

A reward was offered for the return of the scrap. This offer made all of the Turin papers as well as those in Milan . . . but no one responded.

There was a good reason for this.

One of the workers, Antonio Siglia, assigned to clean up the Chapel after the fire, made an interesting discovery. It had been slightly damaged by smoke and water, and could have been almost anything, but rather than relegate it to the trash bin, he put it carefully in his pocket and took it home with him at the end of the day.

His clothing was covered with soot and mud and he was about to toss all of it into a wash tub when he remembered the tiny piece of linen in the pocket. He started to clean it up by rinsing it off but, after examining it, thought better of it and put it in a zip lock envelope for safekeeping.

It was announced on the following Sunday that Papal Honors would be conferred upon the firemen who risked their lives to effect the rescue of the Shroud.

Antonio Siglia knew that the scrap of linen was probably worth a lot more than the reward. An artifact like this could bring a fortune from the right person. He has a cousin who has connections with the Italian underworld. His cousin agreed to get the word out on the streets . . . for a piece of the action. Antonio agreed. His cousin found a potential buyer who thought he could sell the artifact for a very good price and introduced Antonio to the buyer. The cousin did not know the name of the buyer and when he struggled with the introduction, the potential buyer told him to "get lost", while he talked privately with Antonio.

Once the cousin has departed, the buyer asked,"And how did you come by it?"

Antonio told him all about the fire and the cleanup effort including how he found the shred of linen clinging to the shattered polycarbonate.

"Can I see it?"

Antonio was too trusting, "Yes," he replied, removing the envelope from his shirt pocket, . . . thereby sealing his death warrant.

The buyer examined the scrap.

"What will you pay for it."

"This!" replied the buyer.

He withdrew from his pocket a small but wicked looking pistol equipped with a silencer.

There were four "POP"s in rapid succession.

Antonio looked at the buyer in surprised disbelief and crumpled to the sidewalk. He was dead before he hit the ground.

Concerned that Antonio's cousin might remember him, the gunman quickly caught up with him and pressed the muzzle of the silenced pistol against his spine. There were four more barely audible "POP"s.

The connection was cut clean.

The gunman intended to find a well heeled buyer but if he did not succeed, he could always collect the reward. He saw it as a win-win situation.

There had been a lot of press about cloning successes and failures and the killer had taken note of them. In Rome, a team of genetic scientists had a very good track record cloning sheep and other farm animals. They wanted to take the ultimate step and clone a human but most countries had either passed laws preventing research into the cloning of humans or their leaders had taken strong moral stands against it and seemed to have the support of their people. In Italy, they had to face the opposition of both the government and the Pope.

It was in this climate that a man arrived at the office of David Torrelli the President of Geneticraft International. He had already spoken to David by phone and had ignited his interest.

The intercom on the secretary's desk spoke, "Yes, Show him in. I am expecting him."

The killer of both Antonio and his cousin was ushered into the plush office. The man behind the heavy mahogany desk rose and extended his hand. The handshake was brief and clammy, "I am David Torrelli."

"I don't think it matters who I am. What matters is what I have brought you."

"You have it with you?"

"Yes, and I have this." He exposed a bit of the silenced pistol. "It would not be wise to . . . uh . . . do anything you might regret."

"How did you get it?"

"You know how. Didn't you read about the fire?"

"Yes. But . . . "

"It was easy, I got it before anyone knew it was missing. There is a big reward for its return but I figured it is worth a *lot* more than that." He paused to let that soak in.

"Just think, You can use the blood on this scrap to clone Jesus Christ. Doesn't that whet your appetite? I know it does. I can see you drooling over it."

"Clone Jesus Christ !" The thought did indeed make David drool.

"How do I know it is authentic?"

"You will just have to take my word for it."

"Can I see it?"

David was shown a zip lock envelope containing the dirty scrap. It certainly matched the description of the subject of the reward offer.

"Can I hold it?"

David was handed the clear plastic envelope, and the pistol was partly exposed as a less-than-subtle warning.

"What do you want for it?"

"We have already discussed a price."

"It is a *lot* of money for an item of questionable provenance."

"OK, If you are not interested I have someone else who *is*. I am not here to negotiate. Take it or leave it."

David could not give it back.

"The price is one hundred million Lire . . . cash."

David pulled a large briefcase from under his desk and started to open it.

"Not necessary."

"Don't you want to count it?"

"It's all there. If not, I know where you live and where your children go to school. I'm *sure* it's all there."

He cautiously backed out of the office and left the premises.

David Torrelli was elated but at the same time worried that he might have turned over a hundred million Lire for a fake.

He called a meeting of his associates and briefed them on what he had done.

"You all know that the world consensus is that cloning humans is immoral. Most countries have outlawed it and here we have the added obstacle of a Pope who has been quite outspoken against it . . . but this is an extraordinary opportunity. We will be cloning not just *any* human but a *specific* and *special* human. We will be cloning Jesus Christ. The world is in chaos and only He can restore sense and order. We cannot afford to wait for the prophesies of the Book of Revelations to come to pass. The world may not survive that long."

They all nodded agreement with Torrelli.

Torrelli then made assignments closely paralleling some of those made by Natalie when she was organizing *her* team, but his team was more streamlined.

Torrelli took advantage of some of the independent tests that had been run on the Shroud in the last few years. By so doing he was able to appreciably shorten the time that had been needed by Natalie's team to certify the age of the Shroud, and determine the significant characteristics of the blood stains. He obviously got no fallout from Natalie's work. That was all destroyed in the fire, but there were so many other scientists working in this field now, and publishing their findings on the internet that he had almost more information on the Shroud than he could assimilate. He and his team of scientists were completely convinced of the authenticity of the Shroud so they could devote their full attention to the scrap of linen that had come into their possession. They wanted to believe that it was truly stained with the blood of their Savior.

The reward offer had contained a significant bit of information. When the Shroud was examined by scientists in 1978, 50,000 photographs were taken.

Some of these were closeups showing remarkable details. A composite mosaic of four of these photographs was made and the missing piece of linen was outlined. This mosaic was used to identify precisely what they were looking for. A low power microscopic examination was made and after more than a hundred points of correlation were found including details of the weave, the perimeter of the bloodstain, and the detail of the torn edge. It just didn't seem possible that this scrap of linen was a forgery, . . . yet.

The soot and grime that had been deposited on this scrap presented a major obstacle. Carbon 14 dating would unquestionably yield an erroneous date if the scrap was left in its filthy condition. However, if they didn't conduct *some* tests, their entire effort would have to be a based completely on faith, . . . supported by a hundred points of correlation, but even so.

They had to remove that last nagging doubt so they cautiously approached the problem of cleaning the scrap.

The blood stain was so small that they dared not do anything that might jeopardize the precious DNA residing in that stain.

Torrelli suggested that they settle for just two tests. Correlation with known facts would be considered sufficient for their purposes. This was a risky assumption but their blood sample was so small that they really had no other choice.

The first test was to use a very small portion of the blood stain and "type" it. The blood type was AB, the same as the type found on the Shroud. Hopes were lifted significantly with that finding.

The second test was to snip off a small bit of the linen that was not blood stained and attempt to remove all contaminants from it. The latter was harder than it seemed at first.

Others had found a patina . . . bacteria, fungi, mold, organic residues and varnishes, microscopic organisms and other organic contaminants. They had documented what they had done to remove all of these prior to the carbon dating that had yielded a first century date. Torrelli's team also had to contend with the smoke and ash and mud that had gotten on the scrap as a result of the fire.

Torrelli's scientists just followed the road already laid out by the pioneers in this business of cloning.

Their thoroughly cleaned linen threads yielded a first century date.

There was no shout of triumph but rather a lot of quiet back patting. This was good enough for them.

There was nothing more to be done.

Well . . . nothing but develop a viable clone from the DNA hiding in the bloodstains of their dirty scrap, but these were competent scientists; they now had huge shoulders to stand on; and the peak of Everest seemed well within their reach.

It wasn't all that easy. Their sample was so small that every step had to be carefully weighed. They dared not take a chance on wasting so much as a microgram. It took months of hard and creative genetic research but by July, they had developed a minute viable DNA sample from the 2,000 year old blood stain.

They then replicated it using a polymerase chain reaction (PCR) technique to amplify the strands of DNA isolated from the blood sample and thereby provided templates for the rapid replication of the DNA strands. They soon had an ample supply of DNA strands to begin a serious attempt at cloning.

"Well, we've got it, now what are we going to do with it."

A double helix of DNA is not a human cell, but it is the magic ingredient to go *inside* of a human cell and start it on its odyssey of replication, differentiation, and development into all of the complex parts of which a human being is comprised. Their DNA is a blueprint for the manufacture of a specific human being . . . another Christ.

Simply stated but infinitely more difficult to do.

This was work requiring the eyes of an eagle and the dexterity of a . . . what?

Was there any creature alive with the dexterity needed to pull this off?

Torrelli himself had the steadiest hands of any on his team and nerves of steel. It would have to be him.

It was an incredibly delicate task. Under a microscope the chromosomes would be sucked from a human ovum and replaced with chromosomes developed from the DNA derived from the scrap of linen.

Meanwhile, the well documented *dark side syndrome* problem was solved by researchers. The crudeness of the early cloning experiments was damaging a particular gene site. Once the techniques were refined, the problem essentially went away. Dolly, the sheep cloned in Scotland, was among the first to be spared this terrible affliction. Torrelli's team was skilled enough that this would present no problem to them. Their clone would *not* be afflicted by this syndrome.

The peculiar accelerated early growth rate was another matter but it did not appear to adversely affect any of the recent clones. It was, in fact, a welcome phenomenon. The scientists did not have to wait so long for their clones to mature so they viewed it as a non-problem and made no effort to solve it.

THE SHROUD

For Torrelli's team, there were several disheartening failures but their patience and steadfastness in the face of these failures eventually prevailed.

It happened in August. First a single cell, then the unwinding of the strands of DNA, then the separation of the chromosomes and finally the mitosis. Two of them watched through the dual optics microscope as one cell became two and two became four and four became eight. It was a zygote, asexually produced through the sheer magic of cloning.

They thought this moment might never come.

When the zygote was large enough, they implanted it on the Synthetic Placenta (SP) and immersed it in the amniotic tank. The first effort failed. The fetus expired and ablated from the SP after two weeks but they knew they were on the right track and on the next try everything worked to perfection.

In nine weeks (and roughly seven years to the day after Andrew's birth), the clone reached full term and was brought into the world in November 1997.

They named him Christopher.

At the moment of Christopher's "birth", there is an apparent difference of about 28 years in the ages of Andrew and Christopher. However, Andrew is now aging at nearly normal rate but Christopher will be developing at approximately four times the normal growth rate during his formative years and by the time he reaches the apparent age of Christ at his crucifixion, he will have a normal maturation rate. Andrew and Christopher will then be only around seven years apart in apparent age and will stay that way from that time on.

The precious baby that, through the miracle of cloning, has been delivered to them, is worshiped by everyone on Torrelli's team. Each felt himself to be in the presence of God and went into a state of inner peace and serenity when in his presence.

THE SHROUD

Some of Torrelli's team were members of Jews For Jesus. They knew what had to be done with regard to circumcision and took care of the briss properly.

Now, they were faced with the task of bringing up the new Christ child. It was an awesome responsibility.

Moisha Weinberg, the most scholarly of Torrelli's team and a member of Jews For Jesus, was charged with the preparation of a proper course of education for the child.

He would be taught Hebrew, of course, and Italian, the native tongue of all of David Torrelli's team, . . . and he would be taught English. It was the second language of most of the team and becoming the main language of intercourse and commerce among the countries, businesses, and religions of the world. Under Weinberg guidance he would become a truly well rounded scholar.

Moisha took this assignment very seriously. Christopher would receive an education equivalent to that of any other children in the community in which they lived, but, in addition to the three Rs, he would be taught the Talmud, the body of oral Jewish law, consisting of the Mishnah and the Gemara, in addition to the Torah, and would be indoctrinated with the Old and New Testaments of the Bible.

Best to know what the competition is doing, so he would also learn the teachings of the other great religious thinkers . . . . Buddha, Confucius, Mohammed . . . all of them, or at least all of the major ones. There are so many. Moisha would have to draw the line somewhere. With Christopher's expected accelerated maturation, there would be so little time.

From this starting point, Moisha Weinberg would lay out a lesson plan for the schooling of Christopher from moment of birth until he reached full manhood, not just the symbolic manhood of his Bar Mitzvah.

The young child would challenge all of the members of the team to the fullest. The original plan was that Christopher would have as normal an upbringing as possible playing with the children of the members of the team, going to preschool and kindergarten with them. Making the most of youth's precious few moments of play time seemed a small price to pay considering the expected dividends but that part of the plan was not to be. It becomes apparent to the team that while they originally intended that he have a normal upbringing, his accelerated physical and mental growth rate causes him to outstrip the other children in the families of the team. They reluctantly conclude that it will be necessary to isolate him from other children and confine him to the laboratory premises while otherwise giving him all of the freedom accorded their own children.

In just twelve months time, Christopher grew from a helpless baby to a four year old with an insatiable hunger and thirst for knowledge. Most children in that age bracket ask "Why?" . . . but usually do not expect a *real* answer and do not understand it if they get one. Christopher was not like that. He really wanted to know and when he was simultaneously learning Hebrew, Italian and English this posed a significant problem for his teachers who were, for the most part, bilingual, Italian and English being the predominant combination. Moisha Weinberg was trilingual and became indispensable.

Long before Christopher was thought capable of understanding, Moisha would read to him, in Hebrew, the Pentateuch, the first five books of the Bible, generally attributed to Moses.

All of the members of Dr. Torrelli's team became known to Christopher as "Papa".

As usual, Moisha, starting with the book of Genesis, read, "In the beginning . . . "

Christopher interrupted,"What is that, Papa?"

"What is what, my son?"

"What is 'the beginning'?"

There was Moisha, only three words into Christopher's education and completely stumped. How do you explain 'the beginning' to a child who has no concept of none and some, then and now, before and after, or now and later.

"When you are older, my son, you will understand."

"Why? . . . Why must I be older? . . . and what is *older*?"

Each of the team members tried without much success to get him through the first few sentences of Genesis and they despaired that they might ever teach him even the fundamentals.

He was, however, in other classes, learning the three Rs and rapidly acquiring reading skills. With them he achieved a measure of comprehension and, with that, a growing understanding of the words of Moses. Eventually, Moisha was able to work his way through the books of Exodus, Leviticus, Numbers, and Deuteronomy. Then he went through it again in English and in Italian.

Christopher's hunger for knowledge was insatiable. He had many insightful questions about the creation, about Adam and Eve and, where, if Adam and Eve were the first people on earth, and bore only two sons, did Cain and his sons find wives?

Eventually, he reconciled it all in his mind.

Adam and Eve were the start of only one tribe, but, to insure the perpetuation of mankind, God in his infinite wisdom, started other tribes as well and it was from those tribes that they found their wives.

Once the pieces started falling together for him, he moved on through the Bible, and the Torah, and the Koran.

He soon came to realize that while there were many holy places scattered over the world, The Most Holy was Jerusalem. Of all the spots on earth, this tiny city was holy to Jews, Muslims, and Christians alike.

"Why?"

There was that word again.

In Christopher's young mind, the germ of an idea began to develop. It did not spring forth in a blaze of cognition but rather grew slowly until the idea, if not the words for its expression, came into being.

The world needed a single unifying religion and Jerusalem, the most holy of cities should be its home. The ties of all of these religions to Jerusalem might be the very catalyst needed to bring it about. That was why. God wanted all of his people to be one. God wanted it so.

While other children of his apparent age were dreaming of space flight to the moon and Mars, Christopher was dreaming on an entirely different plane.

He, of course, had no way of knowing this because during his first calendar year, the decision had been made to isolate him within the vast confines of the Geneticraft International laboratories away from the other children.

If he thought about it at all, he probably thought that other children thought this way, too.

CHAPTER THIRTY

Gregor Vuchkovitch was beginning to miss Zepp, not personally, because he never did really *like* him, but there were things that he got done without constant supervision. The more urgent of those things were now back on Gregor's plate to take care of himself. The rest were piling up and just not getting done at all.

Gregor did not see a logical successor among the underlings that he and Zepp had recruited in Russia and brought over to the USA, mainly to provide muscle for their various enterprises. They were stupid thugs for the most part, dredged up from the garbage that had once done the dirty work for the KGB.

Should he return to Russia to find a suitable lieutenant or should he take a chance on Andrew? Andrew wasn't Russian but he had diligently and promptly executed every assignment that he had been given. In every test of his loyalty and honesty (to the extent that the word "honesty" has any meaning in these circles) Andrew had never failed a test.

Gregor decided, for the moment, to heap more of Zepp's work load on Andrew." . . . *and we'll see how it goes.*"

He found Andrew and Madeline at one of the roulette tables.

Moving up close to Andrew, he whispered, "I want to see you for a moment, . . . alone."

Andrew was ahead. He pushed his pile of chips over in front of Madeline and said, "Here, I will be back in a minute. See what you can do while I am away."

He followed Gregor to the elevator. Gregor put in the key to his private penthouse and they rode to the top in a matter of seconds.

The elevator door opened and Gregor went straight to his bar.

"I let the bartender go home early tonight."

Gregor reached for the scotch, "Black Label . . . right?"

"Good memory . . . thanks."

Gregor opened one of the sliding doors and they went out onto the terrace, "Andrew, how do you feel about assignments outside of the States? Is your passport in order?"

"I have a valid US passport and I don't think I have a problem with an occasional trip abroad."

"I am talking about more than an occasional trip. How is your Russian?"

"Not too good, in fact, zilch, but I am a quick study. How long before I would start?"

"Right away but I have some assignments where English will get you by. It would be better if you spoke Russian, though."

"Don't worry about the Russian. I will take a Berlitz course and be up to speed in a month . . . by the way, can I take Madeline with me?"

"Sure. Just don't have her around during business and don't discuss it with her . . . ever."

"Gottcha."

"Meet me here tomorrow morning . . . alone . . . and we will talk. Now go back to your lady and enjoy the evening."

When Andrew rejoined Madeline at the roulette table, he said,"Baby, we are going to be traveling a lot from now on, . . . I mean really traveling . . . all over the world. Is your passport up to date?"

"I think so, but I'll check."

"Good. Do it tomorrow. I have to take a quick trip out of the country right now, but, next time, we will go together . . . you and I . . . we are going places."

The meeting the following morning was strictly business. Gregor spelled out a short but very busy trip for Andrew. Each meeting would be with people who were fluent in English. Gregor was so fluent in English that he *thought* in English while conversing with Andrew. This enabled Andrew to put his telepathic capabilities to good use when dealing with Gregor. He always knew what Gregor was *thinking*, not just what he was saying. This gave him a decided advantage because the two were not always the same.

Gregor gave Andrew a list of contacts, addresses, phone numbers, and even blind drops and "mailboxes". He was admonished to commit all of this to memory and then destroy the paper. The next day Gregor gave Andrew a thorough test of his retention of the information imparted the previous day.

Andrew remembered it all and Gregor was impressed.

Andrew was concerned that the people he would be dealing with in Russia would be *thinking* in Russian. He had not met many Russians but the few that he had met were brooding, suspicious, devious, and duplicitous. This was, to Andrew, almost the definition of "Russian-ness" and an obstacle that he would have to overcome as quickly as possible. It was urgent that he get busy on a Berlitz course.

As soon as he left Gregor's suite he signed up and spent the rest of the day studying.

It was near the end of their lease and Natalie and Marc were debating whether to renew it or move on. After the first three or four months of remorse, the idyllic life on their mountaintop near Cancun was beginning to grow on them.

*"If only it could be like this forever,"*Natalie mused, . . . but it couldn't be like this forever and they both knew it. Their 180 day visitor cards were running out and despite their fears, they would have to leave a few days before their lease expired and return to the US to get new cards. The question was,*"Should we renew our lease and return to the villa after we get new tourist cards?"*

Marc vocalized the thought, "I think we should pull up stakes. We would be stretching our luck to stay any longer."

Natalie spoke in hushed tones, as though afraid that Andrew might hear her, "I guess we really should move on. This villa is nice, but . . . "

The next morning they started exploring up the Gulf coast enjoying the white sandy beaches, stayed overnight in Veracruz, and eventually reached the border at Matamoros.

They crossed the border and spent the night in Brownsville. Marc immediately tackled the bureaucratic red tape involved in getting new tourist cards. Every possible obstacle seemed to stand in their way until Marc found that a little palm grease solved everything as far as the Mexican officials were concerned.

New tourist cards in hand, they did not tarry in the States but drove immediately southward, scouting for a new place.

Central Mexico was different from Cancun but quite beautiful and the people were gracious and warm. They eventually found themselves in Guadalajara and then, just a few kilometers away, in the string of villages lying along the north shore of Lake Chapala, 5,300 feet above sea level. Here in Chapala, Ajijic, and San Juan Cosola they were surprised to find the largest English speaking community in Mexico. It soon became apparent, however, that this presented a potential threat to their safety. Americans came and went continuously. Any one of them might return to the US and innocently drop a word that would reveal their location to Andrew.

As much as they would have liked to be among Americans, the risk was too great so they continued southward to Mexico City arriving in an intense smog and during the cleanup after a moderate earthquake . . . Too much like LA. It would be a constant reminder of the danger, a danger they were trying their best to push behind them.

From Mexico City they drove southwestward, eventually reaching the blue Pacific at Acapulco. They fell in love with it immediately.

They checked out the Club Residential of Las Brisas, the four star restaurants, and the lush villas atop the Las Brisas

Hotel with their magnificent views of Acapulco, Acapulco Bay, and the Pacific Ocean . . . but this was not for them. They preferred something more like their villa in Cancun so after a night in the Las Brisas they rose early and explored the nearby hills.

It did not take long to find another villa on the outskirts where they began the cycle all over again.

It didn't seem possible, but the love making was even better than back in their villa near Cancun.

Setting up housekeeping again meant frequent trips into Acapulco for the essentials.

Their Pacific coast idyll was a stay in paradise. But they knew that it would soon be best to move on again. They would do it when their 180 day visitor cards had expired, just as they had in Cancun.

They returned from their regular weekly trip into a nearby village for provisions. Marc unloaded the items they had purchased in the village. Along with the groceries and other supplies was a Los Angeles newspaper. It was several days old but that didn't matter. After dinner, they would divide it between them and devour every word.

Marc took the front page and Natalie took the Metro section. She read the story and then looked at the accompanying picture. The man was not identified in the caption but she had seen that face from the time of his birth. Natalie froze, her knuckles turned white and she started shaking.

Marc looked up from his paper. "Is anything wrong?"

"It's Andrew and look where he is."

Marc had to forcibly remove the Metro section from her iron grip. He looked at the picture. He had never met Andrew but had seen enough of the surveillance tapes to recognize him. There was no doubt as to his identity.

"Maybe it is just a look-alike. They say we all have doubles somewhere in the world," but Marc was not at all convincing and not convinced of what he was saying either.

Seeing that picture brought it all back. Natalie felt the pain all over again.

Someone else saw the picture in the Los Angeles paper. He was the computer graphics expert who reconstructed the image of Christ from a photograph of the Shroud. He scanned the portion of the photo containing Andrew's face, blew it up to the same size as the picture on his disc, and switched back and forth between them. All he could say was,"Remarkable!" and filed the disc and picture together in his desk drawer.

Andrew studied hard and had a rudimentary understanding of the Russian language by the time that Vuchkovitch sent him on his first mission to Moscow.

The crazy syntax of the Russian language gave him difficulty. It would be a difficult language to learn to speak fluently but speaking is one thing, *understanding* it is another. He was confident that he could handle this assignment as long as all of the conversations were in English.

His Russian contacts were covert about everything. He did not see the need for their silly passwords, blind drops, secret visual signals . . . like an empty wine bottle with the neck pointing to a tree where the next message could be found.

He would have found their antics laughable if they weren't so serious about it all.

These were leftovers from the Cold War. Andrew knew nothing about *that* but he went along with it. It was the only game in town.

From time to time, his Russian contacts spoke to him in Russian. He pretended not to understand and before long, they were saying things among themselves that they would have thought better of if they had known, but they revealed nothing of any importance anyway.

What they *thought* was another matter. Andrew picked up bits and pieces that would be really important to Vuchkovitch and he planned to make capital of the information upon his return to the US.

One of the tidbits he picked up was that there was a growing jealousy within the Russian Mafia leadership of the gold mine that Vuchkovitch had fallen into in Las Vegas. Some of the Russians did not consider him bright enough to run so vast an operation and were seriously planning to unseat him and divide up his territory up among them. Ivan Terrikoff approved the plan including the proposed division of Gregor's territory. They would all fly to Las Vegas to survey their new territories.

They had already planned the date of the coup and had chartered a Russian jet to Las Vegas. This would avoid the list of participants from appearing on air line passenger manifests where it might be seen on computers, by anyone, anywhere in the world. They would still have to clear customs at both ends of the flight but that would only be a minor inconvenience.

Andrew caught one of them thinking about his flight and made note of the date and ETA. They were sending in a large team and wanted the takeover to be swift and non-violent . . . except for Gregor and Andrew. They would have to be dispatched.

"I think not!"

Upon his return to Vegas, Andrew laid it all out for Gregor. He told him the date, the names of the conspirators, the number of men they are bringing with them, the firepower they had arranged to pick up once they landed.

"They are all coming, everyone except Ivan Terrikoff, the head of all of the Russian Mafia families. But they will be unarmed and vulnerable until they pick up their weapons. If we can catch them before then . . . we might . . . "

Vuchkovitch's wheels were spinning frantically.

"How do you know all of this?"

"Too much vodka. It loosens the tongue. They thought I was drunk as they discussed it but I heard."

Gregor shook his head in disbelief.

Andrew pressed on, "I think we can turn this to our advantage, I have a plan that I think will work."

Gregor was open to anything.

"Trust me on this. I know how to bring down their plane. No one will survive. Now, what do you think about this? Suppose that you make a surprise flight to Moscow arriving after they are in the air. You go to Ivan's place as though nothing is wrong. Your visit will take him completely by surprise. Before he has had a chance to recover from the shock, you poison him with a rubberband propelled bamboo dart. The gun can be easily disguised and will go through all of the x-ray and metal detectors at the airports. Here it is. Let me show you how it works."

Andrew demonstrated the dart gun for Gregor.

"Yes, It *could* work and if I do nothing, they will terminate *me*."

"Now, with all of the family leaders dead in the crash, and 'Ivan the Terrible' out of the way what is to stop *you* from being the top man in the organization? Do you not deserve that?"

Gregor smiled. His devious Russian mind grasped the irony and the justice of it all.

"I will leave you in charge of Las Vegas until I get back."

"Ivan has snitches everywhere, I suggest that you not discuss any aspect of this with any of your organization here until it is a *fait accompli*."

Gregor said, "I like the way you think. It is so . . . so *Russian*."

Gregor made his plans on his own and had only Andrew accompany him to the ticket office to make his plane reservation for the next day. He did not confide his flight number or any of his planned course of action upon landing in Moscow, . . . even to Andrew. Of course, with his telepathic skills, Andrew knew, but he was no threat, for now. Russian security would know, too, the instant the information concerning his destination was in the computers. There was no way to avoid that and Gregor could only hope that if the Russian Mafia in Moscow had any of the security people in its back pocket, that they would be incompetent, inattentive, or on their day off, or something.

"How will you do it? . . . the plane I mean." Gregor was concerned that the US part of this plan would go off ok.

"Have I ever let you down? You will just have to trust me. I will take care of *my* end of this. There will be *no* survivors."

Before they returned to the hotel, Andrew stopped in an electronics store and picked up a shortwave receiver capable of picking up the air traffic control communications with the aircraft under their jurisdiction. Back in the hotel, he tested it by monitoring the tower traffic at the Las Vegas airport. It worked perfectly.

If they have not found out about Gregor's trip, the Russians would be in the air by now.

Andrew drove Gregor to the airport, saw that his plane departed ok, and then drove out into the desert to the site of a marker beacon for incoming flights.

On the way, he picked up some sandwiches and a large thermos of black coffee. It would be a while. Andrew went over, in his mind, the enormous exertion of psycho kinetic energy that it had taken to bring down Flight 800 . . . but then *it* was more than 2000 miles away. *This* plane will be almost directly overhead.

He could do it.

Andrew set his wrist watch alarm and relaxed.

Even with the heavy caffeine intake, Andrew got drowsy and nodded off but was brought back with a start. The police car loudspeaker blasted him back into reality.

"This is a restricted area! You will have to move out of here immediately!"

Andrew's mind was racing. "*Have they gotten my license number? Have they called it in? Can I bluff my way out of this?*"

"Please step out of the car, What are you doing here, anyway?"

Andrew grabbed a sandwich and his cup of cold coffee and got out waving them at the officers. "I'm having a picnic. It is such a beautiful day and there is no better place for one than the desert."

"Couldn't you find some place closer to civilization for you picnic?"

"Guess I just got carried away with the desert."

Andrew froze the two officers' cerebral clocks.

"Quickly, he moved to the police car and looked inside. The officer in the passenger side was in the process of typing a "Wants and Warrants" request into his computer. He had finished the description of the car but had not yet entered the license plate number. *"OK, no harm done. Lets just sit tight until the plane gets here."*

The officers remained frozen in time while Andrew concentrated on the flow of air traffic control radio transmissions. In about a half hour, the Russian plane checked in with Las Vegas Air Traffic Control and was given an approach vector and altitude. Andrew scanned the skies for the plane.

"Ah! There it is!"

Andrew directed all of his mental energies at the plane. The pilot was talking to the tower. He was cut off in mid sentence and, simultaneously, an enormous fireball erupted in the evening sky. Burning pieces of the shattered plane fell to earth scattering debris over many miles of mesquite covered desert floor. There were small fires everywhere. The officers' radio was soon squawking frantically, now wanting information about the fireball in addition to the incomplete "Wants and Warrants" request. Andrew clouded the minds of the officers and left them with no recollection of their encounter with him or of seeing the fireball. He then drove away. When he was out of sight, he stopped and unfroze the officers who now had over an hour of missing time to account for. They had typed in the description of his car but there must be 10,000 or more black Mercedes Benz limousines in the LA and Las Vegas areas alone.

"Let them chew on that for a while."

Andrew wished he could be there when the officers tried to explain the missing hour to their superiors.

Andrew returned to his suite, showered and he and Madeline had dinner, took in a show, and spent an hour or so in the casino in their hotel. When they got back to their suite there was a prearranged code message from Gregor on his answering machine indicating the he had taken care of his end and had heard the news of Andrew's success.

"All in all, a good days work."

Gregor called a meeting of all of the third echelon Russian Mafia chieftains. They had all heard the news of the fate of Ivan Terrikoff, the boss of bosses, and their entire upper echelon, except for Gregor Vuchkovitch. Gregor proclaimed himself head of all of the families, appointing Andrew as his second in command.

Things were moving a little faster than Andrew had expected. He was summoned to Moscow and informed of his new position. Gregor's impulsive decision caught him by surprise. He thought that he would have to plant and nurture the idea in Gregor's mind, while he was momentarily in charge of the Las Vegas territory. It was apparent that his new job would require that he spend a lot of time elsewhere.

Up until this moment Andrew's only source of income had been the Las Vegas roulette tables. Now, he would not have much time to play roulette. True, he might be able to skim enough of the take to make up for it. Why not? Whether he won it at the roulette tables or skimmed it from the take, the bottom line would still be the same and Vuchkovitch would never be the wiser.

He would need a longer term objective and that meant accelerating his plan to become a "capitalist".

One of the financiers that he had been cultivating was Freidrich Gablein, the CEO and principle share holder of

Deutchteknik, GmBH, a German company that made everything from computers to huge electrical generators capable of powering a large city. Andrew imposed his thoughts on Freidrich and convinced him that he should turn his stock over to him in exchange for an equal number of shares in a non-existent Canadian company.

The next day Andrew had the phoney stock certificates printed up and waited. That night he was approached by Freidrich offering the stock swap. Freidrich indicated that he had wanted to get a foothold in Canada and saw this as an opportunity too good to pass up. After a few social drinks together, there was a handshake agreement and the next morning, the stock changed hands, and Freidrich Gablein had absolutely no recollection of what he had done with his Deutchteknik stock or where he had gotten the worthless Canadian stock.

Andrew needed quick cash so he started dumping the Deutschteknik stock on the European market. The price held at first but as he unloaded more and more of it, the price plummeted. Andrew did not get as much as the stock was really worth but he got it *now* and that was what was important to him. After all, the deal had cost him nothing but the cost of printing some worthless shares.

Freidrich was dazed by what had happened. He had other investments but they were chicken feed compared to Deutchteknik. He was bankrupt. The shock was too much for him. Under Andrew's controlling thoughts, he drove out to Hoover Dam and after looking at the swirling waters for a few moments took a header over the rail. He slammed off the sloping surface of the dam and disappeared into the churning waters below. His body was never found, but tourists had seen him jump and he was identified by his car registration.

When word of Freidrich Gablein's suicide reached the investment world, the bottom fell out of the already low Deutschteknik stock. There were simply no buyers. Many stock-owning employees and families with their life savings heavily invested in Deutschteknik were ruined.

Andrew had expected this. It took only a small part of the money made on the initial stock sale to buy back more than a controlling interest in the company . . . enough to guarantee him a seat on the board of directors and election as chairman . . . and he had cash left over from the deal. The price of a share notwithstanding, Deutschteknik was a sound company with a world wide market for its products. That had not changed.

Now, Andrew had control of a major corporation and his shares had been *legitimately* purchased.

Ownership, . . . that is what stock is all about.

Less than a week of underhanded chicanery had put him on the first step toward his goal of control of the world's finances.

Meanwhile, he had managed to find time, late at night, to make the rounds of the casinos with Madeline and, placing larger bets than usual, grabbed another big bundle of cash for front money for other planned activities, . . . without having to skim the take. *That could come later.*

Madeline was turned on by money. Her financial windfall made her greedy for more, . . . and Andrew had the magic.

She nuzzled his ear,"Andrew, you must be the luckiest man on this planet."

"Do you think it's *luck*?" Andrew was in an expansive mood, "*Luck* has nothing to do with it." Come over here to the slots and I will show you. Pick any machine and play it a few times."

She did and won once out of six times and not very much at that.

"OK, I did nothing on those tries but now do it a few more times."

Madeline played the machine as instructed and coins came spilling out of the tray on every try.

"But, how . . . ?"

"Honey, when you hit the jackpot on the *big* machine did you think that was *pure luck?* . . . Well, it was *me*. I have the ability to control mechanical things with my mind. That's why I play roulette. I can put that little ball wherever I want it. I lose some to make it look good, but the bottom line is *I win*. Can't get *too* greedy you know. Don't want to become *persona non grata* in the casinos. The neat thing is that I don't have to touch anything except my bets."

Madeline nibbled his ear lobe, and whispered, huskily,"Do it for me, . . . again, . . . please . . . "

"Do what?"

"You know, . . . the *big* machine."

"Now what did I just tell you? We can't get *too* greedy. . . . Besides, . . . the *same person* winning *twice* on that machine? . . . Think about it."

Andrew was not about to reveal any of his other mental powers to her and half regretted that he had told her that much.

"But what the hell. We are both cut from the same cloth. This will add to the excitement."

Upon returning to their suite later that night they were both so aroused by their success at the roulette tables that she stripped his clothing from him and he reciprocated. After it was over, he had deep scratches all over his back, the result of a passionate and erotic romp over every piece of furniture in the suite.

"Money . . . that is the key to everything," Andrew and Madeline were of the same thought.

When he awoke the next morning, the light was blinking on his answering machine. *"Damn!"* He must have missed it when he and Madeline returned from the casinos.

It was a succinct message from Gregor, "Collect the take. Put it in the safe. (Gregor's safe worked very much like a night depository at a bank. Anyone could put a deposit *in*, but only *he*, could take it *out*.) Get on the first flight to Moscow. Let me know what flight you will be on. I will have you picked up at the airport."

It was clear that this would be strictly business, there would be no time for Madeline on this trip but they found time for a quickie in the midst of the hasty preparation for departure.

One of the Moscow goons was waiting for him at the airport . . . not so easy to spot here . . . those 1930's vintage suits were everywhere. The goon held a placard with Andrew's name on it. It was printed in the Cyrillic alphabet, but Andrew could make out his name.

I not only have to learn to speak this damned language, I will have to learn to read it.

The main reason for the trip was to introduce Andrew to the surviving members of the leadership of the various families now under the control of the new boss of bosses, Gregor Vuchkovitch.

Andrew could sense the hostility when he entered the room. He was not Russian and all of them felt that the job should have gone to one of *them*. They were not fooled by the events of the past few weeks. It was all *too* coincidental to be coincidence. Gregor must have somehow compromised the plot to unseat him and made a preemptive strike.

How did he find out? He must have an operative here in Moscow. How else could he get the bomb aboard the plane . . . and to take out Ivan Terrikoff at the same time?

They cast suspicious glances around the table.

He might be . . . he must be one of us . . . sitting right here at this table.

They dared not express their feelings to one another. That might prove to be fatal, so they just sat there, listened, and glowered.

Gregor spoke in Russian, "This is Andrew Kreist, my second in command. An order from him is the same as an order from me . . . not to be questioned. Is that clear?"

They all nodded grudgingly, their sullen response punctuated by incoherent grunts. They all glowered at Andrew from deep set eyes beneath bushy eyebrows. Andrew had not noticed that before. It emphasized their Neanderthal appearance.

Gregor looked at each of them for acknowledgment before continuing. "*For now*, each of you will assume control of the family in which you were previously second in command. You will continue to preside over your presently defined territories but I am moving our main base of operations from Moscow to Las Vegas. I think you will find it a less gloomy place than Moscow for our meetings. If there are no questions, this meeting is adjourned."

Gregor made it clear that there would *be* no questions.

"*For now*, . . . " the implication was unambiguous. Screw up, and you are history!

At least he didn't demote any of us.

They were visibly relieved at that.

Andrew imposed his thoughts on Gregor. As the two of them reached the door, Gregor turned and said, "And get some decent suits before you come to Las Vegas. I am embarrassed to be seen with any of you."

Gregor offered to take Andrew to the Moscow airport in his limo. On the way, Andrew asked how Gregor's end of the deal went.

"Like clock work. My appearance at his place took him completely by surprise. I had taped your neat little rubberband powered gun to the inside of my wrist. He was so startled, I extended my hand as though to shake his. At the last moment, I raised my palm as though in a gesture of peace. That tripped the trigger and the dart caught him in the carotid artery. The poison worked so fast; I don't think he ever knew. There was not even a look of surprise on his face. He just crumpled to the floor. I removed the bamboo dart and flushed it. Let the Moscow police puzzle over that for a while . . . and it appears that your end was a crashing success."

Andrew was not sure if Gregor meant that to be funny or not. Probably not. The Russians are not known for their sense of humor.

"Yes, I drove out into the desert to watch. Pieces of it fell over an area of a dozen square miles."

"But how . . . ?"

"Don't ask."

In two quick ruthless moves, Andrew, at an *apparent age* of 32, had moved into the heady upper echelons of both the financial world and organized crime . . . and this was only the beginning. His ambitions went far beyond this.

There is now only one major obstacle between Andrew and complete control of the Russian Mafia . . . Gregor Vuchkovitch.

What was he to do about Gregor?

Andrew opted to maintain the status quo for now. After all, there was much that Andrew did not know about Russia and the roots of their homegrown style of "Mafia". It would take a while to learn all of it and to determine the length of each tentacle of this monster that he was determined to master and control. The tentacles reached further and deeper than he had ever imagined. In the US alone, they reached into the State House of every state capitol, into the Senate, the House, and into the Oval Office, as well. Did Gregor know the extent of his new empire? Probably not, and Andrew had no plans to disabuse him.

Control of the Russian Mafia meant influence in the seats of government the world over and Gregor did not have a clue. The former leaders in Moscow were right. Gregor Vuchkovitch was *not* bright enough to manage *this*.

Gregor did not intentionally reveal the combination of his safe to Andrew, but, on one occasion, Andrew read his mind as he opened it and made careful note of the combination. At some future time, after taking care of Gregor, he might need to know it but maybe not. After all no other lock had ever thwarted him. Even though he was now second in command, he did not want to arouse suspicion by openly asking for it. If Gregor wanted him to know, he would tell him. All in good time. He preferred that Gregor tell him the combination as a gesture of trust.

Andrew also noted that so much money flowed through that safe that Gregor never knew exactly how much was in it at any one time. That bit of information might be useful some time.

———————————————

CHAPTER THIRTY-ONE

"Look what *we* found". The detective dangled a plastic bag in the general direction of Inspector George Bennet, head of the *signature* murders task force. "I think this is yours."

Bennet looked at the bag quizzically. "How so?"

"Well, for openers, Ballistics tells us that this is the weapon that killed John Wilson . . . a 357 magnum automatic, . . . registered to John Pearsons . . . but that is not the name of the guy we got it from."

"Where did you get it?"

"A homeless guy. He tried to sell it on the street and, our good luck, the dummy tried to unload it on an undercover cop on the stolen weapons recovery detail."

"Think he was the shooter?"

"No. Says he found it in a dumpster. We think he is telling the truth, but for a really bizarre reason. He didn't have this gun on him when he tried to peddle it . . . Took our undercover guy to his shack . . . then he dug out the pistol, he was arrested on the spot for having unlawful possession. He got so shook up that he volunteered the rest of the stuff he found with the pistol. There were some files and some video tapes, all relating to a single problem. You have got to see those. They will blow your mind. . . . Here."

The detective handed Bennet a cardboard box containing the tapes and the files. "Like I said, the gun is registered to a John Pearsons. He was president of MAXXX Security where Wilson's body was found. Pearsons has disappeared. We figure either kidnaped or else he is the perp."

"Afraid not. Pearsons came out of the Police Academy with me. We were partners at the precinct before he went into the security business. I can tell you for a fact that he didn't do it, but thinks the perp was after him . . . got Wilson by mistake. He is hiding out until we catch the guy."

"Then the guy you want may be on these tapes. You probably wondered how he got past MAXXX's security to get to Pearson's office."

"Yes we did."

"Well, the tapes don't show *that* but they do show this guy going in and out of the lobby of some building, somewhere, right past the security guard . . . just like he was invisible or something . . . and opening the locked door without touching it.

You can see the lock clearly on the tape. It is unusual. It's made by MAXXX Security and is the same type used on *their* main entrance so he probably 'invisibled' himself just like he appears to do on these tapes and got in and out undetected. Don't know where the tapes were made but since the *signature* killer is your case, this is your problem, now. The pictures are very clear . . . white male . . . medium build . . . late twenties . . . neat haircut . . . clean shaven."

"Thanks for bringing this by. At least it is a start. We've found nothing, up 'til now, on the Wilson killing. Maybe this is the break we have been needing."

Maybe, Maybe not. We'll see.

A quick look through the tapes showed nothing immediately apparent, . . . the lobby of a building, . . . people coming and going and the last tape ending with the fire, . . . spreading with incredible rapidity, . . . and stopping when the flames reached the hidden camera, destroying it.

So! . . . There was a fire, . . . somewhere, . . . but where? . . . At least that is a start.

Bennet's task force played the tapes over and over before they noticed the door latch seeming to open all by itself . . . and the security guard apparently saw nothing . . . Strange.

So that's how he got into MAXXX Security.

Help soon came from another quarter. The task force routinely touched base with Missing Persons on the chance that something there might tie in to the *signature* killings but nothing turned up until a relative reported a missing man who worked as a security guard. His last known employer said that he had left the firm to take a job with MAXXX Security Systems.

Bells went off immediately in Bennet's head.

Bennet obtained a search warrant, opened the MAXXX Security offices and poured through the personnel files. One of the task force officers who was going through the employment applications found one that made him take pause.

"Hey, Inspector, take a look at this."

Bennet studied the application form but his eyes kept coming back to the photo in the upper left hand corner.

"Whaddyathink?"

"I think it's him, the security guard on the tapes."

"That's what I thought. Want me to check the assignment logs to see where he was posted? . . . Just kidding . . . I'm right on it." The officer went to the personnel assignment files and found the guards' duty roster. He returned to Bennet.

"Look at this. He was assigned to that big laboratory building that was totally destroyed by fire. There are no records after the day that Wilson was killed."

"Bring that stuff with you. We are going over to Arson for a talk."

The Arson Squad was completely baffled by the fire at the laboratory. It had totally destroyed *everything*. "We found no equipment, no bodies, . . . nothing but grey ash. We haven't ruled out arson, but there were no traces of accelerants. Forensics has been checking ash samples for months . . . Notta."

Bennet had one of his officers set up the video tape player. He inserted the last tape in the series into the slot and pushed the start button.

Bennet explained, "We think this is the lobby of that laboratory building on the morning of the fire. Notice the number of people entering the building,"

Bennet paused the VCR, "Pay particular attention to this guy, . . . the first one in. It looks like the guard never saw him. He didn't note his arrival on the log".

Bennet resumed playing the tape, "Note that as the rest of the people arrive, the guard checks each of them in. There were a dozen or so of them. Now watch the guard. He jumps up and runs back down the corridor. Now, here comes that guy again . . . the first one in. Watch the latch. He never touches it again but it opens for him like magic. OK, . . . We are still looking at the empty lobby. The guard hasn't returned. Now here comes the fire. It only takes a few seconds to completely engulf the lobby and destroy the hidden camera and transmitter."

The arson team stared at the streaks of interference across the screen of the VCR monitor. They said nothing.

Bennet concluded, "What you just witnessed was a multiple homicide . . . at least a dozen people, . . . killed by arson". He paused as he pressed the rewind button and then still framed the picture of Andrew as he was leaving the lobby for the last time. "That is the killer. We are now pretty sure that he is the *signature* killer as well."

The head of the arson squad said, "My God. A dozen people and not a trace of any of them. Have you checked with the homicide detective handling the Jane Doe found at the bottom of the cliff behind the destroyed building? Definitely a homicide. Maybe she is on one of those tapes."

Bennet replied, "We'll check it out. I've got a feeling this is beginning to crack open."

The task force officers packed up their video equipment and returned to headquarters.

Bennet determined the name of the detective handling the Jane Doe, called him, and requested pictures.

Within an hour, the detective arrived with photos of Sarah.

Bennet again played the tape of that last fateful and fatal day. There was no doubt about it. *There* was the Jane Doe arriving much earlier than everyone else, . . . except the suspect. She departed a few minutes later. So, . . . at least one person killed in this ever expanding mystery was *not* destroyed in the fire. Perhaps something, *anything*, could be found out about her that might unlock another door.

She had slipped to the bottom of the detective's priority list when he got no further than tying her to the laboratory via the serial number on the hypodermic syringe that fatally injected her. Now she was back on the top of his list and he was closely coordinating with both Arson and the signature killer task force.

Reporters and TV crews milled around in The News Conference Room in the Parker Police Center.

Inspector Bennet stepped up to the battery of microphones.

"May I have your attention . . . please dim the lights . . . ok, simmer down, this will not take long . . . I would like for you to watch this tape loop carefully . . . roll the tape please."

The reporters watched quietly as a dubbed loop of a segment of tape showing Andrew in the lobby of the Project building was displayed on the several TV screens around the room. On the tape, there was a profile and then a brief full-face view as Andrew looked at the security guard. The loop showed the same sequence over and over.

Finally, one of the reporters asked,"What is it?"

Bennet answered, "We are looking for this man in connection with a recent series of murders in the Los Angeles area. We do not know his identity. As you can see, he is a white male, slender build . . . best estimates about five eleven and a hundred seventy pounds . . . He should be considered armed and *extremely* dangerous. We do not want anyone to attempt to detain him. If anyone knows him, knows of his whereabouts, or encounters him, in any context, please call the police. We have set up a special task force number. We have a handout sheet showing him full face. The sheet also contains a very limited description, essentially what I just told you . . . and the task force phone number.

We would appreciate any help you can give in the apprehension of this man. For the TV reporters, we have dubs of this tape loop. I won't take any questions at this time because I have just told you everything I know. Let me repeat . . . Please, . . . do not try to detain him. He is *extremely dangerous*!"

Bennet spun away from the microphones and left the room.

The reporters turned off their audio recorders and TV cameras, grabbed copies of the handout and headed for their next assignments.

None of the LA papers gave it front page coverage but all of the TV stations played it the same way . . . a brief scene-setting intro by the anchor . . . the video loop with Bennet's short press statement over . . . followed by the full face picture and task force phone number . . . "so if you see this *alleged perpetrator*, do not attempt to apprehend him. Call the special police task force number shown on your screen."

George Bennet got home late and turned on his TV just in time to catch the end of the news story. He angrily clicked off the TV, poured himself a drink and yelled at the TV set,"We don't ever say *apprehend the alleged perpetrator. Where do they get that garbage?"

The task force number attracted the usual number of kooks looking for their brief moment in the spotlight but there was one call that seemed legit. It was from a Fred Ashton, a computer graphics expert.

After the preliminaries Fred said that he did not know the whereabouts of the wanted man, but that he had a picture that might help the police find him. His was the only decent lead so Bennet took down the address and went to Fred Ashton's office. After the usual introductions, Bennet went straight to the point.

"OK, Fred, Whattayagot for me?"

Ashton took a 3 ½ inch disk from his desk drawer and inserted it into the "A" drive on his computer. He then pulled up on the screen the newspaper picture of the Zepp funeral and pointed to the face of the man at the right shoulder of Gregor Vuchkovitch, Russian Mafia chieftain in the US.

Fred then pulled up his computer-enhanced blow up of the face and said "Check this out".

George Bennet studied the picture.

"Jesus, the Russian Mafia. He is a Russian Mafia hit man." All of the *signature* killings raced through his mind . . . and the fire . . . and the Jane Doe . . . *"What possible connection?"*

"What do you think?"

The question snapped George back to the present, "I dunno. It sure looks like him but . . . "

"It is him. There is no doubt in my mind but how does he fit into this puzzle? A guy well placed in the Russian mafia . . . or he wouldn't be standing next to Vuchkovitch. Who the hell is he anyway?"

"But? . . . what?"

" . . . But, . . . can you make me a printout of this blowup?"

"Sure. No prob."

Fred clicked on the "print" icon on his computer screen and in a matter of seconds, his laser printer spit out a sharp clear copy.

Bennet held it in his hands and stared at it, "Thanks. You've been a big help."

Bennet turned to leave.

"Want to see something that you won't believe?"

"Why not. *I don't believe this.*"

Fred Ashton pulled up the computer enhanced picture that he had derived from the photo of the Shroud.

"Where did you get *that*?"

"I told you that you wouldn't believe this. I made a computer enhanced picture of a guy with a beard and long hair, I took off all of the surplus hair removed various artifacts and got this."

"It's a *hippie*?"

"No, . . . It was derived from the image on the Shroud of Turin."

"Jesus Christ!"

"Could be."

"What?!"

"Know that lab that burned down a while back? They paid me to try to see what the image on the Shroud would look like today. I made this for them. Isn't it an amazingly similar likeness?"

"Of Jesus Christ? . . . or? . . . Jesus Christ!!!!!!!!!!"

Bennet stared at the face in disbelief,"Make me a copy of this, too."

When George Bennet got back to his office, he spread the three images out on his desk . . . the blown up still frame from the surveillance tape, . . . the blown up image from the Zepp funeral photo, . . . and the computer enhanced photo of the Shroud.

"I *don't* believe it", he muttered and just sat there staring."There must be some other explanation."

While the LA TV stations are all available on cable in Vegas, there is so much other activity that television is rarely watched, except for the porno channels provided by the big hotels. This was the case the night the story of the face on the surveillance tape broke. None of the Russian Mafia saw it so Andrew avoided coming under the scrutiny of those who coveted his position in the organization.

Bennet received a phone call from Amanda Withersgate, a researcher in psychic phenomena. Bennet immediately wrote her off as a kook but the woman was insistent so he agreed to speak to her.

She arrived in long wildly flowing garb, and hair looking like it would take at least a thousand brush strokes to restore it to any semblance of order.

Bennet shook his head. *"Is it going to be another one of those days?"*

George asked, "Mind if I record the interview?" He pressed the record button, assuming a permissive response.

She nodded approval and opened the conversation quickly, before he had a chance to dismiss her out of hand, "You don't understand it do you?"

"Don't understand *what?*"

"The things he is able to do."

"*What* things? . . . that *who* is able to do."

"I know all about him . . . a most unusual case."

"Would you please tell me what you are talking about."

"I told you, I am a psychic. I know all about the fire. Ever see anything like it before?"

Bennet did not get a chance to answer.

"He has powers beyond your comprehension. Take the fire, nothing left, absolutely nothing, . . . right?"

"Right, . . . but how do you know about that."

"There are things I know that I don't want to know but I can't help it, . . . it just comes. I don't know if I can help you, . . . other than to make certain you know what you are up against."

Bennet still wasn't sure that he didn't have a certifiable looney on his hands but decided to hear her out. "OK. Go on."

"He's capable of psychopyrolysis."

"Huh?"

"You won't find that in most dictionaries. Pyrolysis is the ability to chemically reduce matter to basically nothing by the application of intense heat. In psychic research we have only *heard* of people capable of doing this with purely mental energy. We call this phenomenon psychopyrolysis. I know of no documented cases, but I receive the vibes from this incredibly evil creature and . . . he can do this . . . I know he can."

Bennet thought briefly about the laboratory . . . *nothing left but gray ash.*

Amanda could see the skepticism in his eyes. She continued, "In the hierarchy of psychic capabilities, psychopyrolysis is at the very top, a giant step up from the next level. Anyone capable of that is capable of any of the psychic activities on any of the lower levels. Almost on the same level is the ability to materialize physical objects using pure mental energy. Christ probably had this ability . . . the loaves and fishes thing . . . Next in line is psycho kinesis, the ability to manipulate mechanical things, then the more common activities like freezing a target's cerebral clock . . . You have heard of the 'missing time episodes' in purported alien abductions, . . . that kind of thing, then, imposing one's thoughts on another individual, and, at the bottom of the list, the ability to read the thoughts of others. This person can probably do all of these things and perhaps things we can't even imagine."

"No, I can't imagine. . . . "

"Beware of this creature. He can cause great harm, wherever he goes, Beware!"

Amanda Withersgate terminated the discussion as abruptly as she had started it and disappeared out the door in a swirl of flowing silk. Looking back over her shoulder she repeated, "Beware!"

"Sure, Sure, . . . beware . . . it takes all kinds."

Up until this moment George Bennet knew, in a sense, *who* he was after but now, although he failed to grasp the full significance of Amanda's remarks, he knew *what* he was after.

George filed away the tape and immediately dove into the pile of work accumulating on his desk.

"Humpf! . . . beware . . . like I don't have enough to worry about already."

Christopher's mentors were elated over his progress. He had reached the apparent age of eight and was a religious prodigy. Recalling the experience of the young Christ, speaking in the temple and impressing the elders with his thoughtful interpretations of the verses of the Torah, Moisha could not resist the temptation to show him off. He took him to a Synagogue and introduced him to the rabbi.

The rabbi knows Moisha. They had been childhood friends and had attended schule together, but when Moisha got mixed up with that crazy Jews-for-Jesus crowd the rabbi's orthodox upbringing forced a parting of the ways.

However, they were still civil to one another in public and even had lunch together on occasion. This was such an occasion and Moisha arrived with young Christopher in tow.

Moisha introduced the rabbi to Christopher. The rabbi flinched at the name. *Christopher, . . . not a Jewish name.*

They ate with some innocuous small talk and were down to dessert before Moisha revealed the purpose for their luncheon date.

"Asa, I would like for you to hear this young man read from the Torah."

"But . . . "

"No 'buts', Asa. You will be impressed, I assure you. You have never seen anything like this before and will never see anything like this again."

Asa reluctantly agreed and they walked the two blocks to the Synagogue.

Asa picked a spot, "OK, start here."

Christopher read it in flawless Hebrew.

"Go ahead, Asa, ask him what it means . . . and, by the way, he can tell you in Hebrew, Italian, or English."

Asa began questioning Christopher at length and the wisdom displayed in his answers was astounding.

"Who *is* he?"

"A student, but a very special person."

"A student of yours?"

"In a way."

"But what about the Jews for Jesus thing? . . . Are you still . . . ?"

"Oh, yes, very much."

"Then why?"

"Because of who he is. Incidentally, he is equally knowledgeable about the New Testament of the Bible."

"An idiot savant?"

"No, Asa, he is not. You would not have accepted him in Biblical times, and, today, you are ready to classify him as some sort of freak rather than accept him. I am certain you do not grasp the enormity of what you have just seen, but you may have just come as close to God as you will ever come. We must leave now, my friend. Shalom."

THE SHROUD

Asa stared in wonder at Christopher and murmured,"My God."

"Yes," responded Moisha, cryptically.

Despite the startup problems, Christopher exhibited extraordinary powers of concentration and it was not long before his education was way ahead of schedule. He wanted to know everything about *everything* and was soon even reading Arabic, a skill he taught himself because none of his teachers could either speak or read the language. This enabled him to read the Koran directly without having to depend upon a translator to interpret it for him. But he, of course, could not speak it or even understand it if he heard it spoken.

It was during this period that Christopher discovered his other mental abilities. He learned that he could tell what was about to happen when one of the Geneticraft team came into the room. It did not take him long to realize that he was reading the minds of the team members. This was a skill that none of them had and he wondered at that. Since each of his mentors thought in their native languages, it made it easier to sort things out when they were all thinking at once. Telepathy, therefore, was an easier skill for him to master than it had been for Andrew who had to cope with more individuals, all thinking in the same language.

Psycho kinesis was a skill that, in some respects, he carried further than Andrew had. He had great fun moving toys and other objects around in the environment but he taught himself to levitate them as well and flew them back and forth across the laboratory. Then he tried it on himself, at first just sitting a few feet above his chair but, eventually flying around the room performing intricate aerial maneuvers. *Nobody* on the Geneticraft staff could do *that*.

CHAPTER THIRTY-TWO

Under the guise of passing on orders from Gregor Vuchkovitch, Andrew took advantage of his frequent trips to Moscow to take personal control of many of the tentacles of the beast known as the Russian mafia, particularly those that reached deeply into the loci of political power and influence of all of the major countries of the world, of the UN, and of the capitols of the larger and richer states in the USA.

His total mastery of the Russian language occurred in a matter of months. He was able to do more than speak the language. He could *think* in Russian, with all of it's nuances, and, at times, even dreamed in Russian.

Every indication of subversion within the organization was quickly ferreted out and crushed.

"How does he know? It is as if he can read our minds."

"If you only knew."

The Russians, being *Russian*, suspected all of the others of being moles and isolated themselves from one another, enabling Andrew to manipulate each of them separately and take firm control of those who were most suspicious of the others. He moved slowly and carefully at first but soon developed a cadre of family leaders who were loyal to him. These one-on-one contacts also gave him entry to many Russian state functions where he was able to cultivate and curry favors from the world leaders.

Madeline loved this part of it. It, no longer, was the *money*. Now it was the *power* and she luxuriated in it.

Most, if not all, of Andrew's operations were on the shady edge but by imposing his thoughts on the thought screens of his powerful contacts he was able to grease the skids for his dubious financial ventures and ruthlessly took over one major company after another. At the same time, he was collecting, in his back pocket, a considerable number of corrupt politicians who were at his beck and call.

When his Russian was perfect; when the core of Chieftains who were loyal to him represented the majority of the Russian mafia families; when his understanding of

Russia and the Russian mentality was adequate; when he was strong enough not only in Russia but in the world, he made his move.

"Gregor, I am going out in the desert tomorrow morning for some target practice, . . . pop a few cans and bottles . . . haven't been out there for a while and I'm getting rusty . . . Interested?"

"When are you going?"

"Early, . . . before it gets too hot. Say . . . five o'clock?"

"I was hoping to sleep late in the morning."

"OK, maybe another time,"Andrew turned to leave.

"Wait. I'm getting stale, too. Ok, I'll go but can you make it six?"

"Fine, I'll pick you up at your penthouse at six sharp and we can go straight down to the garage from there."

"Good."

"Not many people are up that early, we will use his private elevator to get to the garage. and we'll avoid being seen together in the lobby. This will work just fine."

The plan was in place. At 6:00 am Andrew arrived at Gregor's penthouse. They rode down in the private elevator to the garage and walked to Andrew's car. There was no one else in the garage. Andrew drove in silence as they rode together out into the desert.

En route, Gregor seemed uneasy. Andrew could read his mind. Gregor didn't suspect anything, . . . but was generally more withdrawn than usual and nervous. Something seemed to be bothering him. The uneasiness did not crystallize to the point where definite thoughts emerged so Andrew could only sense the inner turmoil.

In their preoccupations, neither was aware of the passage of time until, suddenly, they were there. The trip had seemed unusually short.

They got out of the car and walked toward the arroyo.

Gregor broke his silence, "This isn't the place we usually come to."

Andrew brushed him off, "It's OK. One arroyo is as good as another."

Gregor said,"Andrew, there is something I have been wanting to talk to you about. I . . . "

He turned toward Andrew and looked into his cold eyes.

"Have you figured it out, Gregor?"

The light came on.

Gregor's eyes grew wide with fear when he saw the 22 caliber target pistol pointed at his forehead. Two quick sharp cracks and tiny dark holes appeared in Gregor's forehead. There were no exit wounds. The soft lead bullets ricocheted around inside Gregor's skull making mush of his brains and he slumped to his knees, those terror filled eyes still staring at Andrew . . . *Those eyes.*

Andrew tore them out, threw them into the arroyo, kicked Gregor in after them, and tossed the pistol as far as he could throw it. The gun had been stolen from a gun shop in Billings, Montana. It was not registered; it could not be traced to him; and he had been careful to leave no prints.

He took off the surgical gloves and tossed them into the arroyo, as well, and then drove back to the hotel where he ate a large breakfast.

After breakfast, he was in his room working when there was an unexpected knock at his door. It was the Nevada State Police.

"Mr. Kreist?"

"Yes?"questioningly.

"We believe an associate of yours has been killed. Some teenagers in a dune buggy found him out in the desert, Mr. Gregor Vuchkovitch . . . is that his name? . . . May we come in?"

"Of course."

"We were in the casino together last night. It doesn't seem possible. Are you sure it is Gregor?"

"Yes, we have a positive ID. It's him."

Andrew was subjected to the usual interrogation regarding his whereabouts and activities over the past 24 hours. He answered, or successfully parried, all of their questions and they prepared to leave.

"We may want to talk to you some more, Mr Kreist, after we check out your story. Do you mind coming down to the station with us for a paraffin test?"

"No. But it will probably be positive. We go out in the desert for target practice almost every day . . . but you guys already know that. Give me five minutes and I'll meet you in the lobby."

That's OK, we'll wait right outside the door, take your time.

"I thought he would be out there for a couple of weeks before anyone found him. By then, the vultures would have done a job on him . . . Maybe they found the eyes and will connect this to L A. It was stupid not to bury him. Stupid, stupid, STUPID!"

Andrew uttered an expletive as soon as the door closed behind the officers . . . and repeated it several times.

The murder of Gregor Vuchkovitch went out over the police wire. Neither the Nevada State Police nor the Las Vegas Police knew of the *signatures* in the LA murders, otherwise they might have made the connection right away.

They had no reason to conceal the removal of the eyes in their report so the LAPD soon picked up on it.

George Bennet immediately tied together the *signature* killings, the photo from the LA paper of Vuchkovitch, taken at Zepp's funeral, the mysterious stranger at Vuchkovitch's right shoulder, and now Vuchkovitch's gangland style assassination in Vegas.

"The bastard is a Russian Mafia hit man and a high ranking one at that."

Once again, the questions spun like a pinwheel in his brain.

"How does this all tie to the computer generated face, the probable deaths in the fire at that laboratory, the Jane Doe killing . . . and the deaths of a homosexual, a hooker, a masseuse, and the MAXXX murder, an attempt on the life of the head of the security company, an ex-cop . . . and an honest one at that? They seem to have no connection to each other, . . . and what did the Russian mob have to do with all of them anyway? It just doesn't add up."

Andrew rode to headquarters and, as he had himself predicted, tested positive for gunpowder residue. That by itself proved nothing . . . but there was an interesting anomaly. The residue was found only on his upper wrist. The head of Las Vegas Homicide, Captain Vernon Cosgrove, was not noted for his quick uptake or rapid perception. He puzzled over this. Then it hit him.

"The surgical gloves! That's why!""Have forensics check the gloves for residue."

They tested positive.

Andrew summoned all of the chieftains to Las Vegas.

Knowing what had happened the last time all of the family leaders flew together in the same plane, each opted, this time, to make his own travel arrangements, a smart move, but, in this case, totally unnecessary because Andrew had no motive for terminating any of them.

Andrew booked a conference room in his hotel, expecting that it would be bugged by the police.

When all of the family members were assembled, Andrew stepped to the podium, put his finger to his lips indicating the need for silence and pointed all around the room.

"I am glad you were all able to come to the wedding, The valets are lining up your limos in the garage, as we speak. We don't want any paparazzi hanging around during the ceremony so we booked a small wedding chapel for the event. The lead car will guide you to the chapel."

Andrew again pointed around the room. *"They* think the wedding will be *here* so if we leave quietly, right now, we will catch them off guard."

In the police surveillance room the officer monitoring the bug whipped off his headphones. "Wedding? . . . What freaking wedding? Nobody told me nothin' about any wedding."

"Get on the horn to headquarters and find out about this wedding crap,"

THE SHROUD

At Las Vegas police headquarters they were unprepared for this contingency. Scrambling for information they determined that there were at least a half dozen wedding chapels in the area. Getting married in Vegas seemed to be a popular pastime.

Whose wedding? How do you check up on a wedding when you don't even know who is getting married? Check for Russian sounding names. Get the cars on the streets looking for that damn procession. What the hell is going on here?

It didn't take too long. The police finally located the chapel, set up the surveillance van outside, and aimed their high tech directional microphones at the chapel windows. A regular glass window vibrates in accordance with the sound waves hitting it, but the panes of stained glass were small, thick, and held in place by lead that damped out all of the vibrations, . . . and the surveillance team got nothing.

Not that it mattered. . . . Andrew's meeting had been brief and directly to the point. He bluntly informed the assembled chieftains that *he* was now the boss of all of the families. He then reaffirmed the territories that each would preside over, keeping the US for himself. The main thrust of the meeting was all over by the time the police arrived.

Emulating the Italian Mafia dons, Andrew had purchased a huge gold signet ring which he wore on his right forefinger. Each of the chieftains was required to kiss his ring as a symbol of their fidelity to him. Even Ivan the Terrible had not required *that*.

Andrew felt their reluctance, but they all did it. In a sense, there *was* a wedding, . . . a marriage between Andrew and the Russians.

At the *apparent* age of 34, Andrew had become the head of one of the most powerful organizations on the earth,

---

CHAPTER THIRTY-THREE

Vernon Cosgrove, Captain, Homicide Division, Las Vegas Police Department growled,"That son of a bitch, Kriest. He really suckered us this time. It doesn't matter, This meeting was to consolidate his hold on the other Russian mafia biggies. I know that, and I *know* that he is the one who iced Vuchkovitch, . . . and I am going to nail him for it."

Bennet called the Las Vegas Police, Homicide, "Hi, Captain Cosgrove? This is Inspector George Bennet, LAPD Homicide. I'm calling about the Vuchkovitch murder. Think we both have an interest in the perp. Can we get together and compare notes?"

"I'm pretty sure who did this one", Cosgrove replied, "and we've got the motive but evidence is weak and all circumstantial. Any help would be greatly appreciated. Can you fly up tomorrow? I will clear as much time as it takes?"

"Damn. This is my case and all of a sudden, Cosgrove thinks it's his case. He has one lousy body and we have over a dozen. Gonna have to walk on eggs with this guy."

"OK. As soon as I have my reservation, I will call you with my ETA."

Cosgrove met Bennet as he disembarked at the airport. On the ride into Vegas, Bennet decided not to tell too much. In particular, he planned to keep to himself what he knew about Andrew's extraordinary mental powers.

In Captain Cosgrove's office, Bennet grabbed the initiative immediately, "OK. lets take it from the top." He pulled from his aluminum briefcase a photo derived from the surveillance tape. "Is this your guy?"

"That's him."

"Whattaya know about him?"

"Well, he showed up out of nowhere, cozied up to the top Russian mafia guy here in Vegas, . . . the deceased, Gregor Vuchkovitch. Zepp Grinkoff, Gregor's number two, was the victim of a mob hit and Kreist got even tighter with Vuchkovitch. Then, all of the big guys in the Russian mob, except the top guy, Ivan Terrikoff, were killed on a plane that blew up and crashed in the desert as it came in for a landing here. They were flying in from Moscow. Don't know why."

"I remember that. 'Ivan the Terrible' was offed in Moscow at the same time."

"Right. Convenient coincidence for Gregor Vuchkovitch, Huh? It moved him into the top spot in the Russian mob, and Andrew Kreist became his second in command."

"Now with Vuchkovitch's untimely demise, Andrew Kreist becomes the top dog . . . Need any more motive than that?"

"Sounds pretty strong to me."

"Me too, but the evidence is all circumstantial. We are sure he wore surgical gloves when he took care of Vuchkovitch. He tested positive for powder residue only from the wrist up and one of the latex gloves found at the crime scene tested positive, too . . . but these mob guys all go out into the desert regularly for target practice. On any given day most of them would test positive. Don't think they dreamed this up to protect themselves but it works out that way. It really blew the case we were building up against Vuchkovitch in the murder of Zepp Grinkov."

"Damn, how do you keep the players all separated without a score card? Why couldn't all these guys have English names?"

"Well, the main attraction now is Andrew. That's not too hard to remember." Cosgrove paused, "Now, what have you got for me?"

"We had a string of serial killings in LA, all along the Strip . . . a tootie fruity, a hooker, a masseuse, some kind of connection seemed plausible at first, but the only thing they really had in common was the fact that he tore out the eyes . . . just like you described in the case report on

Vuchkovitch. Then he killed a security guy for no apparent reason but we think he is also responsible for the death of a Jane Doe, who may have worked at a laboratory that was completely destroyed by fire. We have good reason to believe that he was responsible for the fire, too. Probably a dozen people perished in the fire but the destruction was so complete that there was no trace of any bodies. We have him on surveillance tapes. He was there when the fire started. But the strangest thing of all is this."

Bennet pulled out the computer generated picture made by Fred Ashton and handed it to Cosgrove.

"That's him all right."

"*Really?* Care to guess where I got this picture? Don't even try. It so weird I have trouble believing it, myself. The lab that burned down? Well, the people in there commissioned a computer graphics expert to make this for them."

"So?"

"This picture was derived from the bearded face on the Shroud of Turin."

"I . . . I . . . I . . . ", Captain Cosgrove stammered.

"Me, too. Boggles the mind doesn't it?"

"But how . . . ?"

"Yes, . . . but *how*?"

"Beats the crap out of me."

"Exactly."

They both sat and silently stared at the computer generated picture.

The word "clone" never occurred to either of them.

Cosgrove had not revealed all of *his* cards to Bennet.

His Forensics Lab was still working on the surgical gloves, At that very moment, the head of the lab was poring over handout notes that he had brought back from a seminar he had attended in LA. One lecture in particular, given by the LAPD Chief of Forensics, had been on techniques for lifting fingerprints from unlikely places.

"Where is it? it's got to be here somewhere. I'm beat. I've been on this case for days and need a break. I'll pick it up again tomorrow." He headed home for a much needed rest.

On the return flight to LA, George Bennet muttered to himself, "Vegas is nothing but a hick town with a few fancy gambling joints. That hick, Vernon Cosgrove, thinks he will be able to get an indictment on this single new murder with the flimsiest of evidence. Bull. This is *my* case and I am not going to let that S.O.B. snatch it away from me."

Back at LAPD, he called together his task force to let them know what he found out in Las Vegas. After reviewing his conversation with the Captain Cosgrove, he said,"Those hick cops are going to try to steal this case right out from under us. We have more than a dozen homicides attributable to this perp and they have *one*, . . . and a lousy Russian hood at that, . . . but it was a *signature* killing . . . and that ties him to *our* homicides. We have to solidify our case against this guy ASAP. I want an indictment and an arrest warrant as soon as we can pull enough together to justify it. We can start with the security tapes because they tie him to both the laboratory arson deaths and the killing at MAXXX Security. The MAXXX Security case was a *signature* killing and that ties him to the other *signature* cases. At least we have IDs on the victims in all of the *signature* killings. We have circumstantial evidence on the tapes tying him to the Jane Doe we found behind the laboratory, but we don't know who she was, or even a hint at a motive, so lets keep her out of it for now. As far as that goes we haven't established a motive for *any* of the killings except the guy at MAXXX Security. He had the tapes showing the perp, . . . but doing *what*? Whatever it was, it was enough to kill for. This case is just one big freaking unanswered question."

One of the task force members asked, "What about prints? Did the Vegas cops finger print him when they did the paraffin test on him?"

"Damn, I didn't ask. OK, get on the wire to Vegas and have them fax the prints if they have them. If they send us something, check them against all of the recent print files and the *signature* crime scene files. We might have something we either overlooked or maybe we had nothing positive to check against before. Good idea. Anybody else got an idea?"

"What about the pictures?" asked another member of the squad.

"Well, they definitely tie him to Vuchkovitch . . . but that's *their* case. The surveillance tapes tie him to the lab and there is that weird computer picture. I have no idea how that fits in. Any ideas on that one?"

"The computer guy was *there*, inside the lab. He talked to people, he saw them. Somebody there hired him to do that picture. He might remember some names. We need to ID the fire victims. We will look kind of stupid charging him with killing anyone in *that* building when there is not a distinguishable trace of human remains in the fire residue. Maybe the computer guy can help us with an ID."

Back in the recesses of his mind, George had an itch. He mentally picked at it and suddenly it came back to him. "I thought this case was weird enough but we don't want to overlook anything."

He went to his file cabinet and retrieved the tape of his interview with the psychic investigator, "You want weird, listen to this." He played the tape for his team. Don't scoff at this. She is at least partly right about his capabilities."

"OK. Get on it right now. Anything else? . . . Guys, this is all pretty thin. I want it thick enough to stick all over him. So hop to it. . . . Oh, one more thing. The Vegas guys don't have a clue about his mental abilities. If they arrest him they will play hell holding him. You saw the tapes and heard this one. He can open the toughest locks without even touching them. You saw that. He apparently made himself invisible to the security guard. You saw that, too. And maybe he can read minds. . . . So what must *we* do to capture and hold him once we've got him? Think about *that* before you go to bed. I had just one thought on this. *If* we get him into a cell, we can chain the door shut and maybe weld the chain together. After that I don't have the foggiest."

Bennet gave one of his officers the job of checking the *signature* killing crime scene prints against the Vegas prints.

He hit pay dirt immediately. Matches were found *everywhere*.

So, this was not a case of a look alike. It was all the same guy, . . . Kreist.

Kreis, . . . "Christ!" This was becoming more bizarre by the minute.

The head of the forensics lab of the Las Vegas Police Department awoke with a splitting headache. He was having chills and running a fever. With a temperature of 102°, he opted to take a couple of aspirin, called in sick, and climbed back into the bed.

It was three days before the fever abated and he felt well enough to go back to work.

CHAPTER THIRTY-FOUR

After Acapulco, John and Natalie decided not to take a chance on another lease. Better to keep moving in case Andrew . . .

As Mr. and Mrs. Marcel Dupree, they traveled the length and breadth of Mexico, never staying in any place longer than a week. Something new to see or do every day pushed the horrors further and further behind them.

Somehow, the further they got from Los Angeles, the safer they felt.

Their travels extended into Central America as well. They became intensely interested in the cultures that had flourished and vanished and scrambled over the sites of the early civilizations, . . . the ruins of the cities of the Aztecs, the Mayans, the Toltecs, and the Incas.

They became lost in time as they explored the remarkable world of centuries past . . . and in an environment in which time meant nothing, the days quickly stretched into months and then into years. It was a wonderfully romantic idyll, . . . almost like a never ending honeymoon. Los Angeles and everything that it implied was all but forgotten . . . a place where . . . perhaps in another millennium . . . people would explore the ruins and ponder the lives and fates of its inhabitants as *they* were now doing.

Natalie's entire life had been directed toward one goal, the successful cloning of a human being. It could not be totally repressed. From time to time it bubbled to the surface of her consciousness and she thought about what had gone wrong.

Natalie started dreaming more and more often about what might have been, *"If only we had realized that even Christ did not come by it all naturally. He had been raised with a deeply rooted set of values imparted by the rabbis and others. He had been brought up to be a moral man. Was that the only real difference between Christ and Andrew? Could a child's upbringing have such a profound effect? If we could just do it over again what a force for good Andrew might have become."*

Natalie and Marc were regularly exploring the excavated temples and cities of the ancient cultures of Mexico and Central America.

On one such exploration, Natalie wondered aloud, "We know so little about these people. They had a written language and we think that we have deciphered many of these hieroglyphs, but much of it is conjecture. Where did they come from? Their civilizations appear to have sprung into existence, fully developed, in a wink, as archaeological time goes, . . . and the Mayans had a calendar based on the 26,000 year cycle of the solar system around the Pleiades star cluster. This cycle ends on December 22, 2012, . . . by *our* calendar. They believed that time, as we know it, will end on that date. How could an ancient culture conceptualize a *26,000 year* cycle? . . . or the end of *linear* time? We homo sapiens have not even been around that long . . . and imagine, . . . they invented the zero, a number designating . . . *nothing*. It is mind boggling. "

Marc replied, jokingly, "Maybe they are from another world, another corner of the universe. The Maya had a highly complex system of hieroglyphic writing, using pictographs and phonetic or syllabic elements. There are pictographs depicting some of their gods that might be interpreted as space travelers. Or maybe flying saucers landed here and the crews taught them how to do all of these things, or maybe . . . "

"Marc, be serious. What a wonderful thing it might be to talk to some of them and find out for sure."

"And how would we do *that?*"

"Think about it. Their cultures were heavily into human sacrifice to placate their gods, Thousands of men were killed on altars atop these temples. Their hearts were torn out. Blood must have flowed like water up there."

"Well, it is all gone now."

"Maybe not. There are thousands of cracks and crevices up there in and around the sacrificial altars where some blood might have collected and hardened. Virtually all of it has long since washed away, but, perhaps, somewhere inside of those rocks . . . "

"Haven't you had *enough*?"

Natalie ignored the question, "Marc, what if *this* time we did everything right? What a wonderful thing, . . . to turn back the hands of time and actually talk to them. They could teach us so much."

CHAPTER THIRTY-FIVE

It was the regular daily task force briefing, the first after George Bennet's return from Las Vegas. He was becoming impatient,"If we don't move faster, those Vegas hicks are going to try to take him. Whattawegot so far?"

The officer working on the fingerprints answered first,"We have prints that positively identify Kreist as the guy in Las Vegas. There are fingerprint records all over the place but they are all *recent*. They seem to have appeared in a lot of places all at once, his DMV thumbprint, . . . his passport application, . . . like he didn't exist before the *signature* homicides, . . . and all of a sudden, there he is, . . . everywhere, . . . and I *mean* everywhere . . . . His prints are all over the *signature* crime scenes, too . . . except MAXXX Security. . . . He must have worn gloves there. . . . It's like he just blew in from another planet and did all this stuff."

"What about the victims of the fire? Do we have any IDs yet?"The question was directed at the officer charged with getting positive IDs on all of the victims.

"Things are moving very slowly. We have IDd the security guard at the lab. And even though there are no remains, we have a video tape that definitely places him in the building at the time of the fire. We have determined that some kind of genetic research was going on in there. That narrows the search somewhat. Must have been some Ph.Ds in that bunch. At the moment we are showing the Jane Doe pictures to all of the universities in the area in hopes that she was educated nearby. . . . So far no luck. . . . I'm going to check with Berkeley this afternoon, and UCLA tomorrow."

"Well, keep on it. Anything new from the MAXXX Security records?"

The officer on that detail answered,"Yes, the head of the project in that lab was named Natalie Goodenough and her assistant was one Sarah Buckley. Those are possibles. One or both were probably Ph.Ds. I think we will get a break soon on this if they were educated nearby. Meanwhile we are checking with Phi Beta Kappa and the like. My guess is that they were in some honor society or other. We have other avenues to explore, too . . . 'Who's Who' . . . that kind of stuff . . . Also, Goodenough's phone number and address were in John Pearson's Rolodex. A couple of my men are on their way over there to check it out right now, For the first time I feel good about this."

"I hope. . . . Anybody else got any progress to report? . . . No? . . . OK guys, back to the grindstone."

The next day, the well came in. They hit a gusher.

Everyone started talking at the same time. Each member of the task force was bursting with information and wanted to go first.

Bennet held his hands up in a gesture of surrender, "OK! OK! OK! Everyone will get a chance. We'll start with the victim IDs. . . . What do we have from the MAXXX files?"

"Mucho. Mucho. Their files took us to Goodenough's apartment. No answer. We got a warrant. The place looked like it had been unused for a couple of years . . . dust an inch thick. Notes on her calendar indicated that she would be at a conference on cloning in Paris. She was booked on TWA flight 800. Checked with TWA. She apparently boarded, . . . but her body was never found. So, . . . she was *not* a victim of the fire but seems to have died the same day. . . . Strange. . . . We found some files on the project that was in progress. Names of the employees of her firm were listed. Most of them were Ph.Ds but there was one MD and a librarian. The librarian was the only female other than Goodenough and Buckley. We *know* Goodenough was not there. From eye balling the tapes, we figure the younger of the two females who entered the lab that day was the librarian and the one who entered, left, and ended up as our Jane Doe, was Goodenough's assistant, Sarah Buckley. How am I doing so far?"

"I checked out Berkeley. Our Jane Doe's picture matches Buckley's photo in the University records, . . . so it looks like you figured right. Something else, . . . while Goodenough was working on her doctorate, Buckley was her assistant. That further ties the two together. Goodenough's doctoral project was on cloning."

Bennet was thinking out loud, "That guy who reconstructed the image from the Shroud of Turin came up with a picture that is a dead ringer for Andrew Kreist, and I have heard the word 'cloning' a couple of times today. Wait a minute, I'm thinking. . . . Oh my God, . . . he is a *clone*."

What?"

"A clone! They somehow cloned a person from the blood on that Shroud. That explains his extraordinary powers. Two thousand years ago the kinds of things that he does would be called miracles."

"His behavior is not very Christlike to me."

"I don't understand it either, . . . but do I hear a better idea? . . . And two plane crashes that wiped out people connected to him? . . . how do we explain those? . . . Would you like to present *those* to a jury?"

"And the arson victims, I wouldn't want to present *those* to a jury either."

"OK, lets go with what we think we can make stick. Guess it gets back to the *signature* homicides. If you have to work all night, tomorrow I want a true bill on each of the *signature* victims; I want an arrest warrant; and I want extradition papers to bring him back to LA for trial. I want to grab him right out from under the noses of those Vegas hicks. Hop to it guys. Lotta work to do . . . Dismissed."

George Bennet was elated.

"I've got that sonuvabitch now."

When his task force had gone back to work, George called Personnel, "I need a couple of cops with very special skills. Let me tell you what I want and I will be there in about an hour with the proper authorization papers to put them on temporary duty with my task force. If possible I would like for them to be there so we can interview them."

True to his word Bennet showed up with the papers and sat down with the Chief of Personnel.

"Where do you guys come up with these requests. Always something goofy, never just an ordinary police officer. Well, It just so happens, I have three in the entire LAPD who fill the bill."

"OK, I would like to talk to them one at the time. I've brought my own translator."

Bennett was disturbed somewhat by the fact that the first officer interviewed occasionally answered before the translator had a chance to speak.

Bennet turned to the translator, "I hope we have better luck with the other two."

Interviews two and three went as desired and the two cops were TDYd to Bennet.

Bennet told the Chief of Personnel, "I'll take 'em now." and he, the translator, and the two new additions to his task force departed.

Bennet and the translator spent several hours briefing the two officers. They were shown the tapes and Bennet made particular note of Andrew's ability to manipulate locks, and cloud the guard's mind so he couldn't see him.

They impressed upon the two men, the fact that he had extraordinary mental powers. They were not sure of all of his abilities, or his range, but what they knew was enough to cause great concern about how to go about capturing him.

What was unusual about the two new additions to the task force was the fact that they had been doing deep undercover work in the barrio. Neither of them could speak or understand a word of English. They could not be tripped up by a casual English comment.

Due to the nature of their regular assignments, both cops were pretty scroungy.

Bennet spoke to the translator, "Tell them that they will have to shave and get haircuts. They won't have to get it all cut off but it has to be *neat*. They won't be able to get within a block of this guy unless they look like they *belong* . . .

and dress them for Las Vegas. This guy lives in a classy hotel and they should look like *they* are staying there, too. Bring 'em back for me to check out when they are all cleaned up."

Bennet's entire plan depended on Andrew being unable to speak or understand Spanish. He prayed that this assumption was correct.

Bennet took the translator aside,"You won't be able to go into Vegas with these guys. Kreist could read your mind and that will give the whole damned thing away, so, they will have to handle everything themselves . . . getting to Vegas from the airport and back again . . . everything. You will have to wait for them at the plane . . . I doubt that he will be scanning the whole freaking state of Nevada for trouble . . . at least I hope not. I will take care of any necessary vouchers and arrange for the plane . . . and the arrest warrant and extradition papers are in the works."

The plan also assumed that handcuffs would be useless in trying to control him.

Bennet had what he considered a workable plan for this and while the two barrio cops were getting made over, he went over, in his mind, every last detail, again and again.

"Have I forgotten anything? . . . We will have a couple more men, . . . bilingual, . . . on the plane, . . . just in case."

When the translator returned with the made-over barrio cops the transformation was dramatic. They would meld into the Las Vegas scene like cream into coffee.

Bennet blurted out, "Geez, their precinct captain is gonna really be pissed when he sees what I am sending back to him."

Bennet went over, with the translator and the barrio cops, the plan for subduing Kreist and getting him back to LA. They indicated that they understood.

Good. We will whisk that SOB out of Vegas before those hick cops have a clue.

CHAPTER THIRTY-SIX

Bennet went with them to the airport, turned over all of the documents to the translator and instructed him to pass them on to the arresting officers on arrival in Las Vegas.

One last word of instruction,"Have the pilot radio a message to me with your ETA and I will meet you here with a van on arrival . . . and go over the plan again and again during the flight. We don't want any slipups."

The door of the plane was pulled shut, the ground crew pulled out the chucks, rolled away the steps, and the plane taxied toward the runway for departure.

Bennet watched until the plane was in the air and out of sight. He would be in for a nail biting several hours waiting for their return.

It would be a long night. Back at his office he made a fresh pot of coffee and continued to go over the plan in his mind. It *had* to work.

That morning, hotel security called Cosgrove, "The day Vuchkovitch was popped? . . . We were going over our surveillance tapes and found something that might interest you."

Cosgrove assigned one of his men to check it out.

After a quick review of the tape, the officer called in to headquarters. "We've got something here. At 6 am on the day of the Vuchkovitch homicide, the hotel security surveillance camera in the garage caught two guys hoppin' into a car to go somewhere. It looks like Vuchkovitch and Kreist but I can't be sure. Sometime later it looks like Kreist returned alone. I'm bringing in a copy of the tape for you to look at. Coming right in."

After seeing the tape, Cosgrove growled, "He lied to us. He *was* with Vuchkovitch that morning. We've got him now. We can prove he was with him just before he was killed. I think we now have enough for an indictment."

Later, the head of the Las Vegas forensics lab call Captain Cosgrove. "Captain, sorry to call you so late at night but I thought you'd want to know. While I was home sick I got out my notebook . . . you know . . . the notes I took at that seminar in LA last year . . . I took some notes on how to get fingerprints from the inside of surgical gloves. It is a tricky procedure called the cyanoacrylate fuming method. You only get one shot at it so I made sure I did everything right . . . took a while . . . had to go to a pet shop and get an aquarium . . . line it with aluminum foil . . . put in a lamp for a heater . . . put a little super glue in it . . . turned the glove inside out and put it in the aquarium . . . sealed it up good . . . "

"Damn it man! Get to the point!"

"OK, the lamp vaporized the super glue . . . the fumes drew out the prints so they could be photographed . . . the prints were white, almost the same color as the glove so I had to dust them . . . but I got them . . . and they are *his* prints . . . Andrew Kreist's prints . . . He shot him. There is no doubt about it now. . . . We've got him."

"Thanks,"Cosgrove hung up and immediately tried to find a judge to issue an arrest warrant but they were apparently all out for the evening. He couldn't even get an answering machine.

Cosgrove was beside himself with frustration.

OK, first thing in the morning.

Captain Cosgrove had a restless sleepless night and morning was a long time in coming.

Andrew and Madeline were at a roulette table when he glanced at his watch. "Gotta make a quick phone call. I'll be right back,"he whispered in her ear.

When Andrew returned to his hotel suite, the barrio officers were in the corridor a short distance away, waiting for him. They were talking sports when he arrived. Andrew left the credit card room key in his wallet and mentally unlocked his door.

His telepathic abilities were no help as the two officers suddenly pounce on him and handcuff him.

The barrio police have seen the tapes, are aware of his extraordinary mental abilities, and they just got an impressive demonstration when he mentally opened the door to his room. Andrew did not speak Spanish so he could not read their minds.

The officers did not trust the handcuffs to restrain him for long. While one held him, the other jabbed the needle into his arm. Within seconds, he was in la-la land.

They guided his staggering form toward the elevator and zipped down to the garage. After pushing him into their rental car, they hit him with another needle, fully anesthetizing him. One officer drove while the other sat with him, needle ready, watching for any sign of revival.

The return to the airport was uneventful.

The barrio cops were grateful for the presence of the additional officers at the plane. His dead weight would be hard to get into the plane without their help.

Once they got Andrew aboard, they tied him securely with wet rawhide rope, putting more trust in that than in the handcuffs.

The pilot asked for takeoff clearance and within minutes they were airborne.

When Andrew woke up, he decided to bide his time and not to try to free himself until they are back in Los Angeles where he would have more directions in which to run.

When Andrew failed to return to the casino, Madeline got worried. She called their suite. No answer. She rushed back to their suite and found the door slightly ajar. Everything seemed to be in order in their suite but no Andrew.

She called hotel security.

There was not much they could do except review their security camera tapes. Eventually, they got to the tape from the garage surveillance camera. Nothing unusual there except a couple of guys helping a drunk friend into a car. It had Nevada plates and was a rental car.

They showed this tape to Madeline who immediately recognized Andrew. "My God, They have kidnaped him!"

Hotel security was way over its depth with *that*. They called the Las Vegas police. When the officers arrived on the scene they reviewed the tape, took down the license number, and called it in to the DMV. It did not take long to run down the vehicle. It was a rental car, picked up from, and returned to, the Las Vegas airport, . . . and paid for by a voucher from the LAPD.

They called Captain Cosgrove. He was still awake.

"WHAT!" Cosgrove was livid, "He was *mine*, I've got him nailed for the Vuchkovitch job and now he is on his way to LA." He uttered a string of expletives that would shock a pimp.

Cosgrove called all of his key people in from home.

"See what we have to do to get him back. Don't miss any possibility. I *want* that bastard."

At LA International, the incoming plane was met by a police van, Andrew was hustled into it and quickly transported to the holding pen.

Bennet was waiting as the still groggy Andrew was formally booked.

Not taking any chances, he was hit with the needle every time he seemed to be coming out of it.

Bennet said,"I want him in an open cell where we can keep a close eye on him. Is the welder here? Good. I want his cell door secured with several loops of heavy steel chain. Weld each loop, and I want an around-the-clock guard in this area."

Andrew was half dragged into the cell that had been prepared for him, the chain loops were welded and Bennet finally relaxed. "See you guys in the morning when we take him for arraignment."

CHAPTER THIRTY-SEVEN

This was the only flaw in Bennet's plan.

There would be no arraignment.

When everyone but the guard had departed, Andrew started coming around. He shook the cobwebs out of his head and surveyed his predicament. A cunning smile came over his face, *"Who do they think they are fooling with? Don't they know what I did at the lab?"*

When the station had settled down again, Andrew froze the cerebral clock of the guard and then concentrated on the welds. The chains started to smoke, turn copper red, and then a blinding white. Molten steel dripped to the floor and then turned to grey ash as one by one, Andrew cut through the chain loops. When the last of the loops was broken, Andrew addressed the cell door lock, . . . no challenge. He froze the Desk Sergeant, recovered his wallet, credit cards, and driver's license from the personal articles locker and strolled casually out the front door.

There was an unmarked police car in the parking lot. The door and ignition locks posed no problem.

He deliberately left the desk sergeant and guard in a cerebral time freeze to give himself as much of a head start as possible.

The department shrink would face one of his most challenging assignments trying to bring them out of it.

At that time of night there was little traffic. Andrew traveled at the speed limit to LA International, caught the red eye to New York, and then a commuter flight to Washington. He used assumed names and paid cash for everything so there would be no paper trail.

When Bennet was informed of the escape, he immediately deduced his ultimate destination. *He won't be safe anywhere . . . except Russia . . . and he won't risk setting down in any country where he might be taken off the plane. It'll have to be a non-stop.*

He got his task force busy determining the International Airports having direct flights to cities in Russia. There were not that many but it all took time . . . precious time.

Police were alerted in all of the cities having direct flights.

All they could do now was wait.

Before departing LA, Andrew made a quick phone call to Madeline. After getting past the tears, he told her to bring their passports and as much money as she could gather up, to pay cash for her plane tickets and get to Washington by a devious route, buying new tickets at each touchdown, giving a phoney name each time, and paying cash for everything. He named a bar in Dulles International as their meeting place. When he arrived in Washington, he settled into one of the Naugahyde booths and waited.

Madeline's arrival meshed quite well with an Aeroflot flight to Moscow. They waited on standby but managed to get on, . . . the last two passengers to board.

Because of his frequent short-notice flights to Moscow, his and Madeline's passports were always ready, . . . stamped with the proper visas.

They had made it, but not by much. The police arrived at the terminal just as the wheels of the giant Tupolev Tu-144 left the ground and the aircraft nosed into the air.

With Captain Cosgrove beside him, the Las Vegas Chief of Police was on the horn to LAPD. Andrew had been spirited across state lines which took this matter out of the jurisdiction of either the California or Nevada courts. He had obtained a federal court order for the return of Andrew to *his* jurisdiction and was in a gloating mood when he placed the call. After telling Bennet about the court order, there was a brief silence and the chief's jaw dropped.

"He *WHAT*?!!"

It would be a long flight and both of them were completely exhausted. Andrew tucked a blanket around Madeline and put his arm around her shoulder. As she dozed off she asked, "Am I going to have to learn Russian now?"

"You'd *better*."

They slept for more than ten hours in the uncomfortable cramped seats but it was a sleep of relief that it was all now behind them.

CHAPTER THIRTY-EIGHT

Andrew quickly called together the heads of all of the families and informed them that Moscow would, once again, be the headquarters of their world wide criminal activities.

Andrew began by getting the "home team" all on the same page. That was not easy. The suspicions of the family leaders that one among them was a mole, reporting everything to Andrew, hampered a free exchange of ideas and the development of an atmosphere of cooperation.

Andrew hit them with a one-two punch. He came down on them with an iron fist, spelling out in the strongest possible language exactly what was expected of them. He knew that skimming was going on at every level of the organization and ordered an immediate cessation . . . or else.

And don't think for a moment that I don't know *exactly* how much each of you is pocketing. You! Kasikoff!" Kasikoff cringed. "Do you want me to tell you how much? No matter. Next week it will be *zero*. Do you hear me *ZERO*! And that goes for your collectors, too. From this point on, you will share in direct proportion to your returns and I expect an increase each month from the month before. I don't care how you do it but do it . . . and without cutting in on each other's territory."

He came down hard on them about skimming, and indicated that it would be hazardous to the health of any one continuing to do engage in it.

The individuals present could not help but think about how much they would lose if they stopped and this gave him the perfect opening to get specific and personal about the matter.

"Just to make certain we know exactly what I am talking about, I know precisely what each of you is skimming and how much skim you are tolerating from your collectors. The only way to bring this under control is to allow none. Is that clear to you? NONE!"

Andrew than went around the table, addressing each of them by name, and specifying the increase take expected from each of them. Jaws dropped in astonishment as his numbers coincided precisely with their skims.

"Now, shall we continue?"

Andrew looked around the table. They were decently attired in expensively tailored Italian silk suits but they were all bearded.

He stroked his chin for a moment, *"I wonder if they would accept me more readily if I had a beard. NO. I am the boss of bosses. I don't need their lousy acceptance. They will obey my orders, . . . period."*

"We are a business organization now and, will look and conduct ourselves as such. No matter how you are dressed, you still look like a bunch of street brawlers."(which, for the most part, was exactly what they were).

"By tomorrow, I want all of you to look like professional business men . . . neat haircuts . . . clean shaven . . . and *bathed* . . . bathed *every day* from now on . . . and change your underwear every day, too . . . This room stinks."

"Henceforth. when you apply pressure, you will apply it with *class*. Subtlety and finesse will replace broken arms and legs but you *will* produce results. Our pressure will now be economic and political. Am I understood?"

They all nodded. What else could they do?

Andrew's next meeting with his under bosses looked, superficially, like a board meeting at any major corporation but it was clear that they needed a lot of polishing to grind off the rough edges. *"Well, first things first. This is going to take some time."*

It did, indeed, take some time. Andrew realized after the first month that while some of his underlings were coming around, some would never make it. The time for taking the undesirables for a ride was only a footnote in history. The world had changed and criminal activity would have to keep up with the times. Andrew, in another time, would have killed them personally, and not given it a second thought, but now, those who were either too dumb, too recalcitrant, or too set in the old ways were handled in a manner appropriate for a modern corporation.

Andrew brought in professional retirement planners from America. They didn't speak Russian so translators were needed much of the time. Like most outside consultants, they did a study. This is the mechanism by which a consultant finds out by devious means exactly how the management wants their recommendations to be articulated. The final report is then "run up the flagpole". The CEO having seen it already and concurring with its conclusions, puts the recommendations into effect and the inevitable purge occurs. It is all made as painless as possible by means of golden parachutes providing a life of leisure for the dead wood being eliminated. Obviously, the organization did not have a pension plan but the coffers were more than adequate to provide sufficiently handsome pensions to buy a life of leisure in a dacha on the Black Sea for each of the mobsters eased out of the operation.

If anyone objected, there was always the "old fashioned way", so there *were* no audible objections.

This was *not* a corporation, of course, but Andrew was the closest thing there was to a CEO and he was as vicious as a cobra when dealing with his underlings. Everyone toed the line. No exceptions.

He personally called the Offices of Student Placement at Wharton, Harvard, and Yale to recruit the brightest of the new crop of MBAs. His primary criteria were 1) upper five percentile and 2) fluent in Russian. He invited the best prospects to come to Moscow for a personal interview, all expenses paid, and put them up in Moscow's finest hotels. He was pleasantly surprised to find so many qualifying candidates, a fallout from the cold war, and he made the top candidates offers they could not refuse.

It was not long before some of these bright young men moved into important positions of leadership in the areas concerning corporate takeovers but there was still the unions, prostitution, drugs, shakedown operations in the inner cities, and street level gambling. These were too lucrative to let go so the hangers on from the old Russian Mafia still had a place, but it was expected that they would clean up their acts as well, and they did.

Meanwhile numerous attempts were made to extradite him back to the US to stand trial for his transgressions and all failed. Andrew had enough of the European politicians in his pocket to see to that.

Andrew liked his cadre of ambitious young MBAs. Their ruthlessness nearly matched his and they would stab an associate in the back, in a financial sense, with no remorse whatsoever. To financially destroy a man or his company was the source of great personal pleasure for this group of piranhas. Of course, Andrew was the prime mover behind all of the corporate takeovers, utilizing his extraordinary mental powers to determine and thwart the strategies of his opposition. The MBAs were merely the tools of the dismantlement through manipulation of the finances of each target company.

A prosperous and diverse corporation would find itself, suddenly and inexplicably, drowning in red ink and ripe for plucking. Andrew and his raiders would move in and gut the company, spinning off its most profitable divisions and leaving an empty carcass of the unprofitable ones. Many of these currently unprofitable divisions were in development of new products and destined to become the profit centers of the future but Andrew and his band cared nothing for the future. The name of the game was "grab it now".

A corporation must service its debt and pay its employees and that cannot be done without a positive cash flow. The inevitable consequence of this corporate cannibalism was either bankruptcy or the takeover of the remains by another company having the diversity to carry unprofitable divisions if they hold the promise of a major return on investment five to ten years downstream.

Andrew could personally participate in the disembowelment of European companies, and he did not have to confine his activities to Russia. The tentacles of his organization reached deep into the governments of all of the countries of Europe enabling him to move about freely and participate in the direction of these companies. His membership on the boards of directors of many companies gave him personal contact with other board members from whom he mentally derived intelligence about their ambitions. He used his powers to manipulate the other directors and often turned *their* ambitions to *his* advantage.

He operated for a long time without a second in command, but he had Madeline and she learned the ropes quickly. She was a splendid social asset and her sphere of influence quickly widened to include all of Europe. She could often achieve as much by sweet talk as Andrew could through connivance or even brute force.

She was as bloodthirsty for power as Andrew. The manipulation of world financial and political leaders was an impetus that excited her in every possible way. After every state function or corporate affair, in which she mingled with the elite, . . . the elite who were under the full control of her Andrew . . . she reached a peak of arousal. After the festivities, she and Andrew would enjoy an orgy of sexual expression that lasted far into the night. Andrew had it all, . . . and because *he* had it *she* had it. There seemed to be no limit to his endurance, or so he made her *believe*. When it suited him, he froze her cerebral clock and made her believe they had been at it for hours, . . . but most of the time it was the real thing and they made love savagely. They were a perfect partnership.

Andrew made good use of the numbered accounts available in Switzerland and the Cayman Islands to stash away a personal fortune that eventually placed him among the richest people in the world but the magnitude of his wealth was a tightly held secret and even his most astute

MBAs could not possibly imagine it. He also maintained a separate set of numbered accounts for Madeline so she was, in her own right *really* independently wealthy. Her winnings at the "big machine" in Vegas now seemed like chicken feed.

At first, Andrew was undecided as to how much he should reveal to Madeline concerning his extraordinary mental powers, but eventually he told her everything. He had no reason to suspect that she might develop a roving eye and become unfaithful to him but whatever concerns he might have had evaporated when he revealed his telepathic ability to her.

She was skeptical, at first . . . but he *could* control the slot machines, . . . *and* the ball on the roulette table . . . *and* unlock their door without touching it. Perhaps he *could* read her mind.

She devised a complicated test challenging him to *prove* it. He got a perfect score, after which Madeline feared him too much to even think, . . . especially *think*, about it.

In time he demonstrated his other abilities to her. If she got turned on by him before, that was *nothing*, absolutely nothing, compared to now. *He has the power of a God.*

Moisha was discussing Christopher with the David Torrelli and the other members of the Geneticraft team.

"As you all know, Christopher's education is several months ahead of schedule. We have given him a thorough grounding in the Torah, the Bible, and the Koran. Together, we have taught him ethical and moral principals, he has been exposed to the thinking of Buddha and Confucius, and has studied the philosophies of Socrates, Plato, Aristotle, St. Thomas Aquinas and other leading philosophers. He is a skilled logician. We have done almost all we can do to prepare him. I think that it is time to tell him *who* he is."

They all agreed, and Christopher was called before the entire team.

No one seemed to know exactly where to start but Torrelli eventually picked up the ball, "Christopher, you have come to a time in your life when many things should be revealed to you. In your studies of the Bible, a lot of emphasis was put on the life of our Lord and Savior, Jesus Christ, his teachings, his disciples, his death on the cross to redeem our sins, his burial, and his resurrection . . . "Torrelli paused when he realized that he was trying to say it all in one run-on sentence.

Moisha picked it up, "It was Christ's burial in a cave and his resurrection that we want to discuss with you. Something truly miraculous happened that morning. Christ arose from the dead . . . true . . . but an artifact remained behind that told the incredible story of our Savior's crucifixion. It was the linen . . . the burial shroud of Jesus. It was stained with his blood from the crown of thorns, from the nailholes in his wrists and feet, and from the spear wound in his side . . . and on its surface was a remarkable image of Christ."

Christopher was very attentive to what was being revealed to him.

Moisha continued, "Much mystery surrounds the early history of that holy cloth but it is believed to have been brought to Europe by returning Crusaders, emerged in the tiny town of Lirey in France before eventually ending up in the chapel of the Cathedral of John the Baptist in Turin. It is know as the Shroud of Turin and has been in that chapel for several centuries. Recently, there was a serious fire in the Cathedral that threatened to destroy this sacred relic. During the rescue of the Shroud by a group of brave firemen who risked their lives to save it, it was snagged on the shattered case in which it was preserved. We were extremely fortunate that the tiny linen fragment, containing a stain of our Savior's blood, came into our possession."

Torrelli picked up the story again, "Do you know what cloning is?"

"I've read about it."

"It is easy to describe but extremely difficult to do."

Torrelli described the process in considerable detail but then made the leap, "There are many things we still have to learn about the process. One of the puzzles eluding solution for the moment is why a clone matures at an accelerated rate, about four times normal, but eventually slows down to a normal rate when its apparent age equals the actual age of the donor. We know this to be true of all of the clones of *living* donors but do not know what might happen to the clone of a donor who has been dead for nearly two thousand years. Perhaps he will level off at a normal maturation rate when he approaches the age of the donor at the time of his death. Perhaps not. We just don't know."

Christopher had been assimilating all of this and the reality of the situation gelled in his mind, "It is *me*, isn't it? . . . I am a clone . . . "

Torrelli interrupted, "But a very special clone . . . "

And Moisha added reverently, "A clone of our Savior Jesus Christ. You are the embodiment of Jesus. You are the living Christ."

"Somehow, I knew. . . . I can do things that I have never told you about, . . . things that I am certain none of you can do . . . watch . . . "

Christopher levitated David Torrelli right out of his chair, flew him around the room and deposited him gently back in his seat.

Moisha, not a man to be easily surprised, *was* surprised. "Tell us about the other things you can do."

"I can tell you about some of them but I don't know how to tell you about all of them . . . I will just have to show you, . . . and I feel that there may be things that I can do that I don't even know about. . . . I just know that I can do them when the need arises."

Moisha had a lesion on the back of his neck. It had been there for years and would not heal, "Can you heal the sore on my neck."

"I don't know. I have never tried to do anything like that before. Let me see it."

Christopher placed his palm over the lesion and concentrated on healing. The sore was noticeably better. The swelling and the redness were gone and the discomfort as well.

Moisha said, "This is truly the son of God."

Torrelli began a long discussion among the team members and Christopher. The team did not want their efforts to evolve into a circus act. They were concerned that Christopher might use his powers to perform "tricks" rather than use them for the betterment of mankind.

Christopher was already planning a serious evangelical course for himself. He pledged not to reveal his true identity to anyone because he might be considered a magician or, worse, a charlatan and a faker. Christopher had already determined how he would use his powers and vowed that he would only use them for good.

Moisha spoke, "The living Christ once again walks among us. The world can now be saved from the path of destruction that it is on. Praise to God the Father and to His son."

Torrelli bowed his head and whispered a fervent prayer for peace and the salvation of the world.

Moisha *believed* in the new Christ and within a few hours, the wound on his neck had healed completely.

There was much to be done. The uncertainty as to the continuation of Christopher's rapid maturation rate put a stamp of urgency on the evolving plans to launch Christopher's evangelical tour.

Dr. Torrelli's team was clueless regarding the major flaw in Christopher's being. While he has had firm guidance in moral and ethical principals, he was cloned from blood that no longer contained the essence of Christ's soul so despite his training, he is still basically an amoral creature. He may encounter circumstances not covered in his formal education. Here, he could bounce either way, and pure logic, not ethical considerations, might determine his course of action.

The burgeoning economy in the United States was Andrew's next target. He wanted to personally get into the thick of the takeover action in the US but he knew that the outstanding arrest warrants stood in his way, so he attacked with his small army of MBAs who had been given increasing power within the organization. One by one the old line Russian Mafia lieutenants were replaced by these financial wizards.

One of them was Mahail Kirov. Mahail was the product of a family of Russian emigrants who fled to the US a few steps ahead of the purges of the Stalin era. His father, a scientist, recognized early on that he was a mathematical prodigy and guided him toward a career in mathematical science but Mahail had been diverted toward an MBA by a faculty advisor and a cooperative guidance councilor. They convinced him that the corporate world would be far more lucrative than any job a mathematical whiz might otherwise hold down. Andrew was grateful that their influence had overruled the father. Andrew also recognized, in Mahail, a talent far beyond that of the other MBAs and nurtured his development within the organization.

Madeline was his good right arm socially, but Mahail became his good right arm on the business scene.

Eventually, Mahail was formally designated second in command.

During the calendar year in which he advanced from apparent age 16 to apparent age 20, his mentors worked hard preparing Christopher for his ministry. He now spoke several languages fluently but still needed polish in all of them. Language experts were brought in to expand and enhance his vocabulary in each of the languages. He took diction lessons, learning how to enunciate and project his naturally strong voice in order to speak to impromptu gatherings without having to set up a public address system.

He was taken to many of the beautiful parks in and around Rome where he conversed with people of all walks of life. The people of Rome were entranced by his eloquent style and it was not long before he not only attracted those near him in any venue but his magnetism drew people back to him. They made an effort to find out where he would be on the following day and most showed up there. The small gatherings gradually grew into crowds and those into multitudes.

He was soon comfortable in any gathering, large or small, feeling the power that his audience gave to him and which he amplified and returned to them again and again in his messages of peace and love. It soon became necessary to seek out parks having bandshells when the crowds got so large that he could not be seen by his audience. He spoke mainly of redemption through Jesus Christ who died on the cross for our sins but he emphasized the power of love and the healing of minds and souls and bodies through faith in Jesus Christ.

Christopher has become a spellbinding speaker, on the one hand deploring the corruption in business, politics, and even in religion and on the other hand preaching love for one's fellow man and peace. His message is that the world can be made whole again through the power of love and the people of many nations who are tired of stress and strife and killing are receptive to his message.

His following grew and many of the politicians who were in Andrew's pocket began to feel uncomfortable being there. Andrew's lieutenants report back to him that something strange was going on. It was getting noticeably more difficult to get public officials to accept payoffs and bribes. Christopher's influence is beginning to be felt world wide as the news media start to cover his gatherings. Even in Russia he gets coverage on the evening news and it is there, on TV, that Andrew sees him for the first time.

Andrew called his lieutenants around him, "Look at him! Is that the guy who is getting in your way? He is just another religious kook. In America, there is one just like him on every channel, . . . putting hands on people and healing all kinds of imagined aches and pains and illnesses. This guy doesn't even do that. Get your asses back to work and I don't want to hear any more about him. Words, just words. . . . How can he hurt us with words!"

Seeing Christopher on TV *was* a disquieting experience for Andrew *and* for his lieutenants. Most of his lieutenants had not been with him very long so they did not make the connection because of the significant difference in apparent age, but Christopher looked exactly like Andrew did at the same point in his development.

David Torrelli's team was busy organizing a world evangelical tour for Christopher. Meanwhile, *he* started to emphasize his idea that Jerusalem should be the seat of his new world religion. That notion did not sit well in Rome. His "events" in Rome were also becoming more and more troublesome for the Vatican. Miracles had always fallen into *their* domain and he was clearly invading it.

It was not really Christopher's fault. He had vowed not to use his incredible mental powers to perform miracles, but faith cannot be denied and when there were healings of terrible afflictions . . . many of them . . . with hundreds of witnesses, some caught on television cameras, it seemed like the prudent thing to do to get him out of Rome. A world tour was the obvious answer so plans were set in place and Christopher and a small entourage left Rome for the USA.

His first appearance in Madison Square Garden was a sensation. When he raised his hand in benediction at the end of his address, cries of disbelief spread through the building as the blind were made to see, the lame to walk, and the disfigured made whole again. Even Christopher was astonished at the results of his appearance. This was an opportunity that he could not reject.

Christopher, knowing who he was cloned from, subtly changes his evangelistic message from "peace and love and

Salvation through Jesus Christ" to "peace and lover and Salvation through *me*."

Christopher's objective became a single truly ecumenical world church with himself, a clone of, and therefore, truly as much the Son of God as Christ had been, as its leader.

———————————

If there was one thing Andrew intuitively understood, it was cash flow, . . . positive cash flow, and many American corporations were experiencing it in an unprecedented manner.

The Justice Department was still fuming over the way he escaped punishment for his earlier crimes in California and Nevada. However, when his mergers of banks and of major corporations triggered anti-trust action, Andrew reached deeply into his bag of connections. To the chagrin of many members of Congress and the Wall Street community, all of whom wanted to see him stopped, the Attorney General called off the dogs and he was free to pursue the same paths he had followed in the European takeovers.

In the US takeovers his band of MBAs did not have the advantage that they had maintained in Europe as a result of his mental intervention. What they did now took longer, but they all knew his mode of operation and regularly conferred with him over their heavily encrypted communications system. Under Mahail's watchful eye and under Andrew's long distance guidance they did a thorough job of bringing the American economy to its knees and the government was powerless to defend against further incursions from the streamlined new Russian Mafia. The stock market needed only a sniff. The slightest hint of Andrew's interest in a company would start its stock bouncing up and down like a yo-yo . . . and the entire market would have a bad case of the shakes for weeks.

When a law got in his way it was of little consequence. His hold on the State Houses, Congress, and the White House resulted in legislation that cleared the way for him.

At apparent age 36 Andrew's ruthless forays raiding and cannibalizing corporations clouded the world's financial scene but his domination of the corrupt politicians in all major countries prevented action by any government to stop him.

Andrew was now essentially in control of the global economy and he was running out of worlds to conquer.

Forgetting how restless *he* had once been to be number one, he unwisely plans an extended vacation with Madeline.

CHAPTER THIRTY-NINE

It was at this point in his life that Andrew began to ruminate on his extraordinary mental powers.

Where had they come from?

While he had not thought much about it for years, With Mahail picking up a lot of the load. Andrew now had a few leisure moments to just relax and think.

"Madeline what do you say to three or four months on the Riviera?" The question caught her by surprise.

"I thought that you are all tied up. It never occurred to me that we might . . . I would love it. When can we leave?"

"Not right this minute. I have some loose ends to tie off . . . but soon."

"I will need new clothes. It is warm down there."

"Be sure and get a bathing suit that will make me the envy of every man on the beach."

"I will only get a couple of items, now. Everything in the stores here is so glum. I want to wait 'til we are there and then get some really chic and fashionable things . . . especially a sexy swim suit. I will get you so excited that . . . "

"You do that already," Andrew pulled her to him and covered her with little nibbles, gently unbuttoned her blouse and continued nibbling.

"Oh, Andrew . . . you are getting me so . . . Oh, I need . . . it . . . now," she reached for him and grabbed him, possessively.

"You know, we will have plenty of time for this on the Riviera."

"I know."

Madeline was a woman of enormous passion, will, and talents that were not to be denied. She persisted.

Andrew *found* time.

Their plane gently descended into the Nice-Côte d'Azur International Airport. After clearing customs, they had baggage handlers transfer their luggage to a Lear jet to take them to Cannes. After the vast expanses of the United States and Russia, neither Andrew nor Madeline were prepared for the diminutive French Riviera. Their chartered jet was barely airborne when it started its descent into Cannes.

Their limousine was waiting at the airport and despite the unexpectedly heavy traffic they were soon being escorted to their suite atop the four star Hôtel Majestic. The Majestic, an elegant palace, located in the heart of Cannes on the Croisette boulevard, and facing the sea, offered everything that they could possibly want.

The gastronomic restaurant, Villa de Lys, and the Restaurant de la Plage offered gourmet cuisine the equal of any in the world. The Hôtel Majestic also provided a private beach, night club, . . . and the Casino Croisette.

It had been a while since either of them had been in a casino and both looked forward to a relaxing dinner followed by a profitable evening at the roulette tables.

Madeline got turned on by her winning streak. Andrew just stood beside her and let her do the betting. He, of course, controlled the outcome and Madeline raked in the plaques. They did not expect to stay long enough in Cannes to give the house time to become suspicious, . . . not that they could do anything about it anyway.

Madeline loved winning even when it was "fixed", *especially when it was "fixed"*.

Afterward, Madeline rewarded Andrew for his part in her winning streak and left him too exhausted in the morning to get up before noon, . . . but it was the tiredness of satisfaction, and he *was* satisfied, . . . and then some.

When they tried to *do* Cannes, it was clearly impossible. The nearby Palaise des Festivals was the center of activity of the Cannes Film Festival. When they opted to start their time on the Riviera in Cannes, neither had realized that the Film Festival would be in progress at that time or what a circus Cannes would become because of it. Strolling around the city was a most disquieting experience for both of them. There were so many people and uncomfortably close to them. There could be no rest and relaxation in Cannes except in their hotel where they were virtual prisoners.

"Thank God we have the limo and driver booked for our entire stay. These crazy movie people will be tying up everything on wheels for the next few days," Madeline was exasperated that neither of them had thought of the festival when making their plans because Cannes is synonymous with the Film Festival. "Why don't we drive up the coast to Antibes and spend a couple of nights there?"

Andrew was agreeable so the following morning they made the drive. Antibes was a pleasant surprise. It is the home of the largest English-speaking population on the Riviera. Andrew was very fluent in Russian and Madeline was becoming so because, in Moscow, he had spoken to her only in Russian . . . but to hear English spoken again. It was the sound of home, . . . a home to which they could never return. There were even English language television channels, and after a full day, it was a treat for Andrew to just prop up his feet and enjoy it. They settled into the Hôtel Ambassadeur and made it their base of operations for their daily excursions.

Initially, Andrew called Mahail every night to check on things but Mahail was so competent that the calls became less and less frequent. In time, the entire operation was in Mahail's able hands and Andrew did not bother to call at all.

Moving from resort to resort every few days had a decidedly calming effect on Andrew and Madeline noticed that he was more relaxed and carefree than he had been since they first met in Las Vegas.

At dinner, she whispered in his ear,"I *loved* you the way you were, but now I *like* you, too. Do you understand the difference?"

"I think so."

"If you don't, I'll show you when we get back to our room," . . . and she did.

Over the next several weeks, they made excursions to Nice, Cagnes sur Mer, Grasse, Beaulieu, and Monaco where the magnificent Monte Carlo Casino beckoned. Each had an incredible "lucky streak" every time they stopped at a roulette table.

Back in their suite Andrew wondered aloud, "I wonder what it would be like to break the bank here at Monte Carlo. . . . I could do it, you know."

It would have to remain an unfulfilled fantasy. The publicity might prove deadly . . . but both Andrew and Madeline wanted it so much they could taste it.

Nearing the end of their vacation, they found themselves gravitating back to the English speaking environment of Antibes more and more often.

It was there that Madeline excitedly called Andrew out of a warm bath to see what was on the TV. "Hurry, hurry, it's about you."

He rushed out, still wet, in one of the terry cloth robes provided for hotel guests.

It was a program, one of a series produced in the US, about the world's most wanted criminals. This program was about Andrew.

Andrew watched intently as Inspector George Bennet explained what he had done in LA and Las Vegas.

"That's the bastard who kidnaped me out of Las Vegas."

"I didn't know you did all those things he is saying you did," said Madeline, with a quiver of fear in her voice.

"Well, you know how they blow things up." Andrew brushed it off.

The narrator of the program cut back to Bennet from time to time.

There were pictures of him on John Pearson's video tapes, and the news photo taken at Zepp's funeral.

Bennet then showed a side by side image of him at the funeral and a still frame from Pearsons' surveillance tape.

"These pictures show that he was present when the fire started and he is with the Russian Mafia."

Bennet saved the most puzzling for last.

"The people who died in the fire at the laboratory commissioned a computer graphics expert to determine what the image on the Shroud of Turin might look like with a modern haircut, and no beard."

Andrew stared at the reconstructed picture derived from the photos of the Shroud, an incredible likeness.

Finally the narrator interviewed the computer graphics expert who reconstructed the image.

It suddenly hit Andrew. He had long ago figured out that he was a clone, but of *whom*. Now he knew.

"I was cloned from blood on the Shroud of Turin."

Andrew doubted that the image could have been that of Christ . . . but how else could he have acquired his incredible powers? Regardless of who had been wrapped in that Shroud, the idea that anyone might clone another individual having powers equal to his was unthinkable. The Shroud would have to be destroyed.

Andrew left his plans for domination of the worlds financial and political scenes on the back burner and in the capable hands of Mahail.

He made the destruction of the Shroud his top priority. Turin could be reached by car and they had a limousine and driver. It was the only thing to do and it had to be done now.

Andrew should have remembered what happened when *he* was the number two man in the Russian Mafia. The itch to become number one had to be scratched . . . and Mahail Kirov was getting the itch. He should have been tuning in on Kirov. An oversight like that could be very dangerous, even fatal.

Mahail was getting very comfortable in Andrew's slippers and would not give them up easily upon Andrew's return but Andrew was becoming too comfortable himself and had his mind on everything but business.

Mahail Kirov was quick to take control once Andrew was out of sight. He would not have been so eager to do so if he had know that Andrew had the power to tune in on his thoughts but Andrew was, for the first time in a long time, disengaged from the daily operation of the mob and enjoying every minute of it. Mahail was free to plot and scheme without fear of reprisal.

The reckoning would come when Andrew returned. Best to take care of matters now, . . . and not wait for that day.

Mahail gathered those of unquestioned loyalty to his side and proposed that a hit squad be sent to find Andrew and terminate him.

Let the old KGB leftovers do the job. They all disliked Andrew anyway, for edging out the Russians for control.

Mahail sent out agents to determine Andrew's initial destination. They reported back that he had taken an Aeroflot flight to Nice and had chartered a Lear jet to Cannes. It should not be hard to pick up the trail there.

The six man hit squad headed by former KGB muscle man, Alexi Duchokov, could not carry weapons aboard their plane but they would need them on arrival, so the advance agents made arrangements with the French black market for the purchase of six Uzis for the squad. Mahail was informed as to the pickup point and this information was passed on to Duchokov. After picking up the Uzis, they would prepare an ambush and catch Andrew in a withering crossfire. There would be no escape.

The hit squad staked out Andrew's suite in the Hôtel Majestic. That was as close as they would get to him for now. The excursions that he and Madeline were taking to points all over the Côte d'Azur were all based on spur-of-the-moment decisions. There was absolutely no way the hit squad could find out where they were . . . and now they were about to depart France for Italy.

Eventually the realization struck Christopher, *"What if another person were to be cloned from the Shroud of Turin, another person with powers equal to mine?"*

It would not do to have two equally powerful world religious leaders. More people had been killed in the name of religion than any other cause in history. The Shroud would have to be destroyed. This matter was too urgent to delay a single moment.

Christopher broke off his evangelical tour and returned to the headquarters of Geneticraft International in Rome. David Torrelli was surprised to see him. David and his team had launched Christopher's tour with high hopes that the word of Jesus Christ would be spread far and wide and here he was, . . . back, . . . and so soon.

Christopher explained his reason for returning, expressing fear that a calamitous religious war might break out if there were to be another clone from the Shroud.

Torrelli asked Christopher to wait in his office while he consulted with the other members of the team who had cloned and nurtured Christopher. As they discuss the problem, Torrelli points out the fact that if his accelerated aging rate continued, Christopher would have a very short life. And what if something happened to him before his work was completed? It had really just started and he *must* complete Christ's work.

No. They might need a backup so they would have to protect the Shroud at all costs. Christopher was eavesdropping, using his telepathic powers, this was one of those situations for which all of his moral training had not prepared him. His decision was based on pragmatic logic.

The greater good must be served.

Christopher walked out of Torrelli's office, stopped in front of the building, . . . turned, . . . and watched the building burst into intense flames, . . . just as Andrew had done at The Project Complex.

Destruction was complete. There were no survivors and nothing was left but grey ash.

Destruction of the Shroud was now an imperative for Christopher.

He set out immediately for Turin.

———————————

CHAPTER FORTY

Alexi Duchokov, leader of the Russian hit squad was becoming impatient. He and his men had the Hôtel Majestic under careful scrutiny. From time to time they checked out the casino, the dining rooms, and other possible locations but there was no sign of either Andrew or Madeline. Alexi took a calculated risk that Andrew might learn of their presence and guess why he was there. He warily approached the hotel desk manager, "I am a friend of Mr. Andrew Kreist and I understand he is registered here."

The manager pecked at the computer and replied, "I'm sorry, he *is* registered here and *is* still, technically, a guest of the hotel, but about a month ago he had all of his belongings and luggage removed from his room and shipped to the Hôtel Ambassadeur in Antibes, Juan de Pins. He did not indicate when he plans to return to Cannes."

Alexi muttered an invective under his breath.

"I beg your pardon?"

"Sorry, just talking to myself."

Alexi hurried back to his group and laid it all out for them. They had been watching the wrong rabbit hole and must waste no time getting to Antibes. All six of them grabbed their belongings and weapons and piled into their rented Peugeot.

As he had been directed to do, the manager of the Hôtel Majestic called the Hôtel Ambassadeur and left a message for Andrew Kreist, but it arrived too late. He and Madeline had already departed.

Andrew was in a serious mood as his limo left Antibes. He had determined that Turin did not have a decent hotel but Milan was not that far from Turin. Perhaps they should stay in Milan and make a side trip to Turin to do what had to be done. By the time their limo reached the decision point, Andrew's mind was made up.

"Pull into the next rest stop."

The chauffeur complied.

While Madeline was fixing up her face, Andrew called the Hilton in Milan and made the necessary arrangements.

———————————————

Once again, in Antibes, Alexi opted to risk an inquiry at the desk.

"Sorry, Monsieur, Mr. Kreist checked out yesterday."

"What? . . . Where did they go?"

"I do not know, Monsieur, he did not leave a forwarding address."

A whispered string of Russian invectives.

The clerk ignored the profanity," . . . But, I marked up a map for him to show the routes to Torino and Milano. He might have gone to *one* of them, Monsieur."

Alexi turned to leave and as an afterthought turned back to the desk.

Do you have another one of those maps?

"But of course, Monsieur."

"Then mark it up for me," it was more of a demand than a request.

The desk clerk retrieved a map of northern Italy and marked the routes to Turin and Milan.

Alexi rudely snatched the map from the clerk's hands and stormed out of the hotel.

The gang piled back into the Peugeot while Alexi glowered at the map as only a Russian can glower. *Two choices, . . . which to take?*

The routes are identical for a while. I will make up my mind before we reach the fork.

"Ok, just drive."

The wheel man gives him a puzzled look.

"That way, you idiot, that way," Alexi gestured in a generally easterly direction,"That way," and scrunched down into his seat.

THE SHROUD

After a shower and a brief nap, Andrew and Madeline decided to have their dinner in their room. Room Service food is never very good and especially after the wonderful French cuisine to which they had become accustomed. It was overcooked and cold, but Madeline was not put off by it. Andrew had hardly tasted his when Madeline began offering delights that took his mind completely off of food. She relentlessly pursued her sensual satisfactions and they took a lot of satisfying. When it was over, Andrew was too exhausted to do anything but sleep.

The following morning, they got away early, grabbed some coffee and croissants en route and arrived in Turin in plenty of time to reconnoiter the cathedral. There were many people there to see the Shroud. That would present a problem. He could not control all of their minds at once and someone might recognize him. Not that it really mattered. After all. He was one of the most wanted criminals in the world   .   .   .   but he just didn't want any unnecessary complications.

Andrew had to think this over.

Perhaps the evening might be better.

Andrew did not care one way or the other if innocent people were killed or injured. The only thing of import was that the Shroud be destroyed. He walked all around in the cathedral, making note of anything and everything that might affect the outcome of his attack on that mysterious piece of linen.

He checked out the bulletproof case in which the Shroud was displayed. That would present no problem. By this time tomorrow it and its contents would be nothing but a pile of grey ash.

He and Madeline decided to explore the sights of Turin to kill some time.

"Alexi!" the mobster was out of breath, "You won't believe this. What are the chances that we would find him so quickly?"

"Where? Where is he?"

"Just strolling along right over there, . . . by the big church. Come. I'll show you."

"Where?"

"Right there," he points, "See, he has his woman with him."

"OK, keep an eye on him. I will get the rest of the guys and get the Uzis from our place and be right back."

Alexi brought the rest of the gang, now heavily armed and they all sat in the sandwich shop watching.

"Where is he now?"

"Back inside of the church. They come out and walk away from time to time but keep coming back to the church."

"There must be something *real* interesting in there."

"OK, here is what we will do. Stanislav, you go in the church and find out what he is doing in there and then come back here."

Stanislav returned a few minutes later,"He and the woman are just sitting there looking at that big glass box at the front of the church. It looks like they mean to stay there for a while."

"Anyone else in there?"

"Just a bunch of priests and nuns over in one corner, praying."

"Lets just hope that he stays there. We will go at him from all sides and get him in a crossfire."

"What about the woman?"

"Screw her. If she gets it, it's her fault for being with him."

As the mobsters worked their way down the side aisles, Andrew started to sense danger. He began getting telepathic signals that all was not well.

There are several of them, . . . thinking in Russian. They are planning to ambush me.

Christopher arrived just as the evening vespers began. He wished that the priests and nuns would get through the vespers and leave. He did not wish to harm *them* but the Shroud, that abominable scrap of linen, had to be destroyed. Hopefully, they would leave soon so he could get to the business of destruction. Christopher sat in a pew that gave him a good view of the protective case that held the Shroud.

Christopher, of course, could sense the nervous thoughts of the Russian hit men but, while multilingual, he had no experience with the Russian language and was unaware of the threat that these men represented.

Andrew glanced around the cathedral trying to pick out all of the assassins. He whispered to Madeline, "We are in danger. When I tell you to get down, *get down.*"

It wasn't the way Alexi planned it. It just happened. The hit men were not all in position when one of them, nervously fingering the trigger of his Uzi, accidentally fired a short burst that knocked out one of the stained glass windows. Suddenly bullets were flying everywhere. Andrew shoved Madeline down on the pew and pointed his finger quickly at each of the assassins. Bolts of purple lightning crackled across the room and the assassins crumpled to the floor. He got all of them but one.

That one saw Christopher, and mistook him for Andrew. Christopher was quicker. He took out the last assassin with a similar lightning bolt from his fingertip.

Christopher and Andrew both jumped to the same conclusion. Up to this point, each had been unaware of the others existence, at least as a Titan of enormous powers. In the confusion of the moment, each concluded that another clone had been generated to protect the Shroud and each concluded that the *other* was the protector.

Each thought the protector had to be destroyed.

Andrew formed in his hand an immense ball of electrical energy and hurled it at Christopher. Luckily for Christopher, Andrew reverted to thinking in English, a language in which Christopher was very proficient, so he knew Andrew's every thought.

Recognizing his advantage, Christopher did his thinking in Hebrew, a language totally foreign to Andrew.

As Andrew hurled the ball of energy at him, Christopher levitated himself. The ball surged beneath him, vaporized a stained glass window, and brilliantly illuminated the darkening sky over Turin. Christopher responded with a ball of fire that struck Andrew's left arm leaving it a dangling chunk of well done meat.

Andrew, in shock, did not feel the pain of his injury, but, driven by pure instinct and rage, developed a huge crackling ball of energy in front of him and directed it at Christopher who was not quick enough to retain his advantage. In a last desperate act, he unleashed a similar packet of electricity at Andrew just as Andrew's projectile enveloped and totally incinerated him.

On this level playing field it could end only one way, Andrew was vaporized by Christopher's missile.

Yellow, blue, purple, and green electrical discharges continue to crackle and sputter inside and outside of the cathedral for several minutes, then gradually subside.

All that was left of Andrew and Christopher was two small piles of grey ash.

The assassins were all dead, as was Madeline who was struck by a stray bullet.

The bulletproof polycarbonate case protecting the Shroud had been hit by several rounds from one of the Uzis but the Shroud was unharmed.

When the Italian police arrived, the priests and nuns were blabbering unintelligibly.

What had they witnessed, . . . miracles or something else? They were not at all certain *what* they had seen. It was too much to try to describe.

Within a week, the Italian police had identified Madeline and quickly assumed, with the help of the LAPD, that one of the piles of ashes had been her lover, Andrew Kriest. They had no idea who the other pile of grey ash might have been.

Pictures of Andrew Kreist used in the TV program about the world's most wanted criminal were sent to Italy and the nuns and priests identified *both* of the deceased from these pictures. They said that they appeared twins or perhaps brothers with a small age difference but the pictures could have been of either of them.

Christopher's followers were baffled by his disappearance from the world's religious scene. The most fervent of them truly believed that he was Christ reborn and that He alone could bring love and peace to a torn and troubled planet. What had happened to their Savior?

When the television specials on the demise of Andrew, the world's most wanted criminal, hit the screens, they recognized Christopher in the computer enhanced photo of the face on the Shroud, . . . and knew. Christ had indeed returned and saved mankind from the most vile and evil creature ever to walk the earth, and again, had paid with His life for man's transgressions. Nothing would ever convince them otherwise. Twice in two thousand years He had died for us.

What greater love . . .

CHAPTER FORTY-ONE

Bennet is discussing the events of the previous day with the Signature Killer Task Force, "I know that several credible witnesses positively identified them from the photos and the computer-enhanced picture that we provided but there were *two* of them. The woman who was killed in the gunfire was positively identified as Madeline Belvoire, Andrew Kreist's lover, so one of them probably *was* our man but I am just not comfortable with it. My God! *Two* of them? What if there are *more*?"

One of Bennet's Signature Killer task force is completing his report, "Inspector, when we checked out Dr. Goodenough's apartment we found a frozen test tube of what appears to be blood. Remember? They still have it over in the Cryogenics Lab. The label on it says 'Andy'. What do you want me to do about it? Maybe it is important."

"Just leave it there for now. When the word spreads that he is dead, she will probably surface again. . . . We can check with her then and find out what she wants us to do with it."

When Natalie and John learned of Andrew's death, they returned to Los Angeles.

Natalie returned to academia and became head of the new Department of Genetic Engineering at Berkeley.

She learned of the recovery of her suitcase from TWA Flight 800 and arranged for it to be shipped to her. Everything in it was moldy, . . . smelly, . . . ruined.

She threw it all into the trash, . . . all except her diary of the cloning effort. She cleaned it up as best she could, carefully separated the pages and started reading it. *"How could I have missed this? . . . and this? . . . what we should have done was . . . so many small things that went unnoticed . . . if only we had done it differently . . . but what's done is done . . . no way to go back."*

John reopened MAXXX Security.

John and Natalie are planning marriage to finally formalize the arrangement under which they have lived since the disastrous events at the Project Complex.

All appears to be back to normal. But, . . .

The Shroud survives.

And, . . .

The phone rings at Natalie's desk at Berkeley.

"Hello, Dr. Goodenough?"

"Yes."

"Inspector Bennet, LAPD, here. We are still holding, in our Cryogenics Lab, a test tube of frozen blood that we recovered from you apartment. It is labeled 'Andy' . . . Hello? . . . "

"Hello? . . . "

"Dr.Goodenough? . . . "

"Are you there? . . . "

FINIS
?